Dirty Dancing at Devil's Leap

But her face was turned up toward his, luminous and unguarded, close enough for him to count her freckles. She was listening, softly enthralled, her eyes brilliant, intent, in that way he remembered from when they were so hungry to touch each other.

And just like that it felt like someone was playing racquetball with his heart.

His hand closed around her arm. He tugged her up against him.

Her mouth was there to meet his, all softness and yielding hunger. Everything he knew her to be—the sweetness, the ferocity, the fearless pleasure seeker—was in her kiss, and any plans he had for finessing it were swept under by a greedy panic of want. They kissed as though they'd

By Julie Anne Long

JULIE ANNE LONG

DIRTY DANCING AT DEVIL'S LEAP

A HELLCAT CANYON NOVEL

AVONBOOKS

An Imprint of HarperCollinsPublishers

DIRTY DANCING AT DEVIL'S LEAP. Copyright © 2017 by Julie Anne Long. All rights reserved. Printed in the United States of America. No part of this book may be used or reproduced in any manner whatsoever without written permission except in the case of brief quotations embodied in critical articles and reviews. For information, address HarperCollins Publishers, 195 Broadway, New York, NY 10007.

First Avon Books mass market printing: September 2017

Print Edition ISBN: 978-0-06-267288-9
Digital Edition ISBN: 978-0-06-267289-6

Cover design and photo illustration by Nadine Badalaty
Cover photographs: © Shutterstock; © 123RF (people)

Avon, Avon & logo, and Avon Books & logo are registered trademarks of HarperCollins Publishers in the United States of America and other countries.
HarperCollins is a registered trademark of HarperCollins Publishers in the United States of America and other countries.

FIRST EDITION

17 18 19 20 21   QGM   10 9 8 7 6 5 4 3 2 1

*To every bookseller and librarian
who ever put a book in a reader's hand
and said, "You will love this."*

ACKNOWLEDGMENTS

My thanks to my wise, witty, and wonderful editor, May Chen; to the brilliant folks at Avon Books who work so hard and ingeniously to make sure books find their way into the hands of readers, especially Jessie Edwards and Shawn Nicholls; to my stalwart agent, Steve Axelrod; to bloggers and reviewers who write so passionately and eloquently about the books they love—you're the best, and I adore you; to the dedicated, discerning booksellers and librarians who lead us to our new favorite authors; to all the warm, enthusiastic readers who've embraced Hellcat Canyon; and a special shout-out to Josh Morgon for bike expertise.

CHAPTER 1

Avalon Harwood nudged the wheel of her BMW with her forefinger and it did exactly what she wanted it to do. Which officially made it unlike everything else in her life.

The speedometer quivered on up to fifty as she eased it into the first S turn.

She'd passed a 40 MPH sign a while back.

But she knew this network of back roads that laced through Hellcat Canyon, California, as instinctively, say, as she knew how to get to the bathroom in her apartment in the pitch dark when clothes and shoes and books were strewn in her path. Which was all to the good, because for the past three hours she'd been preoccupied by the images crashing and pinging inside her skull like a handful of change circulating in a hot dryer.

For some reason, she kept coming back to the sparkly orange toenails.

This time she imagined the gas pedal was her boyfriend Corbin's windpipe.

The speedometer quivered up to fifty-five.

Threaded through all those ghastly images were important philosophical questions. Such as: What would her life be like if she didn't always *wonder* things?

Like that time when she was nine years old and she'd wondered whether her big toe would fit up inside the faucet of the bathtub.

And as it turned out, it could.

It just wouldn't come back out again.

She'd panicked and shrieked and her brother Jude had called the paramedics, mostly because he'd always wanted a reason to call the paramedics, and when they arrived something like five minutes later Jude had run out the door to greet them screaming, "Get the paddles!" because he'd seen it on a TV show. (To this day, "Get the paddles!" was family shorthand for any emergency.)

And then there was: What would her life be like if she didn't always feel as though she had something to *prove*?

Like the time when she was twelve and she'd built a ramp and proceeded to jump her bike over the narrowest part of Whiskey Creek. Because back then she would have done anything to impress Mac Coltrane, and when she was twelve, jumping Whiskey Creek on a bike seemed the logical way to do it.

That jump, however, had been worth it for two reasons.

For those three glorious seconds during which she was fully airborne.

And for those three seconds after she came to: flat on the ground, dazed but unbroken, half in the creek, half out, bike half on her, half off—Mac Coltrane kneeling next to her, saying her name.

And she knew that even if her heart had stopped for good, the expression in his hazel eyes would have jolted it back into pounding, joyous life again.

Sometimes she thought it had never quite beat the same way again.

But then she'd always kind of experienced Mac as a series of jolts. Every summer between the ages of ten and sixteen, her heart was a pinball in her chest, pinging whenever she saw his bike thrown down in front of someone's house or chained to the newspaper rack in front of the Variety Store downtown where everyone went to buy candy, or when she caught a glimpse of a dark-haired boy of a certain height in the grocery store or library or anywhere, really.

Right on cue around the next S turn, she caught a glimpse through the trees of the old Coltrane summer home at Devil's Leap. It was what her dad called a Victorian pile, but it had starred in her fantasies from the moment she'd laid eyes on it when she was about eight. How could it not? It had a turret, for God's sake. The turret was shingled in curving tiles like the body of a dragon, and the whole thing was painted a sort of deep, dusty rose, a singular color that glowed like something you'd find at the end of the yellow brick road when the sun hit it at this time of day. It had seemed entirely reasonable when she learned that Mac Coltrane lived in it, because she'd never before or since seen anyone like him.

The one and only time she'd been inside it occupied a unique fixed point on the graph of her life: it was the best and the worst day to date.

Though in light of today's events, she might just have to review the rankings.

Three hours ago she'd been all but airborne with happiness. An old friend from her San Francisco State teaching program days, Rachel Nguyen, had invited Avalon to tell an audience of a hundred-some-odd young entrepreneurs in San Jose her story: how four years ago, she'd been an exhausted full-time student who paid for classes by working full-time as a cocktail waitress at a bar frequented by Ivy League computer nerds. Then came the night she'd wistfully wondered out loud to the nerdy-cute Dartmouth computer science grad who kept hitting on her: What if there was an online game or app that gave you the full college experience—football, the student union, part-time jobs, dates, competing for the classes you wanted—and made it all fun and no work?

Five years later, GradYouAte had eight full-time staff members, a couple of interns, a dozen-some-odd contractors, a few investors, a little board of directors, and shareholders and was closing in on actual, albeit slim, profits. SilliPutty, the Silicon Valley news and gossip site, had recently run a photo of her perched on a desk in a vintage slit pencil skirt, a funky orange pump saucily dangling from her toe; that Dartmouth grad, all curly hair, too-big-but-somehow-just-right nose, hip-nerdy glasses, and dimples, had his arms looped around her from behind. The headline read *GradYouAte's Avalon Harwood and Corbin Bergson Talk Success, Vision, and How They Make Mixing Love and Work Look Like Child's Play*. She had a title (CEO), a nice chunk of cash in the bank, an adoring live-in boyfriend, and life, for the most part, was like skipping, la la la, through that pleasant green meadow where the Teletubbies lived, apart from the challenges of parking in San Francisco, maybe. And the expense. And maybe that one time she'd been mugged at gunpoint.

Secretly, no one was more bemused about all of this than she was. There were days, in truth, when it felt more like something that had sort of happened to her rather than something she'd actively engineered.

After she'd soaked up the applause and basked in the light of all those inspired faces, Rachel told her, "Damn, girl, you knocked that presentation out of the park. Any time you want to do any workshops, say the word. I'll set you up." While Avalon had quit the teaching program to create GradYouAte with Corbin, Rachel had gone on to build a leadership training business so gloriously successful she was now looking for the perfect North State headquarters for seminars and retreats.

Somewhere on the road between San Jose and San Francisco Avalon became aware that her happy glow was shot through with a sort of restless wistfulness.

She found herself putting off returning to GradYou-Ate's offices on Van Ness and Market for the same reasons she might not want to immediately follow up, say, an excellent chicken piccata with a bag of Doritos (though both had a place in her culinary repertoire). She'd stopped instead and impulsively bought a tiny jar of limp flowers an ancient Russian woman pur-loined from yards around her neighborhood and sold off a blanket on the sidewalk near her apartment, and she decided to go upstairs to her apartment to drop them off. Corbin would love them because they had a quirky origin story. "The only thing I'm allergic to is the mundane," he'd told that SilliPutty reporter the day of their interview. He was probably saying things like that in a marketing meeting right now over a cut-throat game of ping-pong in their offices. Corbin often refused to like something if he suspected even one other person had liked it first.

She trotted up two flights and was about to slide her key into her door lock when she paused.

And laid her ear against the door.

Bam . . . Bam. Bambambam. Bam . . . bam bam.

The muffled sound was a little like a shoe going around in a dryer, or a loose shutter slapping the out-side of a house in a storm. Except that they didn't have shutters and it wasn't even drizzling.

Which led to the next philosophical question: What if she wasn't the kind of person who moved away from mysterious thumping noises, instead of toward them?

She gingerly turned the key.

Gently, gently poked open the door with a fingertip.

She left the door open a crack in case she needed to flee. But surely a burglar would have left the door open, too?

She delicately put one foot in front of the other all the way down the soft hall runner. Along the way she discovered the sound wasn't coming from the kitchen . . . Or the bathroom . . . But it *was* growing louder.

She stopped at the threshold of her bedroom.

And . . .

It was like the time she'd been mugged. A guy had materialized out of nowhere on Oak Street, pointed a gun at her, and said, "Give me all your money." She'd looked up at him half smiling because . . . surely this was someone's idea of a practical joke? Surely this wasn't *actually* happening?

But no, as it turns out, she really was being mugged.

And no, the white butt bobbing up and down on the bed really did belong to her boyfriend, Corbin.

Ten orange toenails sparkled at the base of his spine.

They were attached to the feet which were attached to the legs which were locked around him.

In the middle of those ten toes were little white blobs. Avalon knew those white blobs were meant to be skulls, because she'd squealed over the adorableness of the Halloween pedicure at the office just a day ago. Because, you know, sisterhood.

In short, Corbin was banging their intern, Grace.

Not only banging her, the intermittent headboard bamming meant he was attempting to be *fancy* about it.

And to think, for all his evangelizing about originality, Avalon could never even really get him to do it in a mirror.

She was mesmerized. She couldn't feel her limbs or her face. It was as though shock had squeezed her consciousness from her body and she was watching the whole thing from overhead.

She finally jumped when Corbin suddenly yelled, "Holy shit!"

As this wasn't what he normally shouted when he came (though he'd once shouted "Wow oh wow oh wow!" in wonderment, like a dying person moving toward dead relatives in that proverbial bright light), Avalon figured he must have caught her reflection in the bulbous chrome base of their (artisan) bedside lamp.

He shot upright, yanking fistfuls of the sheet with him like a magician attempting that tablecloth trick, and Grace spooled like a rotisserie chicken right off the side of the bed and landed with a dull thud on their lovely, thick Flokati carpet.

And all was silence.

Apart from . . . was that some sort of car alarm outside?

Avalon realized the ghastly high whine was in her own ears.

Corbin pulled the sheet up to his clavicle. His fist was

clenched white over it. This struck her as the second uncharacteristically stupid thing he'd done today (the first being banging an intern in their bed). She'd *seen* him all the way naked plenty of times before.

Absurdly, he looked the way he did when he'd just showered after racquetball. His curly hair was glued to his forehead with sweat.

Corbin always looked peculiarly unfinished without his glasses.

Suddenly knowing all of these little intimate things seemed intolerable.

As she stared at his blank white face she could almost see the thought balloon over his head filled with his own unfortunate realizations: yep, that really is my girlfriend of five years standing in the doorway.

"I'd give that dismount a six," she said, brightly.

"Christ . . . Avalon . . . I . . ." His words were frightened gasps. He stopped.

"Wasn't done yet?" she suggested.

She didn't recognize her own voice.

For some reason Corbin glanced uneasily at her hands then. She remembered the little vase. She gently, gingerly put it down on the dresser, like it was a bomb and she'd just set the timer on it.

In her peripheral vision Grace shifted very slightly.

"Freeze, Grace," Ava commanded, like she was Deputy Chief Brenda Leigh Johnson on *The Closer*. She had no idea why she wanted Grace to freeze. It was just that giving interns orders had become a reflex.

Grace obeyed like it was Simon Says.

Corbin—glib, motormouth, brilliant witty blah blah blah Corbin—remained silent.

And that was somehow the eeriest thing of all. It was like the deep silence of a power outage. A silence caused by a grave malfunction, like an earthquake or a nuclear attack.

She wasn't the sort to shove a stiletto into his sternum, even if they'd owned a stiletto. And if they had, it would have been an artisan hand-forged one-of-a-kind stiletto, because he would have insisted.

But she *did* know how to cut him in the worst possible way.

"I always knew you were a cliché, Corbin." She'd never sounded so bored.

She didn't quite remember leaving the apartment and finding her car and getting in it. She only knew her inner GPS was taking her home to Hellcat Canyon as if she were a creature fleeing for its burrow. She hadn't been there since last Christmas. Almost a year.

Who would have guessed the smooth green Teletubbies meadow of her relationship had a tiger pit in it? FOOSH! Down she'd gone.

Shouldn't there have been some sort of trajectory of transgressions before she found him banging their intern? Some clue other than the sort of selfishness common to guys like Corbin—hypereducated Ivy League nerdy-cute guys who were charming and witty and casually brilliant and benignly certain that everyone would happily just enjoy the gift that was their mere presence, because that's generally what people did?

Her speedometer quivered up, up, up to sixty.

She was just about to really gun it through the next set of delicious S turns, when from out of nowhere red lights flashed in her rearview mirror.

"Fuck." Her voice startled her: it was a dry caw, thanks to three hours of silence. She heaved a sigh so gusty it ought to have blown her doors open, slowed it on down, and pulled over to the next verge.

She draped her arms across her steering wheel and tipped her forehead onto them. She drew in a long, hot, shuddery breath and sighed it out. This was going to be one monster of a ticket.

She lifted her head, which felt so heavy it was like trying to jack up a car, and watched in her rearview mirror as a big, big sheriff's deputy loomed and trudged over the verge toward her.

The guy ducked down, pushed the sunglasses up off his face. "License and registra . . . *Avalon*? Avalon Harwood? What the hell? Why the hell you speeding?"

Ah, small towns. Sheriff's Deputy Eli Barlow had just gone from Cop Voice to Friend Voice in three seconds flat. He sounded worried and pleased and affronted all at once.

"Oh, *hey*, Eli. So how are things?" She tried an apologetic, ironic little smile. Eli was an old high school friend of her older brother Jude's. He was always such a nice person, big and quiet. He knew all about her toe up the faucet and jumping Whiskey Creek and probably nearly everything else she'd ever done, because, well, small towns.

Eli snorted. "Why the hell are you speeding on *this* road? BMW or no BMW, you know better. Everything okay?"

"*Such* language, Deputy. I'm so sorry. I really am. I just . . . I got . . . I'm not . . . everything's fine."

She wasn't precisely a *glib* liar but she could usually do better than that.

As it was, he was studying her with cop eyes: sympathetic laser beams. "I call bullshit on the 'everything's fine,'" he concluded.

She twisted her mouth wryly. "Are those X-ray shades on your head, Eli? Because, you know, that's what Google ought to be working on. Not Google Glass. They could issue them to cops. Shades that see right into the souls of transgressors."

This, quite understandably, resulted in his bemused silence. She wouldn't blame him for thinking she was on some exotic big-city drug.

"Where are you going?" he asked shortly.

"Home."

He nodded once, thoughtfully. Mulling her fate, perhaps.

"Seriously, how are you, Eli?" she said into the brief silence. More reasonably. "It's good to see you, regardless."

"Well, I'm great. I'm getting married."

His words were evenly inflected, but they had a soft rosy glow all around them, just like the top of Whiplash Peak had right now.

She'd never in a million years thought she'd be one of those people who would feel diminished by someone else's happiness. But right now, the rays of his joy felt like heat on a sunburn.

"Wow! That's great! Congratulations." That last syllable was cracked and delivered in a pitch probably only dolphins could hear.

She meant it, and he really deserved to be happy. But she didn't like realizing she was still a long way from being the person she yearned to be: invulnerable, evolved, serene as a nun.

Eli was frowning in earnest now, thanks to her cracked dolphin squeak.

She'd forgotten how fast the night happened here in the county. In just a few minutes, the sky would be full dark. The sky would explode with stars.

"Do your folks know you're on your way home?" he said finally.

She probably looked like someone who had fled the scene of a crime. There was a gym bag in her back seat and her purse on the seat next to her, and that was it, apart from those cutting-edge, not-yet-on-the-market Bluetooth speakers she'd received as a gift from a friend who'd meant for her to give them to Corbin. She couldn't even remember what was *in* her gym bag, apart from sweaty yoga pants and maybe a fossilized M&M.

She shook her head no.

He pressed his lips together. "You're not, um, impaired in any way, right, Avalon? Because I know you'll tell me the truth and I'll give you a ride to your folks' house."

"Nope. Not impaired. Unless you count my judgment in men."

His head went back a little, then came down in a sort of nod of comprehension. Then his mouth quirked wryly at one corner and he shook his head to and fro slowly. She was pretty sure she'd just answered his why-are-you-speeding question.

She tried an insouciant "what are ya gonna do?" one-shouldered shrug, but her body felt stiff from all her held-in emotion and she was a little worried it looked more like a death spasm.

"Call your parents now," Eli ordered. Albeit kindly. "Tell them you're on your way. And swear on your mom's bright red head and your dad's Glennburger that you won't speed again around here, because I know a lot of people kind of like you and it would ruin *my* day if I had to pull you out of an accordioned BMW."

She half snorted, half sighed. And obeyed.

"Call Mom," she told her car.

CHAPTER 2

Eli was smart, she thought dryly. Just the sound of her mom's voice shaved the spiky edge from Avalon's mood. She gave her mom a capsule version of today's events and then drove like a responsible citizen into town the back way all the way to the Harwood House.

The family homestead, an unprepossessing farmhouse built around 1940, was painted a muted periwinkle blue, which meant that around twilight its edges tended to blur right into the sky, and thanks to a competent but no-frills addition a few decades ago it was shaped a bit like an L, or as her father liked to joke, a boomerang, because the grown kids did have a tendency to return. (Except for maybe Jesse. Who was off gallivanting God knows where. The Himalayas?) The front window threw a rectangle of warm light down onto the porch.

She parked her car on the verge, seized her gym bag from the back, climbed out, and sucked in a huge draught of startlingly brisk, woodsmoke-flavored country air. And paused. A million stars jostled each other in a black sky. You really couldn't see them in San Francisco. Somewhere a dog barked, doing its job of warning off raccoons or deer, and the sound made her yearn. She'd had dogs, cats, mice, frogs, even once, for about three hours until her mom found out, a snake, and one darling squirrel, all of them rescued. But Corbin didn't see the point of keeping a pet in their tiny apartment when they both worked all the time.

She'd lived without a lot of things a little too long.

The house was almost precisely between downtown and the hills, and Avalon knew that if she really craned her head in one direction, she could just about see the neon glow of the Misty Cat Tavern sign at the foot of Main Street. The restaurant and music venue had provided a comfortable living for her family for a few decades and a sort of heartbeat for the town.

And then . . . there was the other direction.

But even now her heart skipped with an echo of that old delicious agony of anticipation. It was a bit like when that pinky toe she broke when she was eighteen twinged now to signal approaching rain.

Long ago, beginning the first day of summer vacation, she'd begin looking in that direction for a light at Devil's Leap that would signal Mac Coltrane was in town.

She didn't look that way now. She resolutely headed up to the porch instead.

Of course it was dark up there at Devil's Leap. It had been dark for eons.

"Here, honey."

Her mother thrust a soft bundle into her arms. Avalon unfurled it to find a blue flannel nighty that could have sheltered a dozen Bedouins if propped on sticks.

Avalon held it to her nose and inhaled.

"Snuggle, white lavender scent," her mom informed her.

While Avalon sniffed the nightgown, her mom had been watching her face as if it were a drive-in movie screen, and apparently what she saw there made her pull Avalon into a long squeeze which concluded with a kiss in the middle of her forehead, where Greta from the New Age Store in downtown Hellcat Canyon would say her third eye resided. Her mom had named her kids Jude, Jesse, Avalon, and Eden, all names inspired by a bygone time of peace and love.

"And turmoil. Let's not forget the turmoil, Mom," Avalon always wanted to say.

"Do you want to talk about it?" Her mom wasn't known for her circumspection, but she knew Avalon was less comfortable with gushing than frankness.

"I . . ." Suddenly Avalon felt as though she needed an entirely new language to talk about what had just happened. It was utterly outside her realm of experience. "I don't know. Not yet. I feel a lot of things. And nothing. I haven't really run it through the Mass Spec yet."

Her whole family enjoyed watching *Bones*.

"You might be a little numb," her mom suggested

cautiously. "It's nature's way of giving us a grace period before the annihilating rage sets in."

This was interesting. Her mom was the cheeriest, most unflappably no-nonsense person she'd ever met.

"Wow, Mom, how often do you feel annihilating rage?"

"Oh, every five years or so. Lasts seconds. For example, remember when Jesse's soccer coach called him an idiot and made him cry when he missed that goal when he was eleven? I wanted to disembowel him."

Avalon mulled this. "Huh."

"That wasn't meant as a suggestion for how you should handle Corbin, by the way," her mom added hurriedly. "Maybe leave that part to your dad or your brother Jude. He wields a mean scalpel."

Avalon managed a smile at this. Her brother Jude was a surgeon in Black Oak.

"It might be best to be a little careful during this stage, Ava. Maybe . . . don't give in to impulses."

"Since when have I ever given in to impulses?" It was a wan joke.

"Mmm," her mom said, one of those syllables that could mean anything at all. Four kids had taught her to pick her moments. "Oh, here's your dad."

Her dad was indeed hovering behind her mom. The hall light gave him a misleading halo. It was funny how age seemed to fade some people, but her parents only got more vivid. Her mother's red hair bordered on scarlet now, assisted by whatever box of color happened to be on sale; her dad's was gleaming silver, and his mustache would have won Best in Show in any mustache pageant. They both took up a little more space: both a little softer, a little broader, a little more imposing, perhaps, with a sort of seen-it-all, can-handle-it-all, usually enjoy-it-all dignity.

Sherrie Harwood gave her husband's arm a little squeeze and he gave her bottom a reflexive, affectionate pat as she retreated.

Her dad propped a hand on the bedroom door frame. "If you need help sleeping, Avalon, I can get you a shot of brandy. I think I have a bottle around here left over from last year's Chamber of Commerce Christmas gift exchange."

"Good parenting, Dad."

"Only the best for you, pumpkin."

She managed a little laugh.

He hovered there in the doorway, as if he could body block anything else that might want to get in there and hurt her. "So . . . do you know what you're going to do yet about . . . ?"

"Nope. But we have a company together, so . . ."

Funny how they were talking in ellipses about Corbin. Kind of like he was Voldemort, suddenly. Her dad wasn't one for long, heartfelt, girlish talks.

"I'm doing fine, though, Pop. Really."

Right on cue, a text pinged in from Corbin. She seized her phone and squeezed it like a KGB assassin strangling an enemy spy. The little screen finally went black.

Then she slapped it punishingly down on the night-stand.

Her dad watched all this wordlessly.

"Yeah, you seem fine," he said dryly, finally.

She sighed.

"Hey, I was talking to Lloyd at the feed store today. He says that that old Coltrane house at Devil's Leap is finally up for auction. Tomorrow morning, nine o'clock, courthouse steps."

Her heart lurched.

She couldn't say a word for a few seconds.

"I'll be damned," she said, almost stammering. "I was just . . ." Just what? Reviewing the ignominy of her romantic past? "I just saw it through the trees on the way here."

"Yeah, Lloyd checked out the photos on the auction website. Says it's pretty much unchanged inside. Won't sell, though. No one around here has that kind of money or needs a house like that."

"I suppose you're right. Kind of a shame, though."

In her memories, the inside of that house glowed like a burnished romantic flashback in a movie. Golden hardwood floors and about a half dozen crystal chandeliers and an extravagance of windows, many of them trimmed with William Morris–esque stained glass. Its beauty had been an ache.

Sometimes it seemed that as long as that house remained empty, it was like a snow globe around that time with Mac.

"Well, it's kind of a ridiculous house," her dad said

with typical pragmatism. "It has a damned turret. Beautiful grounds around it, though. Remember how you guys loved jumping off that rock into that swimming hole at Devil's Leap? Those summer days when your mom and I could get away when you all played with those Coltrane boys."

She couldn't speak for a moment.

"Vaguely," she lied. Her voice frayed.

The Coltranes had bought the house the summer when Avalon was about ten years old. She and her siblings and Mac, and sometimes his brother Ty, had all run about together like little forest creatures up at Devil's Leap, summer friends.

But she and Mac had competed with each other in every imaginable way from the moment they met. She'd had no idea what to call that sort of exhilarating hybrid of fear and wild joy she'd felt in his presence, but she did know it was almost exactly the same way she'd felt that first time she'd jumped off Devil's Leap into the watering hole.

By the first time Mac kissed her—coincidentally right after she'd beat him in another race to the rock—she'd fully understood what to call those feelings.

"We loved taking you out there," her dad said. "You kids had such a blast, and you all were so damn cute. I remember like yesterday watching you flying off that rock right into the swimming hole that day you raced young Mac Coltrane."

"I won that day, too. And a lot of other days."

Funny, though. Mac almost seemed to enjoy her wins as much as his own.

"Yeah, you sure did." Her dad said this with relish. He was every bit the competitor she was.

"I beat him at least half the time. Bike races, checkers, foot races, burping."

"That's because everything you ever did, Avalon, whether it made any sense . . . well, you've never half-assed a thing in your life."

She gave a short, surprised laugh.

She also often tried too hard and overshot her mark. Her dad refrained from saying that.

She sat down on the bed, cradling the flannel nightgown.

"Dad . . . what made you think of that suddenly? Devil's Leap and all of that?"

He paused. And then one side of his mustache hiked with his rueful, crooked smile. "I was just thinking you never were afraid of a damn thing."

His tone was richly complicated: loving and wry, proud and resigned. It contained everything he knew about her and everything he suspected she'd go on to do.

It was his way of telling her that she would emerge triumphant, even if they had to pick her up and bandage her first. Or get the paddles.

So like her dad to compress a long, heart-searching, girlish talk into just one sentence.

Suddenly she couldn't speak over the throat lump.

He gave the door frame a brisk, conclusive pat,

"Night, pumpkin. We'll feed you breakfast tomorrow morning at the Misty Cat if you don't have to head back to work right away. Want the light off?"

"Not yet."

He pulled the door most of the way closed and flicked off the hall light.

She sucked in a long, long breath and blew it out again, then she stripped off her sweaty, crumpled clothes and pulled the giant nightgown over her head, where it settled over her like a fragrant hug. She was too physically drained to contemplate a much-needed shower and still too wired from shock to actually sleep.

Should be a fun night to get through, she thought dryly.

Her eyes darted to her silent phone and her stomach knotted violently at the notion of texting Corbin, as if it was literally attempting to shrink farther away from him. But the GradYouAte staff would expect to see her tomorrow, and doubtless a hundred some-odd emails awaited her, too.

She could leave the phone off for the night. But she was going to have to face it all tomorrow, regardless.

She could handle it. She was a big girl. She'd just turned thirty.

And yet whenever she visited her parents she always felt as though this twin bed was gradually molding her into her teenage self, the way a mouthful of braces had reined in her overbite just inside a year back when she was twelve.

She finally burrowed under the covers, shoved her feet down, and discovered her mom had put the purple-flowered sheets on her bed. They were percale and worn to soothing, buttery smoothness with age and a decade's worth of kicking Harwood feet, and like hot tea with lots of milk and Graham Crackers, they were whipped out when someone had the flu or a broken bone. Her mom had clearly decided the pain of her condition warranted it.

Did it? While she could practically *feel* the outline of a sort of icy, furious shock extending from her clavicle to her belly button, shouldn't she feel . . . devastated . . . right now? Shattered? Destroyed? Or other words that featured hyperbolically in her teenage diary?

Maybe her mom was right: maybe she was numb.

Or maybe she just didn't feel things *seismically*, anymore.

Maybe age and the march of time just naturally leached potency from emotions, flattened the peaks and filled in the valleys. Maybe a relentless inflow of reality on the way to adulthood diluted magic the way she and her sister, Eden, had once sneaked water into their parents' bottle of whiskey until they'd inevitably gotten caught.

"Mac Coltrane is a wizard," she'd once gushed to her diary. His eyes were the green side of hazel, and in them flecks of gold floated like autumn leaves on the Hellcat River. No one else she knew had eyes like those. With just a *look* he could turn her blood to sparkling cider, or make her breath go short and shuddery, or make her feel . . . cherished. It had certainly felt like alchemy then. He could say so much without saying a word.

Like the day of the squirrel funeral. They'd wrapped Trixie in a velvet shroud, which was really a Chivas Regal bag he'd stolen from his dad, and put her in a shoebox, and she and Mac had silently hiked out deeper onto the Devil's Leap land to a spot Mac had scoped out earlier, where two tall, beautiful blue spruces grew surrounded by smaller ones, like a little tree family. He'd produced from his pocket a perfect heart-shaped rock he'd found, gray, like Trixie's fur, a little smaller than Avalon's palm, and they laid it on the grave. Somehow no church or hymn could ever hope to be as comforting as the quality of his silence and presence.

But his personality had edges, too, like a jewel, or a blade. When he liked things, he *really* liked them; when he hated things, he was funny about it, but deadly earnest. He claimed to loathe children ("Why?" he said simply, usually when a toddler was screaming nearby), the song "Don't Cry Out Loud" ("the *worst* song in the world"), restrictions on his freedom, and anything that smacked of "romance," which he claimed was a construct designed to make *everyone* feel inadequate and to divest idiot men of their money. He'd had nothing but good-natured scorn when she'd told him about her fantasy of slow dancing on Devil's Leap to what she thought of as her namesake song, Roxy Music's "Avalon."

"Oh, Avalon. That's just ridiculous. No one actually does that kind of thing in real life."

She wasn't offended. She was amused. Nor was she swayed. She was no fragile flower. And she'd always sensed that at his core was unequivocal regard for her, no matter what she said or did.

Things he loved: his Ritchey P-29 mountain bike, freedom, Devil's Leap, and, she'd thought, her.

He'd never said that last one out loud, though.

And Mac Coltrane had cratered her heart when she was seventeen.

So maybe "magic" was just another way of saying innocence. And innocence was another way of saying "pain."

And so in the end she supposed the death of magic was a mercy visited upon adults, because she never wanted to feel that kind of pain again.

She supposed she had herself to blame, though maybe that was a mercy, too: an unworthy curiosity had led to her being somewhere she wasn't supposed to be when Mac had uttered words that, much like the meteor that had supposedly wiped out the dinosaurs, changed her entire world.

As for Mac, well, his whole life had cratered rather spectacularly—and publicly—just a few years after that.

Google had never been forthcoming about what had become of him—he didn't even have a Facebook page. Though that could be for privacy reasons, given that he was Dixon Coltrane's son. If he Googled *her* today, he'd find the SilliPutty photo of her perched on a desk dangling an orange pump from her toe, her devoted boyfriend beaming over her shoulder, the very personification of modern love and success.

So she supposed that meant that she'd won in the end. She'd showed *him*.

Why then did her entire life feel so . . . haphazard?

She lay musing, one cheek under her hand, and mulled. She'd had dreams. How was it that she wasn't living any of them? She craved, suddenly, to do something *deliberately*. From the very beginning to the very end. Like her brother Jude, who had planned to be a doctor and was now a doctor, or like her friend Rachel, who was now looking for property to expand her burgeoning leadership training empire.

Avalon levered her torso slowly up from the bed like a mummy rising from a sarcophagus.

She sat like that, in the dark, her elbows on her knees. Animated not by a curse . . . but by an idea.

She leaned over the side of the bed and yanked her laptop from its case. She cradled it in her lap for an instant. As if giving herself an opportunity to change her mind.

Tentatively, she powered it on.

Then typed a few words in the search engine window.

Her palms were already damp.

When she hit Enter, the bright rectangle of the screen in the dark of her little room was a window onto her past.

And maybe a window onto her future.

Once she knew what she needed to know, she exhaled the breath she didn't know she was holding. And then powered the laptop off and clapped the lid closed.

The old digital alarm clock next to her bed read two thirty a.m.; she set it for seven.

And when she lowered herself back to the bed, her heart was pounding exactly the way it had the first time she'd taken that jump off Devil's Leap.

CHAPTER 3

Mac Coltrane's sheets were a little bit scratchy, which also described his mood.

They were about a three hundred thread count. And cheap. He liked that they had body and heft and didn't cling to him on hot nights or tempt him into lingering in bed, and they had cost practically nothing, and these days he knew the cost of everything.

He didn't like anything that clung. Or tempted him to linger.

And that included nearly every tie of every kind.

Except, well, maybe the goats. He was pretty committed to the goats.

But his bed was vast, because he was a restless sleeper. He often woke up diagonally across it, limbs flung out, like he was afraid someone would steal his territory. Once upon a time, a lifetime ago, it seemed, when he was test driving the kind of lifestyle one expected of a billionaire's son, he'd slept on satin sheets. Until that night he'd rolled over and his shifting knee had accidentally punted his date out the other end of the bed. She'd emerged with a soft plop onto the floor as if she'd gone down a waterslide, astonished. They'd laughed like giddy fools. That was a few months before his whole world caved in.

He'd gone from knowing exactly who he was, where he was from, and where he was going to feeling as blank as the checks his dad used to give him.

And just as worthless as those checks would be now.

He'd shifted the rubble painstakingly off himself, one piece at a time, as strategical as a Jenga player and as methodical as any crew sent in to free survivors of earthquake wreckage. The hard way, step by step, he learned exactly who he was.

Someone who got what he wanted.

In some ways, the apple didn't fall far from the tree. As the saying went. Even if the tree was in prison for fraud.

"When the bidding starts, put me on speaker. I want to hear it."

"Of course, Mr. Coltrane." His attorney's tone didn't at all betray that Mac had said this to him a hundred times. Mac liked to subtly tweak Graybill, who was English, starchy, correct, and possibly the most literal man Mac had ever met.

Because, well, frankly, "smartass" was another of the things Mac Coltrane definitely was.

"Have you changed your bidding cap, sir?"

"Well, I checked the dryer, the sofa cushions, and

all the pockets of my clothes, and came up with nada. So no."

He'd also checked the mailbox, and no promised big white envelope from Mike was there, either. He wished he was surprised by this.

"Ha ha. Ha. Very well, sir."

Graybill was humoring him. Mac suppressed a grin.

Like his father, Mac had the knack for turning virtually nothing into something, and then something into something big. Methodically and skillfully, but not as quickly as he would have preferred. Because unlike his father, he had a little *thing* about doing it the right way.

Graybill had worked for Dixon Coltrane and was perhaps the only person on staff who'd managed to remain untainted by the scandal. And Mac knew Graybill shared some of his own life philosophy about how to stay on the straight and narrow.

And he, just like Mac, knew of one possible way Mac could significantly change his bidding cap. He also knew it would be a cold day in hell before he took that route. Because it would involve forgiving.

How about that. There was yet another way Mac was his father's son: he was implacable when he decided not to forgive.

"Okay then. To reiterate: the bidding cap is still three hundred. And that's firm because it has to be. But I doubt we'll even hit two hundred."

He didn't mention all the reasons he didn't think

they'd hit that cap: the grounds were gorgeous, but Hellcat Canyon was in the middle of Bumfuck Nowhere, California; the house was immense, idiosyncratic, costly to maintain—beautiful but ridiculous. It needed updating. Rumor had it there was also a ghost. He'd never met the ghost, but then he'd lived there during the summers only, sometimes not even a whole summer, for just short of eight years.

But there were other ghosts. These were more of the figurative kind. For instance, sometimes when he closed his eyes after staring into the sun an image would hover for an instant behind his lids: a girl with big mahogany eyes filled with gold lights, her hair a few shades deeper in color, impossibly gleaming. But there had never been anything ethereal about her. He knew, because he'd held her. She was the realest person he'd ever known. The truest thing he'd ever felt.

She'd wanted to be an elementary schoolteacher and she loved animals, and he supposed that described millions of girls. "A common little person," his dad had called her. Among other things.

It took Mac years to fully understand now how definitively untrue this was.

She *had* disappeared, however.

So she had that in common with a ghost.

And maybe all of that had been an illusion after all, like everything else in his life had turned out to be.

It took him a long time to adjust to her absence. He hadn't realized that she was the lens he'd begun to see nearly everything through. That even though she was kind of a secret, she was also, in a way, his center of gravity. And when it was clear he was just never going to see her again, life had taken on a peculiar, almost dreamlike quality. What he did had ceased to matter because nothing had consequences in a dream.

Hence the foray into satin sheets. Life in general had become a satin sheet. Superfluously decadent; nothing of substance adhered.

He was aware he didn't like to say her name in his mind. Which meant it had more power over him than he preferred any soul to have.

That was a helluva long time ago, though. A fair number of women ago. His parents' divorce ago. His father's indictment ago. The national guard ago. Backpacking through Europe ago.

Somehow all of that had led him back to here about three years ago, thanks to Morton Horton and the goats.

For about two decades he'd been untangling the skein of his life as if it were a wad of Christmas tree lights, all of them burnt out save one.

That light was the house at Devil's Leap.

And he knew Graybill thought he was nuts. Mac hadn't done an irrational, unplanned thing in about two decades.

But he didn't feel the need to explain to Graybill why this was, in fact, the most rational thing he'd ever done in his life. If there was one thing Mac loathed, it was revealing anything that might be construed as a vulnerability.

Publicity came in a close second in the loathing department. He'd had enough of that for a lifetime.

Which was why Graybill would be doing the bidding for him tomorrow.

"Yes, sir. I understand the cap."

"Until tomorrow then. Thanks, Graybill."

"Until tomorrow, Mr. Coltrane."

Mac signed off and stood up abruptly from his perch on the end of the bed and opened the door to let in The Cat, who laced himself around his shins without quite touching them, The Cat's version of an air kiss. The Cat had showed up one day about a year and a half ago and never left. Mac poured some kibble into the bowl, then turned around for a last look at the room, at all the minimalist decorating at its finest. The shotgun over the door. The vast bed. The shelf alongside it holding all of his i-gadgets.

Next to those, a collection of neatly stacked tie boxes.

Mac couldn't forgive, but he couldn't seem to get rid of those, either.

Through the transom window of this cottage the big old Victorian house seemed etched into the night sky, just a few shades less dark. For three years now it had been a hundred-some-odd feet yet two hundred light years away.

He doubted he'd sleep tonight.

Tomorrow at nine a.m. was the hour when that gap

would close and he, like every Coltrane had stretching back at least a century, would do the inevitable: get exactly what he wanted.

A valon roared into the courthouse parking lot at about three minutes to nine, skidded to a sideways halt, yanked her seatbelt out of its socket like it had taken her hostage, and all but toppled out of the car, scrambling gracelessly upright and ramming her hip but *good* on the door frame in the process. She took three leg-dragging, whimpering, Quasimodo-esque steps to adapt to that little mishap, sucking air in between her teeth against the pain.

Fuck fuck fuck.

She had three minutes. Elbows tucked into her side, head down, morning air whistling through her ears that had always stuck out just a little more than she preferred, hoping the little butt nudge she'd given the car door was enough to swing it closed, but not staying to hear the click.

If only everyone in Hellcat Canyon wasn't so freaking *nice*. She'd planned to be the first person in line before the credit union opened this morning; she was the second. The first was Mrs. Corcoran, who was eighty-seven and had brought with her a coffee can full of dimes.

"Boy, you must have been saving these for decades, Mrs. Corcoran! If dimes could talk, I bet they'd have a tale to tell. Let me get those wrappers for you . . ."

To keep from hyperventilating and frightening

both Mrs. Corcoran and the sweet, helpful clerk, Avalon multitasked.

To her current assistant (Kenneth? Daria! No! It was Enrique—staff turnover among young, flaky, skilled tech workers was so high she sometimes forgot who was on deck), she sent a text:

> I'll be out of the office thru end of week due to family emergency. Defer all decisions to Corbin. Pls overnight anything currently in my inbox to the address I'll send soon.

"Okay, now you have five dollars, Mrs. Corcoran . . . I remember when I could get a whole breakfast down at the Misty Cat for five dollars, don't you . . . ? I like the Hellcat Scramble myself . . ."

Then it was time to put a stop to Corbin's thirty-five texts:

> I've told Enrique I'm out of the office for the rest of the week due to a family emergency. You'll need to handle things. I'll be in touch in about a week. DON'T text me again until you hear from me.

"Handling" things was basically Corbin's worst nightmare. The administrative day-to-day decision-making was so so so so *torturous* for someone of his genius caliber.

How fascinating to live in a world where people ended up doing things for you just because you didn't want to. How very like a *Pasha*.

The anger was almost as good as the coffee she desperately needed.

Almost.

"Okay, now you have fifteen dollars, Mrs. Corcoran . . . whoopsie! This is a Canadian dime! Ha ha ha! Now, how did that get in there? Did I tell you I went to Vancouver over the summer . . ."

Avalon was officially hyperventilating now. She shot Rachel a quick text:

> I may have exactly the property you're looking for in the North State! Stay tuned.

Finally, a yawning clerk opened another window. Perhaps alerted by a manic gleam in Avalon's eye, she dispensed with pleasantries and got right down to it.

A few minutes later Avalon bolted out of the credit union like she'd just robbed it with an all-but-drained personal bank account and a stack of cashier's checks. Which is what the website had instructed her to do.

And she was going to be on time! She was going to make it! She might even be a minute earl—

Fuck.

She came to a screeching halt. The Hellcat Canyon courthouse had been built around 1870. It was handsome, modestly scaled, white domed, Doric of column and marble of foyer.

And it was situated at the top of at *least* thirty fucking granite steps.

Why, Hellcat Canyon? *Why*? To make rash brides

and grooms think twice before getting hitched by a justice of the peace? To make criminals think twice about making a break for it?

She whipped her sunglasses off and wiped the sweat and surrendered to a split second of crushing doubt, her lungs already burning and heaving. Maybe the universe was trying to protect her from yet another metaphorical bike jump across Whiskey Creek.

She tipped her head back and stood on her toes. About a half dozen people were milling about the courtyard fountain, each of them limned in the rose-gold of an early morning autumn sun. Her competition.

Suddenly a big guy in suspenders and a denim shirt stretched tautly over his barrel torso burst from the courthouse double doors like a cuckoo from a clock and bustled over to the fountain. He flourished a clipboard. The little crowd surged toward him.

Her phone pinged.

Ava, at least tell me WHERE you are!

Another freaking text from Corbin.

She growled ferally, jerked her head away from it exactly as if he was forcing her to stare at his bobbing white butt again. Her back teeth clamped down hard.

The anger was a gift. It was all the adrenaline she needed.

She took a deep gulp of air like a deep sea diver and all but hurled her body forward.

Bam Bam Bam. Bam. The hard fall of her feet on the steps vibrated her teeth; her breath roared in her ears. She was reasonably fit thanks to San Francisco's hills, but her only goal in life at this moment was to not throw up before she reached the top, and hopefully not even then.

The entire group pivoted to stare wonderingly at her.

She managed to stand regally erect for three triumphant seconds, hands planted on her hips, smiling enigmatically, the breeze whipping her ponytail sideways.

Before she buckled in two like a two-by-four sliced by a karate chop. Black spots danced before her eyes. Wheezing, she waved away the concerned feet she saw from her bent position. A couple of pairs of John Deere work boots, a pair of Nikes, a pair of handmade loafers so shiny she could see herself in the toes.

She levered herself upright a few seconds later. Sweaty and more than a little nauseated, but then, she was an old hand at both of those conditions.

Everyone was still staring at her. They now, to a man (they were all men), seemed faintly alarmed.

She smiled placidly back at them.

Handmade Loafers was Los Angeles–thin and his gray hair was ruthlessly barbered. She would bet all of her cashier's checks that he smelled like expensive aftershave. His charcoal-gray suit was meticulously tailored if unadventurous (though arguably, any suit in Hellcat Canyon would have been noteworthy). He looked like a G-man or a lawyer. Her money was on the latter.

She knew instinctively this was the guy to beat.

She scanned them and summed them up as Overalls, Cardigan, Timid Guy, Button-down Shirt, and Handmade Loafers. A fly had begun orbiting all of them. Avalon was a little worried she was the attraction. She needed a shower.

She was the only woman, the only one in black, the only one in yoga pants; the only one in sunglasses, a sweaty T-shirt, messy high ponytail, and a cardigan speckled with lint. These were all the things she'd found in her gym bag. The blazer she'd worn to speak to the young entrepreneurs yesterday was hopelessly crumpled.

But one thing she'd learned in her by-the-seat-of-her-pants school of business was when you're feeling underdressed, too young, too . . . *female* . . . in a room full of men: hold yourself as if you own the place. As if you've graciously granted everyone present audience and they are there on your sufferance.

"Good morning, folks!" The auctioneer boomed into the sleepy silence, which made everyone give a little start. "I'm Chuck Beasley, and I'll be your ringmaster for today's proceedings. Today you'll be bidding on the *beautiful* fairy-tale Victorian manse at Devil's Leap, once belonging to the storied Coltrane billionaire dynasty, whose history stretches back a few hundred years and contains heroes and rogues alike. Three thousand five hundred square feet, ten rooms, five bathrooms, breathtaking grounds, glorious hardwood parquet floors, nine-foot ceilings, and as if that wasn't enough, it also comes with a groundskeeper under contract through the end of the year. Presumably you've had a chance to review the photos online, yes?"

A sort of assenting murmur rustled through the little crowd. Avalon had spent the good portion of last night perusing all those photos. And the house looked the same inside as it had the last—and only—time she'd seen it. It did need some updating, a little TLC, and paint.

"Excellent!" Chuck Beasley was clearly a force of nature. "All bidding is at your own risk! Bid early, bid big, bid often, and bid at your own risk! Do we have an opening bid?"

"Fifty thousand," said Overalls. Avalon had pegged him as the sort who was here for the spectacle, given that entertainment options in Hellcat Canyon ran the gamut between A (bingo at St. Anne's) and B (whatever was going on at the Misty Cat or The Plugged Nickel). If you wanted to elevate your pulse at all in Hellcat Canyon you had to get creative.

"Do I hear fifty-five, fifty-five. Fifty-five," Chuck Beasley ratta-tat-tatted in auctioneer cadence. "Fifty-five is *peanuts* for a magnificent house, are you clever people going to let this gentleman outsmart you and outbid you and take home a bargain? Give me fifty-five, fifty-five."

Avalon raised her finger coolly.

"Lady in the shades bids fifty-five!" the auctioneer crowed. Every head whipped in her direction again. "Do I hear sixty thousand? Sixty thousand is pocket change for a Victorian palace, do I hear sixty thousand?"

Out of the corner of her eye, Avalon saw Handmade Loafers nod subtly.

"Sixty from the well-groomed gentleman!" Chuck Beasley bellowed with pleasure. "Do I hear sixty-five? Sixty-five thousand, you know you want it, you know you came to play, don't be coy or it'll get away. Who'll give me sixty-five?"

"Sixty-five?" said Timid Guy in a little voice. Avalon was pretty sure that would be his first and last bid.

"We have sixty-five, and I know the rest of you can beat that. Do I hear seventy, seventy?"

"*ONE HUNDRED*," shouted Button-down Shirt.

It caused a unanimous momentary blip of astonished silence.

"One fifty," Avalon said coolly. Taking pains to sound bored. She glanced at her fingernails and frowned a little distractedly, as if dropping tens of thousands on property was something she did every day, so commonplace it was all she could do not to whip out her cell phone and start playing Words with Friends.

The auctioneer whistled low. "One fifty to our Lady in the Shades, who reveals herself to be hard-core. Now we got ourselves a horse race. Do I hear one fifty-five? One hundred fifty-five thousand for the house at Devil's Leap?"

"One sixty," Handmade Loafers said evenly. He had an English accent. That was interesting.

Avalon would love to beat out an Englishman.

She would love to beat *any* guy today.

"One seventy-five," she all but drawled.

"Two hundred thousand," he countered with great disinterest, before the auctioneer could even say a word.

Thus launched some swift-bidding ping-pong between the two of them.

Up the price went, up and up, with Chuck the auctioneer, who clearly could not believe his luck, merely shouting out their bids as they were made, until:

"Three hundred thousand dollars."

Handmade Loafers laid those words down like crisp little bricks.

Overalls clutched his heart. Avalon hoped this was merely theatrics.

But sweet Jesus. She was tempted to do the same.

Three . . . hundred . . . thousand . . . dollars.

It sobered her into startled silence. The great weighty roundness of that number cut right through her buzz of defiance and determination. How had it come to this?

She *did* have the money.

And she'd have a little left. But it was everything she'd meticulously saved over the past two decades.

It was just definitely a lot higher than she thought she'd need to go. She and Corbin always kept money in reserve in case they needed to forego a paycheck, or cover an emergency contingency. Once or twice, early on, she'd dipped into her savings to help cover the GradYouAte payroll.

Clearly it was a lot higher than the auctioneer thought anyone would go, because it took him a good thirty seconds to recover his aplomb.

He cleared his throat.

"Do I hear three hundred five thousand dollars? Three five? Lady in the Shades, I know you don't want to leave without this magnificent prize. Three hundred five thousand dollars is *still* a steal and I know you know it. Be the envy of all your friends, not to mention all these people standing around you. Be the enemy of this well-dressed gentleman. Are you going to let him get the better of you?"

Are you going to let him get the better of you? It was like the universe talking directly to her.

Her heart was slamming like bass in a disco.

"All right, then," Chuck said matter-of-factly, rather sadly. "Three hundred thousand. Going . . ."

Avalon darted a glance at Handmade Loafers.

He was looking steadfastly straight ahead. His posture was indolent. But he had a tell: his face had gone white.

It might just be adrenaline. It might be tension. It might just be because he was English.

But Avalon definitively knew: he wasn't going to bid higher than that.

Because he couldn't.

"Going . . ."

Her fingers laced together. "Three ten."

Had she really said that out loud?

Everyone was looking at her, so she must have.

There was a collective gasp, then someone coughed violently. It was safe to say a circling fly had been siphoned in.

Her words hung in the air, thrumming with insane bravado. Her will had hijacked her senses.

Handmade Loafers's face was now as gray as his suit.

"Turns out we have three hundred ten thousand dollars." The auctioneer sounded subdued yet gleeful. "Do I hear three fifteen?"

For a millisecond everything in the world seemed locked rigidly into place. Nothing moved. Not time. Not her lungs or her heart or her eyelids.

"Do I hear three fifteen?" Chuck Beasley coaxed, "Will the well-groomed gentleman sweep the prize away from the lady for three hundred fifteen thousand dollars, or will he suffer defeat today?"

Handmade Loafers was as motionless as the fountain. His lips were parted slightly. Avalon suspected he was struggling for breath.

"Going . . ."

Avalon's own breath shuddered in and out, in and out. The blood rang in her ears.

"Going . . ."

She knotted her sweat-slick hands and pressed her lips together to prevent her silent, desperate prayers from escaping. She struggled not to close her eyes.

"SOLD! The House at Devil's Leap sold to the Lady in the Shades!"

A great collective whoop went up.

Avalon had fainted once before in her life, and the moment preceding it had felt a *lot* like this one: the light-headedness, the black spots dancing before her eyes. So she didn't trust herself to move just yet.

She did close her eyes briefly and indulged in an exhale so lengthy it ought to have deflated her two sizes.

"Congratulations on your exquisite taste and your triumph, my lady, and thank all of you for coming today. Why don't we give her a hand? Come have a chat with me, if you would." Chuck Beasley beckoned her forward.

She took a long, low, slow bow to acknowledge the applause. Her head swam on her way back up, another reminder that she'd slept maybe two hours last night. When she was upright she glanced around her as if she was seeing the world for the first time. Once again, everything had changed, and she'd done it. The sky seemed to have acquired a sort of rippling haze. She distantly knew this was because she was drunk on euphoria and bravado and fury and fatigue.

She moved, as though borne on a magic carpet, toward the beaming, beckoning auctioneer. She couldn't feel her feet.

Handmade Loafers rotated slowly to watch. She was

distantly aware that his expression suggested she might be a creature he'd never before seen, something cute but perhaps rabid. He was holding his cell phone a few inches from his ear, as if it was perhaps too hot to hold it closer. A peculiar high-pitched whine seemed to be emanating from it, as though it was picking up outer space signals, or an incoming fax, or perhaps preparing to explode.

And as she drew nearer to him, she nodded gently, and became aware that the whining sound was, in fact, a word: *"Noooooooooooooooooooooooooo . . ."*

CHAPTER 4

"**W**HAT THE FUCKING HELL HAP-PENED? Who the hell was that woman? Where did she *come* from?"

Mac was in his cottage. Graybill was still on the courthouse steps.

"Mr. Coltrane, may I ask if you intend for me to attempt to answer these rhetorical questions, or are you venting?"

Oh, for God's sake.

"Well, obviously the latter, Graybill," he said through gritted teeth. "But if you can address the former, you'd have my utmost gratitude." He mimicked Graybill's clipped English.

"She went off with the auctioneer, Mr. Coltrane. If I'd known you'd wanted me to give pursuit I might have."

Mac sucked in another breath, as if he hoped oxygen would behave like Ativan. His equilibrium remained thrown. "What did she look like?"

"She was about five feet five. A bit sweaty and

disheveled. Frankly, she looked a bit as though she might have slept in her clothes. I at first took her for one of the homeless women who camp out here, or for someone late for a meeting with her parole officer. Then I realized she was wearing what I believe were lululemon yoga pants and Armani sunglasses."

Mac was momentarily speechless. "What in the . . . how in the . . . *lululemon*? Are you kidding me with this, Graybill?"

"I wouldn't presume to kid about this, Mr. Coltrane, given how important the matter is to you. You may thank my wife for my knowledge of lululemon."

Mac rubbed his forehead with his hand. "Is that all you've got on her?"

"She had a very determined air. Hysteria channeled in a very goal-oriented way. Knew exactly what she came to do and wasn't going to leave without accomplishing it."

Mac was momentarily distracted by wondering about Graybill's marriage, given the things he noticed about women.

"And she wasn't *un*attractive, Mr. Coltrane. Her hair was a sort of dark red. Her form was pleasing. Her face was covered mostly with the aforementioned sunglasses. Though I thought I saw freckles. It of course might have been, er . . . dirt."

The word "freckles" pinged somewhere in the vicinity of Mac's heart, which he used these days strictly as an organ for pumping blood. Certainly no woman had seen the inside of it, to be euphemistic, in eons.

But the word was like a little pinprick puncture. Oddly, he felt the anger seep out of him.

And for a vertiginous millisecond, a slippage in time, he was that uncertain kid again. Hurt. Inwardly flailing, outwardly frozen.

For just a second, however. He might as well be made of rock these days.

"I do wish I could be of more assistance, Mr. Coltrane," Graybill said into the silence. Graybill was starchy, but Mac believed him, because he was a decent guy.

"What a pity I'm not a police sketch artist, Graybill. Or a psychic. Or both."

"All viable career alternatives, Mr. Coltrane, should you wish to abandon the agrarian life. A psychic works downtown in Hellcat Canyon, I'm given to understand."

"Thank you, Graybill. I, too, have seen the giant palm over the New Age bookstore on Main Street. That was more humor on my part; please don't bill me for it."

They remained connected in a sort of commiserating silence.

"Mr. Coltrane, I would be happy to act as your agent should you wish to contact Tiberius in New York."

That was about as delicately put as any human could put anything. Graybill knew exactly how Mac felt about the house. And about his brother, Ty. It was a testament to how well he knew how much this meant to Mac.

"No," Mac said shortly. "Thank you," he added a moment later, after a pointed delay, to punish Graybill a very little for even asking.

"Very well," Graybill said evenly.

Mac cleared his throat. "That woman was attractive, huh? At least that gives me something to work with."

"I've every confidence in your eventual success, Mr. Coltrane." Admirable dryness, that.

"And your bill will reflect today's efforts, no doubt."

"We do understand each other, Mr. Coltrane."

Mac pressed the call to an end and stalked out to stand at the threshold of his cottage. He sucked in a long, cool, deep breath.

He'd stop by his mailbox to see if that promised envelope had appeared. His instincts told him he'd come up empty yet again.

Then he'd go burn off his frustration with a hike downstream from Devil's Leap, take his fishing pole, maybe.

And work out a new plan.

One thing he'd learned over the years: a perverse elation often followed on the heels of a defeat. It was like discovering a little sliver of light indicating a window in a room you'd thought was airless. All defeat meant was another opportunity to prove himself yet again. And then again. Until he won.

One day, maybe, he'd be invincible.

He especially liked to win when the odds were stacked against him, especially if he had a worthy opponent. It was such a delicious feeling it was a wonder his father had bothered cheating.

Unless you counted that whole choir of cheerful birds singing their heads off in time to the wind soughing through pine boughs, not another soul in the world knew she was standing here right now, at ten thirty in the morning, in front of a house that looked like a giant pink birthday present. She was cleaved between a sort of exultant terror and a strange relief.

It felt like she'd just rescued something in the nick of time. Though she couldn't quite say what or why.

Clean, hard lines—the slant of the roof, the long narrow front porch—met gentle bulges—the turret, the four sets of vast, multipaned bay windows that let in glorious amounts of sunlight, each of them trimmed in a rectangle of dazzling William Morris–esque stained glass across their tops. Two balconies and two wide decks—one above and one below. French windows led out onto the top deck, and she'd once imagined herself bursting through windows like those while she was wearing a gossamer nightgown, the wind whipping her hair out behind her, like a heroine in a Gothic romance. From that deck you could see Devil's Leap, the namesake rock rucked up through the magic of tectonic plates eons ago. It rose twenty feet or so in the air, and in her mind, the smooth granite surface was the size of a Broadway stage.

She was as breathless as the first time she'd heard *Clair de Lune*.

Also . . . kind of like someone had dropped an anvil on her chest.

The driveway was sandblasted smooth, spotlessly white, crack-free and swept clean of leaves and pine-cones and the various animal droppings that tended to wind up anywhere you went in Hellcat Canyon. Her beautiful blue car looked right at home in it.

She finally ventured forward. Glossy, well-established azaleas and camellias hugged the walls of the house and the rails of the porch. A silvery cluster of venerable but still lissome birches arched up from the corner of a lawn which undulated moat-like around the house. It was lushly green and neatly barbered. Ancient oaks with huge heavy branches already naked of leaves for the season now mingled with a full dozen or more other trees, pines and a young redwood, liquidambars, and dogwoods, in a planned yet casual disarray.

She saw nothing that could be construed as super-fluous flora, a miracle considering how opportunistic Scotch broom and Indian paintbrush and firethorn were in Hellcat Canyon. The Harwoods had once found a potato, a carrot, and a little rose growing out in their front lawn. It was always a surprise come spring to see what had gone wayward.

The groundskeeper under contract clearly took the job seriously.

Avalon became aware of a stabbing pain in her hand. She uncurled her fingers and found a perfect imprint in her palm of the house keys she'd been squeezing. They were all hot as little brands and damp with her own sweat.

"Here goes," she breathed. She took a decisive step forward.

Something white darted in her peripheral vision. She spun about.

A white-and-brown tabby cat was staring at her in astonishment, frozen midstride, its front paw in the air. Clearly, he or she had been going about its usual rounds and Avalon was obviously unexpected.

"KITTY!" She realized she sounded for all the world like her niece, Annelise, when she'd first met their cat, Peace and Love, when she was three years old.

The cat turned around and trotted down the flagstone path that made its serpentine way across the lawn. It had a startled rather than a low-to-the-ground terrified gait. It glanced over its shoulder once. Almost as though it *wanted* her to follow it. Or so she told herself.

So she followed.

The flagstone path terminated some ten yards later, and she was now on a sort of paved red-dirt drive liberally sprinkled with gravel. It stretched on for about a hundred feet or so, ending in a barred metal gate about the length of her dad's old blue pickup truck. The gate divided the drive from another long narrow road that led into Devil's Leap from Old Canyon Road.

That was the way her parents had driven them into Devil's Leap during that summer.

Now she realized what a symbolic divide that barred gate was.

Disappointingly, the cat seemed to have vanished. Which was very catlike of it.

Outside of the gate a pair of mailboxes were mounted on wooden posts, which was a bit odd. Surely there was only one house on the property?

She jiggled at the latch of the gate to free it, and then gave it a hearty shove, which made it groan and creak in protest, and walked its considerable weight almost to the far end of the road, until it was most of the way open.

There. *That* was better.

The freshness in the air hit her like a wine distilled from childhood and freedom. From here, she could probably find her way to the Devil's Leap swimming hole with her eyes closed. She'd get there by texture: the scratch of the blueberry vines when you dove down the dirty path, the stones, some smooth, some coarse, arranged by nature, that formed a risky sort of staircase up to the top of the rock—

A text interrupted her reverie. It was Rachel:

The house looks gorgeous! I'll be in Sac tomorrow—how about if I come by around two?

Avalon texted: Perfect!

A little rustle and a thud next to her feet made her jump.

"Well, there you are!"

The cat had long white legs and a brown tabby saddle and its homely face was the sort a child might draw—comprised of spheres and triangles. He was also missing about a third of his tail. But it had a certain rakish nonchalance that conferred presence. He reminded Avalon of Humphrey Bogart.

"Well, hello, Humphrey!" She knelt to get closer to cat height. "Do you come with the house?"

He wasn't wearing a collar but he was plump and a quick peek told her he'd been divested of testicles, so maybe he was someone's pet roaming far afield.

"*Prrrrrp!*" He bumped her hand with his hard little noggin. His eyes were as yellow as doubloons, but little shavings of darker gold floated in there, lending him an air of mystery.

She scratched him under his chin until he purred. She was vaguely aware of other ambient sounds. Squirrels making their scolding chuckling sounds from up in the trees. Was that bleating off in the distance? The creak and scrape of metal. She didn't pay much attention to that last one.

The cat was much smarter.

Its eyes flared hugely and—VROOM! It was out of there.

"*What* the—" Avalon gave a start and turned to look behind her.

Just in time for that long metal gate to collide with her forehead and smack her flat.

CHAPTER 5

She opened her eyes a second later.

She could feel gravel digging into her thighs through her yoga pants.

"Mother *fuck*," she half muttered, half moaned.

"Oh, thank God you're alive. I thought someone might have dumped a body."

She gave a start and turned her head. A pair of denim-clad knees filled her field of vision.

The voice was male, lusciously deep, husked at the edges, familiar in a strange way, Maybe it was the voice of God.

If it was, for just a millisecond there, she hadn't minded being dead.

"Does that happen a lot around here?" she said to the knees. A little woozily.

"Not as often as you'd think, given the remote location."

She hoped he was kidding.

She hoped he wasn't a vagrant or the type that liked to hide from the law in the thick woods here.

She touched her hand to her forehead to check for blood or dents.

She held it in front of her eyes. It came away clean. It sure was stinging, however.

"I saw that gate heading at you and I ran like hell but I couldn't get here in time to stop it."

"There was a cat . . ." she began woozily. "I got distracted by a cat . . ."

"Yeah, that's The Cat."

That really didn't clear things up at all.

"So how are you feeling? How many fingers am I holding up?"

She turned her head to look up.

Just as the owner of the voice bent over her.

Her heart jolted as if battery cables had been applied to it.

Surely only one person in the world had eyes like those: like looking into the shallows of the Hellcat River, through to the fool's gold and river rocks.

She was certain she'd stopped breathing.

"Wait . . . am I . . . am I dead?"

She hadn't meant to say that out loud. In a whisper, no less.

Two straight dark eyebrows made a V when he frowned.

"I have a hunch you got clobbered harder than we thought. Maybe I ought to call an ambu . . ."

A series of subtle emotions whipped across his face like scenery outside a train window.

He stood up abruptly.

And then two swift steps back as if she were a ghost.

Or maybe he was just getting old and needed a little distance to see clearly.

She propped herself up on one elbow. The vertigo she felt when she did that wasn't entirely because she'd been banged in the head. It was because she'd been dragged backward through decades.

For an absurd moment, suspended in time, they stared at each other. The sensation was weightlessness, of all boundaries being kicked away. Like taking an underwire bra off after a long day, only infinitely better.

"Avalon?" He sounded like a spy whispering a password to an enemy guard.

She toyed for a mad millisecond with denying it.

In the end, she said nothing. Mainly because she couldn't speak. Her every cell was preoccupied with singing a sort of ill-advised "Hosannah."

It was resoundingly clear that the proverbial years hadn't simply been kind to him. They had pretty much crowned him their king.

Mac towered now, though. And while his shoulders were doing a pretty good job of blocking the sun, he was still lean as a runner. His dark hair was shorter but still waved a bit up off his forehead; she saw a couple of silver threads.

Finally, his mouth quirked at the corner. "I always knew animals would be your downfall."

He instantly dropped back into a crouch and rummaged about in the little cooler he'd been carrying, then handed her a plastic bag knotted around ice.

"Here. It's been keeping a steelhead trout and a beer cold but I think you're going to need it. Can you sit up all the way?"

She demonstrated that she could sit up all the way by sitting up all the way. She remained on the ground, however.

She wordlessly took the pack and held it to her head. Oh, the bliss.

It did indeed smell like fish.

They still didn't speak. And then he cleared his throat. "It's been a while, huh? I thought for a moment there I slipped through some sort of time portal, Harwood. It's still . . . Harwood?"

She nearly did herself another injury by keeping her neck motionless in an effort not to inspect his hand for a ring.

"Yes." She hated that she sounded subdued. That her voice still sounded dazed and wondering as he'd materialized just like the wizard she'd once thought he was. She didn't trust it yet to tackle multisyllabic words without shaking.

Not a single one of the fantasies she'd had about running into him again had featured her in rumpled yoga pants staring up at him from the ground.

"You kind of disappeared a few years back, Harwood." His tone was light. But there was something a little too careful about it. The way he was holding his body suggested that maybe his breath was held, too.

So. He'd noticed she'd disappeared.

There was no way in hell she was going to reveal to him why.

She shrugged with one shoulder. "Huh. Did I? It was such a long time ago." She gave him a remote little smile.

Something jaded, guarded, and cool moved across his eyes then.

And it was silent.

She gave a start when two squirrels suddenly began chasing each other around and around a pine trunk. Either fighting, playing, or about to have noisy squirrel sex. One never knew with squirrels.

"So how many pets do you have now?" His voice was wry. But a little uncertain.

So he remembered that day, too.

She was shocked by a sudden sense of violation that a person who'd caused her so much pain still walked around knowing the contents of her heart. Her precious memories. The vulnerable parts of her.

"None," she said shortly.

He said nothing. He frowned faintly, as nonplussed and uncertain as if she'd just uttered a word in Turkish.

She craved to know and yet feared to know. But she knew she would have to ask, because if she didn't, it would seem as though it mattered.

"So what have you been up to, Mac?"

She kept the words as offhand and neutral as possible. She didn't want him to think she cared in the least.

"What have I been up to for the past decade and a half?" he said ironically. "Oh, nothing much."

The whole world pretty much knew what became of his dad, so he probably assumed he didn't have to fill her in on that.

His answer was limned in a faint bitterness.

That was the moment she was certain Mac had no idea why she'd disappeared that day. She'd always wondered.

If he'd suffered, that was as it should be.

And she sure as hell wasn't going to illuminate him now.

So they'd established there wasn't going to be any sharing.

"So what brings you back here, Mac? Are you the Phantom of Devil's Leap?"

"I was just about to ask you the same thing. Kind of off the beaten path of any given nature walk. And it's private property."

"Yes. *My* private property."

His whole body went rigid as a fence post. "Come again?"

She rocked her hips a little and fished the keys out of her pocket and dangled them. "I bought the house this morning at auction."

He stared at those dangling keys, transfixed. "*You* bought the house?"

"Yes."

Another wordless moment ticked by.

"*You* bought it."

"Did you drink away the intervening years, Mac? Yes. I bought. The house."

His silence suggested he was struggling mightily to process this.

"So you're the . . ." He pressed his lips together over the colorfully profane word he genuinely wanted to use, though the emotion with which he would have delivered it rather throbbed in the air. ". . . who bought this house out from under me."

I'll be damned, Avalon thought. *Karma might be a bitch, but turns out she has a sense of irony, too.* He must have sent that guy in the suit. Who looked like a very expensive lawyer.

"You know . . . that guy in the suit went as white as his dress shirt when I outbid him. Or rather . . . I guess I mean when I outbid . . . you."

She locked eyes with him.

She wanted to raise one eyebrow like a cartoon villain. She was pretty sure that would hurt, though, so she didn't attempt it.

Mac's eyes narrowed.

And then he shook his head to and fro, sorrowfully, almost paternally. "Avalon. You paid *way* too much."

"Or . . . maybe you just didn't have enough money to outbid me?" She suggested this sweetly, oh so gently, with a sympathetic tilt of the head.

He blinked. His eyes widened in surprise.

Damned if that didn't make him smile faintly, in what looked like genuine pleasure. "Maybe I have a particle of sense. I gave Graybill an explicit cap for a *reason*."

"Maybe I just know what the house could be worth. Some of us have vision."

"Vision, huh? I'm guessing yours is double right about now. You know, kind of like that time you tried to jump Whiskey Creek on your bike. Ava Knievel. Interesting, but I guess not surprising, to learn you've made overreach a life philosophy."

She was perilously close to scowling at him.

She tried that brow arch instead. It worked, but it hurt, and it turned into a wince, which also hurt.

He crouched down next to her instantly. "Look at me," he demanded softly.

The words somehow bypassed her reason. She obeyed him instantly, as if she'd simply been waiting for permission to do that and only that. She looked, and her heart hurt, as if it was unfurling after being curled in on itself, as she took in that familiar, once beloved terrain. The dimple she could nearly always see because he had a way of smiling crookedly, even in repose, as if everything was eligible to be amusing and he wanted to be ready to laugh. That little dent in his chin she could press her thumb into.

A surge of something like wonder, maybe even joy, tensed his features, gone in a flash. She wondered what he saw when he looked at her.

"Just wanted to see if your pupils are the same size and they are. You probably don't have a concussion. You seeing spots, Harwood?" His voice was soft.

"Nope." One frayed, woefully delayed syllable. She wanted to trace those new lines raying from the corners of his eyes with a finger.

As if they were the lines that connected the last moment she ever saw him to this one.

"I am. Thirteen of them. Six on one cheek, seven on the other. I remember, because for some reason I counted them the last time I found you flat on your back after doing something reckless."

Her heart stopped.

The words "flat on her back" instantly conjured that day in his parents' bedroom, the two of them lying side by side, the sun glinting off the hair on his arms, her head against his shoulder. Drunk on a surfeit of slow, endless French kissing. Their hands never wandered much and buttons didn't open but their legs twined and their groins sure did chafe. That was the day she'd made up her mind to let him touch her boob if he tried it.

She scooted back from him now like a hermit crab. As anyone would reflexively retreat from a potential source of great pain. Or a cliff edge.

"Well, this has been an interesting reunion, Mac, but I'm afraid you'll need to excuse me. I have a lot of things to get done this afternoon."

She pretended not to see the gentlemanly hand he extended as she attempted to get to her feet. She managed it with a certain amount of grace. She only staggered a little. She swiped one hand all over her butt and little bits of gravel fell to the ground.

He watched all of this in apparently rapt silence.

She held on to his ersatz ice pack with the other hand, though.

They stood together in silence. It felt reluctant, dense with unspoken things, with grief and joy that felt all of a piece.

"When you open the gate and push it to the side, you need to lock it into place next to the drive. There's a loop there for that purpose. Otherwise gravity will get you every time and it'll swing shut."

"Okay," she said. And then she added, "Thank you."

"Every couple of hours with the ice," he said shortly. "Fifteen to twenty minutes at a time."

"I know," she said, crossly.

"I bet you do."

She did scowl, then.

"You can keep the ice."

"Thanks. It's mostly water now."

"You can keep that, too."

And then another silence ensued.

It occurred to her that he didn't want to move from her any more than she wanted to move away from him. Perhaps it was born of nostalgia for a time when they didn't know all the things they knew now about men and women and hearts and truth.

Though she couldn't, of course, read his heart. After all, she'd been wrong before.

A hick from the sticks, he'd said to whoever called him on the phone that day. Avalon? *She's just a hick from the sticks.*

She realized now, as he stood here, that a part of her had always refused to believe he'd actually meant those words. This part of her, she knew, was not to be trusted. She'd learned that the world was a safer place when you cleaved unto a "what you see is what you get" philosophy. It wouldn't protect you from every shock, of course, like finding your boyfriend in bed with the intern. But it was a pretty good guiding manifesto and the only way she could explain the gulf between what she felt was true and what he'd actually said.

"Mac," she finally said quietly, evenly, "if you've finished with your . . . what is this? A farewell lap of the property? . . . I'm going to take a stroll over to Devil's Leap and climb up there to take in the view."

He hesitated. "Um . . ."

"What?" she said irritably.

"There's just one little issue."

". . . What?" More tersely now.

"Technically you'd be trespassing on private property if you do that."

Foreboding prickled at the back of her neck. Which was the only reason she didn't shout, "YES MY PRIVATE PROPERTY."

"What are you talking about?" She took pains to sound bored.

"Aw, don't tell me you didn't *know*."

She didn't have a smart-ass answer prepared for this, so she opted to remain enigmatically silent. She had a sneaking suspicion she really wasn't going to like the next thing he said, and that Mac, on the other hand, was really going to enjoy it.

"The land here at Devil's Leap is in *two* parcels, Avalon. It always was. The eight acres with Devil's Leap and the swimming hole and the groundskeeper's cottage is over there." He gestured down the road to what looked like a sturdy, weathered box with a roof. She'd thought that was a shed. "The other parcel is the house and the two acres surrounding it. *You* bought the house and the two acres surrounding it."

He said this with the maddeningly patient cadence of a kiddie show host.

"I knew that." She'd tried for insouciance. Her voice emerged a little cracked, however, and a beat after she preferred.

And it was a great big fat lie. In the thought balloon over her head, a cartoon Avalon was kicking another cartoon Avalon over and over.

"Yeah?" he just said, with mild interest.

"I just figured the swimming hole owner would cut his new and closest neighbor some slack and not object to a little nostalgic stroll. Especially since I'm a Hellcat Canyon native and my family has deep roots here."

"Well, I'm sure that all depends," Mac said genially.

"I'll just make him or her an attractive offer for the property." She shrugged as if this was no big deal at all. She wasn't entirely certain how she'd go about doing it, unless she sold a big chunk of GradYouAte stock. She'd spent almost all of her savings.

"Attractive, huh?" Mac mused. Unnervingly, he wasn't blinking.

She didn't say a thing.

"*Why* do you need a house this big, Avalon?" he asked suddenly. "Going to install a husband, kids, a Labrador, a few forest creatures?"

He was fishing: an irrational, reflexive happy stab of gratification.

"Why do *you* want it? Do you plan to install your third trophy wife and a legion of spoiled and ungrateful stepchildren who have run-ins with the law?"

He was amused. "I'm going to fill it with hookers and blow. And rock stars and rappers. I'll have non-stop parties. I'll have limousines and ambulances and helicopters going in and out with equal frequency."

There was a beat of silence.

"Sounds like a good time," she said evenly.

He grinned at that, a slow-spreading, wholly delighted grin, and for a moment time slipped again. At one time her definition of happiness was simple: Mac Coltrane smiling at her.

She'd managed to finally shoot a glance at his hand. No ring.

But that didn't mean there'd never been a wife. Somehow, given his previously outlined views on romance and kids, she didn't think so.

"It's a *house*, Avalon," he said patiently, very reasonably. "I'm going to use it exactly as if it's a house. I'm going to live in it, put my feet up, read Malcolm Gladwell books and listen to NPR."

"Sure you are. Next you'll be trying to sell me the Golden Gate Bridge."

"Given how much you paid for this place, I like my chances of selling you the Golden Gate Bridge."

She heaved a world-weary sigh. "Mac," she said slowly, with as much lofty condescension as she could muster. "Mac, Mac, Mac. What you are failing to understand is that I *did* get a bargain. It's all about being able to see the potential."

She in truth didn't actually think this was quite a bargain anymore, given that it didn't include the swimming hole or the actual rock named Devil's Leap, or the rumored hot springs she'd never seen. Unless they were going by San Francisco standards, in which case the price was practically on clearance.

"Okay. I'll bite, Harwood. You could buy property pretty much anywhere in Hellcat Canyon and build a bigger house from the ground up for half the cost. Why did you have to buy this particular house? What *is* your"—he made air quotes—"'vision' for it?"

She contemplated hedging. It wasn't any of his business, really. But the instinct to impress Mac Coltrane with her maturity and sophistication and cleverness overrode strategy.

It was either that, or challenge him to a footrace to Devil's Leap.

"It's simple, Mac. The house is big and utterly distinctive, there are gorgeous views from nearly every window, and the grounds and the land around it are spectacularly beautiful. All of which makes it an ideal location for a conference retreat and seminar center for Silicon Valley tech executives. The downstairs layout is perfect for workshops and breakout sessions, and the upstairs main rooms are large enough to partition into several additional rooms. Nature hikes and the Devil's Leap swimming hole will be a huge lure. And there's that private airfield nearby at the edge of town, which makes it all that much easier to reach, and adds just a touch more exclusivity to the whole thing. I'm going to do some updating and repairs, and then I'm going to sell it. I actually have a prospective buyer coming in tomorrow."

Mac took this in thoughtfully, nodding along, his eyes going abstracted as if he were watching all of these conferences take place in his mind's eye.

"Corporate retreats? Like . . . tech and gaming douches doing trust falls, and . . . and . . . shit like that? Former frat bros running around this property?"

She opened her mouth. Then closed it again.

Because frankly, despite herself, she thought that was a little funny.

Mainly because it wasn't entirely inaccurate. And Mac never was much of a word mincer.

"Yes. Though"—and she made some air quotes of her own—"'shit like that' is quite a broad umbrella for a lot of other useful activities. And women will be involved, too, of course. CEOs of companies, like myself. It'll be perfect for annual business planning, contract negotiations, takeover talks, seminars . . ."

A faint little dent appeared between his eyes.

Almost but not quite a frown. He held this expression in silence until:

"Over my dead body." But those words were strung like little beads on a filament of steel.

Her jaw dropped.

"*What* the . . . It's not like you have any kind of say in it. IT'S MY HOUSE."

"Right." He said that mildly enough, too. He smiled slightly.

But he wasn't blinking.

He suddenly reminded her unnervingly of his dad. And to this day, Dixon Coltrane remained one of the scarier men she'd ever seen, including the guy who'd pointed a gun at her on Oak Street in San Francisco and demanded her money. Her one and only encounter with him on that fateful day lasted for only the time it took for her to ask where the bathroom was and for him to tell her. He'd told her, so politely it was only later she realized he'd dismissed her as of zero worth to him, the way it was said you barely notice it when a stiletto is first inserted.

She forcibly reminded herself that Mac had gone on to confirm exactly those sentiments in that phone call she wasn't supposed to overhear.

This steely-eyed, coolly smiling man in front of her now made her uneasy. Despite the seductive glimpses of the boy she'd once known—the glinting, decisive wit, the suggestion of gentleness—she was reminded that she knew nothing about the adult Mac.

And it was probably best to keep it that way.

"Well, thanks for the ice, Mac. If you don't mind, I'd like you to wrap up your farewell tour of my property right now. I've got a lot of emails to answer and I need to track down the owner of the Devil's Leap tract and make him the proverbial offer he can't refuse."

"Avalon . . ." he said gently. With just the faintest whiff of exasperated pity. "You're talking to him."

Her silence was almost a tribute to his exquisite timing. She was absolutely certain he'd planned this revelation for this very moment.

For the second time that day she was reminded of who his dad was.

And as she stared at Mac, who appeared calm, and nearly bored, waiting out her next move so he could get the process of vanquishing her over with, a suspicion plinked into her mind like a quarter flipped into a plastic cup: maybe, just maybe, her mom was right: she'd been virtually *inebriated* by fury and shock, and maybe, just maybe, it had resulted in a little madness like any bender. Maybe she was indeed in over her head.

"Well played, Mac. If I hadn't been banged in the head by a metal gate I would have seen that coming a mile off."

The corners of his eyes creased ever so slightly in amusement. Those gold flecks seemed to spark as though they were struck from an anvil.

"Would you have?" All soft sympathy and grave, grave doubt.

Bastard.

"Well, then, Mac, let's discuss the sale of your property. To me. I'll make you a fair offer."

"A fair offer, huh? That's mighty big of you. And you know, I'd be happy to let you use the Devil's Leap property any time you'd like."

"You would?" It was easier than she'd thought.

". . . As long as you sell the house to me."

She heaved a sigh. She'd walked right into that, too. Boy, she needed to get a good night's sleep.

"Mac," she said with great, great, exaggeratedly tender, entirely feigned patience. "That's not going to happen. And ironically, you're kind of trespassing on private property right now. So . . ."

"About that." Mac leaned toward her chummily, as if confiding something he'd overheard at the water cooler. "This is funny, Avalon. You're going to like this."

Which of course meant she wouldn't.

"I have a contract that says I'm allowed to be on this property."

"Why would you have a . . ." She clued in just before he said it out loud.

"Because I'm the groundskeeper."

CHAPTER 6

"**Y**ou're the groundskeeper?"

"Yes."

"You're the *groundskeeper*."

"Funny coincidence, huh?" He smiled at her happily.

The cognitive dissonance was profound. *Coltrane* and *groundskeeper* weren't words anyone had ever included in a sentence, possibly ever.

"So . . . you mow the lawn and trim the hedges and rake and . . . and things?"

"Excellent grasp of the job," he said somberly. "And I'm not only the groundskeeper." He pointed down the road to that little box of a house. It was about as modest as a Craftsman cottage could get. She supposed she'd seen that before, but she'd thought it was a charming toolshed, or some kind of pump house, maybe. "I'm also your neighbor."

He turned back to study her for the impact of this statement.

A teeny part of her couldn't help but think this was funny.

She was speechless, though. About fourteen of those little cottages could have fit into any of the Coltranes' previous homes.

Her first thought was: *my teenage self would never have slept a wink if I knew Mac Coltrane was sleeping nearby.* Her hormones and her every cell would have been permanently set to "vibrate."

Good thing this was not going to be her permanent residence.

"Is that what you, um . . . do? For work? Grounds-keeping?"

"Mainly."

Mainly? It was another way of saying no. She wondered if his side business involved hookers and blow and rappers. Maybe it involved helicopters. The money he'd bid on this house must come from *somewhere* and nobody got rich mowing lawns.

"I keep hearing farm animals," she said suddenly. "Sounds like sheep or goats."

"Those would be my goats."

"You have *goats*?" She rubbed at her hairline. Right about now she would love to be able to blame the blow to her head for the surreal nature of this conversation.

"Well, the goats are my subcontractors. They eat some of the taller grass around this property and mine. And contribute ingredients to some pretty great cheese. I rent out their services locally, too, before fire season."

She was quiet, because what she really wanted to say was "What the *hell*?"

She suspected she now knew how he'd felt when she'd told him she didn't have any pets. As if she was no longer certain this was Mac Coltrane and not an imposter or a hallucination.

As if this were an actual dream, she decided to play along.

"So . . . um. How . . . how did you become the groundskeeper?" It was pretty hard to say that sentence without sounding like Lady Chatterley.

"There was an opening here. I applied. Really, the goats were already here, and they were the selling point."

He was clearly enjoying her discomfiture a little too much. It was pretty apparent there was a lot he was leaving out, and he was doing it just to watch her squirm.

Back in the day, she'd thought he'd told her everything. She'd certainly spilled her heart to him.

But back in the day she'd loved without question because why would anyone do otherwise? She'd thought that if it *felt* like love, then it was. She'd thought that if it seemed like someone loved you, that if someone kissed as though their whole soul was in it, that if they touched you as if it were a privilege and also as if you were beautiful and precious, then they must in fact love you.

Discovering that just because *she* felt something powerfully didn't make it true was one of the most brutal—and probably useful—lessons of her life.

She supposed he'd taken her innocence that way.

Livestock farming, weed-pulling . . . who's the hick now, Mac?

But that wasn't what she actually felt. She felt no triumph or vindication.

From all reports, the bones of the Coltrane family fortune had been picked clean and the marrow sucked out. Every single thing in every one of five grand homes was dismantled, carted away, sold to strangers, the proceeds dispersed to the victims of his father's financial crimes. The houses had gradually been sold off. This was the last one.

She wondered if his Ritchey P-29 was sold off, too.

Something ferocious reared up in her at the thought. As if she could put herself between him and anything that might hurt him. It wasn't rational. She wondered if that made her weak.

"Well. Um. You're doing a great job." Her voice had gone a little hoarse. "The grounds look so clean and pretty."

His eyes went wide with amazement.

Then some emotion she couldn't decipher, something so soft and so fierce her breath hitched, flickered across his features.

And then he pressed his lips together in what looked very like stifled hilarity.

He tugged his forelock sardonically. "Welcome to the neighborhood, Avalon. Guess I'll see you around."

When he bent to scoop up his cooler and turned to walk away, she knew a wayward, surprising stab of panic. As if she were an astronaut out for a spacewalk and her tether had just been cut.

That was how it was with Mac, she realized: to-

gether they'd somehow created an atmosphere of
their own that felt both more real and more intoxicating than the mundane one here on earth.

His shoulder muscles moving beneath his T-shirt
as he walked away were a poignant poetry. New, yet
familiar. She fancied she could still see the outline of
the boy he used to be beneath that big man. And she
could still remember vividly how it felt to hold his
body against hers.

And then he turned around and walked backward
for a few seconds. Even from where she stood she
fancied she could see that dimple, and for an odd
moment, it seemed as significant as the first star in
the night sky. Something you could wish on.

"Every two hours," he called, and pointed to his
head.

Mac stopped just short of his cottage door and
stared at it with some surprise.

He barely remembered walking the hundred-some-
odd yards up the road back home.

He dropped the cooler. He headed for his coffee
pot and dumped the lukewarm brew he found there
in a cup and slammed it into the microwave like he
was wrestling a prisoner into a cell. The days when
he was a snob about coffee were long gone.

Then he retrieved the cup and took a gulp. He literally felt as if he needed sobering after a bender.

And as he held on to it, he realized his hand was
actually shaking a little.

He gave a short, half-astounded, half-scornful laugh at his own expense. But it wasn't every day a guy time-traveled. That moment when realization kicked in his mind had felt scrambled like a satellite transmission at the mercy of a solar flare. No thoughts could get through, only a swarm of emotions, and he'd all but forgotten what to do with most emotions.

He supposed there was a certain poetry in *Avalon Harwood* of all people buying that house out from under him.

He'd never been a big fan of poetry.

Well, sure, there were the ones about the Man from Nantucket that he and his brother had sniggered over when they were adolescents. But poetry often went hand in hand with that shell game people liked to call "romance." It purported to illuminate, and in his estimation it often obscured instead. He was deeply suspicious these days of anything and anyone that didn't come right out and say whatever the fuck they actually meant.

He took another hit of coffee. And winced.

In that article he'd found via Google, her boyfriend, that Tech Doofus who'd gone to Dartmouth, had said things like "The only thing I'm allergic to is the mundane," and she'd said things like "I *love* working all the time." Mac had muttered, "You have *got* to be kidding me," when he'd read that. It was nearly impossible to imagine this was the Avalon he'd known, who'd reveled in her freedom and who had once slaughtered him in a burping contest and had once collapsed, crippled with laughter, when her brother Jude had accidentally farted in the middle of pontificating about some scientific principle.

But there was money in that game she'd helped invent if she could buy this house out from under him, so he had to hand her and the Tech Doofus as much.

She'd wanted to be a teacher because she loved kids and she loved telling people what she knew, and she'd *loved* animals and running around in the wild outdoors. But as it turned out she wasn't a teacher and she had no pets and she was going to turn this beautiful place into a refuge for the kind of people most of the world needed a refuge *from*.

So he'd laid that "I'm the groundskeeper" on her as a sort of little test. Because he was crafty that way. It was true, of course: he was the groundskeeper. But it wasn't the only truth about him.

She could have shoved a snarky dagger right in if she'd wanted to. Her eyes could have registered shock at how far the mighty had fallen.

But no. She'd been kind instead.

He closed his eyes and gave a short laugh. He didn't know what to call that feeling that had been growing in his chest since he'd seen her, like something in him was expanding, the way the universe was said to during the Big Bang. He might have called it happiness except that he'd thought he was pretty happy already. Or, all he'd needed to get all the way to happy was the house.

She'd been tough and dazzling and hilarious back then, but even all of that was fed by a compassion he'd wanted to wade into like a warm sea. It was the lens through which she saw the world.

But he still wasn't going to let her overrun this property with corporate schmucks.

If he'd been brave enough, if he'd really wanted to throw her off her game a few minutes ago, he could have said: I remember exactly what it felt like to pull that soft, soft lower lip of yours between mine, very gently. How we turned kissing into an art form, because it was all we had or, more accurately, all we dared, and like a couple of maestros we found infinite little variations and pleasures in it. But mainly it was pleasurable because we were kissing each other, because the yearning had been like nothing I've ever known since. And I *liked* you so much. And how you smelled a little like strawberries, and laughed so easily, and cried without shame when your squirrel, Trixie, died but never any other time, and never backed down from an opinion when it was something you cared about. And how badly, badly I wanted to have sex with you, so badly I spent a lot of summer nights staring at my ceiling tortured by my imagination, because those were the days long before internet porn. And how I didn't dare press you or me, because I guess I knew all along how easily you gave your heart away to things bound to crush it. Like a squirrel. Or like me.

Because I didn't believe in anything.

And I thought back then that, in the end, I couldn't have you.

He couldn't have pulled that off with any bravado. He wasn't the sort who said that kind of thing out loud. Avalon was the only person who had crept past every single one of his defenses, and judging from how he was indulging in hand-trembling navel-contemplation right now, apparently she still could.

There was also the fact that she was just so damn *pretty*.

So maybe the free and funny and kind Avalon he knew was still in there, layered over with corporate bullshit the way the walls in his parents' bedroom had been layered over with that hideous black-and-gold wallpaper.

It might actually be kind of *fun* to find out.

That was the thing about Avalon: competing with her back then was some of the most fun he'd ever had in his life.

It was pretty clear he couldn't win this particular round through financial means.

But being a Coltrane *did* come with a certain genetic degree of cunning.

He leaned back in the chair in front of his cottage, latched his hands behind his head, and mentally sifted through his conversation with her until he lighted on one critical piece of information.

Didn't she say she had a potential buyer coming tomorrow?

A slow smile spread all over his face. He pulled out his phone.

First, he checked the weather report.

Excellent. Couldn't be more perfect.

He flicked through his contacts and pressed Morton Horton's number.

"Game on, Harwood," he murmured.

CHAPTER 7

BING BONG *SQUONK*!

Avalon jumped and clapped a hand to her heart.

She craned her head and through the beveled glass of the front door she saw a pair of shadows shaped like her parents.

She quickly entered a note on her phone: *Fix squonky doorbell.*

Then she opened the door and her parents stepped wordlessly in the foyer. It was filled now with hazy gold sunshine thanks to a skylight that dizzied with views of blue skies and pine tops above. Below, a black-and-white checkerboard of marble gleamed. The little fang-like crystals on a nearby chandelier sprinkled tiny rainbows on the walls, the floor and, incongruously, her dad's nose.

She'd called her dad a few hours ago to tell them the news, including her plans to flip the house quickly, hopefully to her friend Rachel, to whom she'd texted photos.

"But . . . that place has a *turret*," her dad had finally said in an aghast hush after a long silence. He'd made *turret* sound like *black mold*. "Do you have any idea how much it costs to replace those curved windows in aMMMPH."

His grunt was followed by a lot of crackling and rustling.

"We'll be by around three, honey," her mom said brightly, bravely, resolutely. She'd wrested the phone from her husband.

And now her dad was holding a big box full of things that clinked and clanked. A pot lid was balanced on top. Her mom was carrying the gym bag Avalon had left behind at the house this morning. It was now mysteriously plump.

"We brought you some things we thought might be handy," her mom said.

Their expressions, however, suggested they were picturing her with her toe stuck up the faucet.

"I *swear* to you I did not pull an Oy Vay. I can handle this," she reiterated by way of greeting. "I'm a great project manager and I'm pretty persuasive. Rachel is already excited about it, because it's the kind of space she wants and she doesn't want to do the work. I *know* I can flip this for a profit, even after renovations."

There was a little silence.

"Guess you're going to have to now, eh, pumpkin?" her dad said with mordant resignation. He gave her a shoulder pat.

She took the box from him and the bag from her mom and carried them off to the main room to deposit them on the floor. Her parents followed gingerly through at first, like people trying virtual reality goggles for the first time.

The scale of all the rooms seemed so *profligate*. Ceilings soared up to rounded corners, trimmed all around with stucco carved into birds and fruit and vines. Right smack dead center of the small ballroom (it had a freaking *ballroom*) was a crystal chandelier with as many tiers as a tycoon's wedding cake. The floors were a sea of golden parquet. They really needed refinishing.

She and her parents fanned out like a SWAT team.

Her dad peered into the toilets (most of them tall, old, and rather grand) and flushed them; he tried all the faucets in the bathroom and kitchen (water gushed forth, a little rusty at first); he bounced on the floors to see if they squished around the (clawfoot!) bathtubs. None did. He used a little device to check whether the outlets were working. Three weren't.

Then her dad wandered in one direction and Avalon trailed her mom as her mom poked around.

They were quiet for a while. She knew her mom was starting to relax; she was smart enough and experienced enough to recognize the quality of the place.

"You know, I remember how you used to look at him," her mom said suddenly, running a finger along the grout in the kitchen. Avalon made a note in her phone: *Replace kitchen grout.* She did like the tile, though.

"Who . . . Corbin?"

His name in her mouth felt strange, like she'd been pronouncing it wrong, or misunderstood its meaning, all these years. She'd spent all of fifth grade pronouncing "superlative" as "superlaytive" and had been scorchingly mocked by her siblings when she'd said it out loud at the dinner table.

"Mac Coltrane."

Avalon went still. Hearing his name in her mother's voice was like a sudden little shock, both delicious and painful. Like when she was a kid and rubbed a balloon on her hair and then poked her brother in the arm. She wondered if her mom had any inkling of what she and Mac had gotten up to during the summers between the ages of fourteen and seventeen. Her parents *had* been working pretty hard at the Misty Cat those years.

It wasn't until that day that she realized that Mac had kept their affair a secret because he was *actively* trying to hide it, not because secrecy was more romantic.

"Probably I'd never seen a rich kid before. I probably stared at him the same way I stared at a three-story building the first time I saw one. Or that huge motor home Mrs. Morrison once drove into downtown."

Her mom snorted. "You *were* pretty captivated by that thing. Maybe you should have bought one of those instead of a house. But oh my goodness, look at that *garden*!" She stood on her toes and peered out the huge window over the kitchen sink.

If she let this moment go by without mentioning that Mac Coltrane himself was responsible for how pretty that garden was, it meant she was still keeping him a secret, which meant whatever she felt about him was still raw.

Surely she could handle an offhand mention.

Funnily enough, she let the moment go by.

"I was just thinking about that poor child on the way here." Her mom fingered the doorknob on the kitchen door that led to the garden, her face alight with wistful delight. Brass, carved in scrolls of flowers. She turned it; it came off in her hand.

Her mom shrugged and handed it to Avalon.

"Who, Mac? Poor was the last thing he was."

"Avalon, I think you know what I mean," her mom said with the faintest hint of reproach, which Avalon rather liked, because she frankly liked being known well enough to be called on her bullshit. It perversely made her feel loved.

They both toed at the kitchen linoleum where it was peeling up near the back door. Avalon made another note in her phone.

They heard another flush and the thrum of water rushing through pipes as her dad progressed with thumping feet through the upstairs rooms. Mac's mother's taste was enshrined up on that floor in the form of that hideous black-and-gold metallic wallpaper in the master bedroom and light fixtures on chains, that sort of thing.

"We can ask Truck and Giorgio to help bring the mini-fridge and the sofa from the rec room for you to use in the short term. Oh, and the twin bed from your room and the bean bag chair."

Truck Donegal sometimes played bouncer for the Misty Cat, and Giorgio was the grill savant.

"That would be awesome, thanks. I'm going to sleep in the turret."

"Of course you are," her mom said.

Avalon grinned. She fetched the clinking box to unpack (plates and glasses, potholders, that sort of thing) while her mom wandered back into the laundry room behind the kitchen. Her dad's footsteps thumped directly overhead now. Thud thud thud creak.

Scraping that wallpaper off the walls in there was going to be cathartic. *That's* where she was going to start. After she washed the walls downstairs.

"Mac was sweet." Her mom's voice was kind of muffled because she was peering into the dryer. "And kind of fundamentally lonely, even when he was with you kids. A mom notices these things. I always wanted to hug him but I don't think he would have stood for it. He and his brother were so close, even with the age difference. They always struck me more as allies."

Don't worry, Mom. I hugged him kind of a lot, she thought. *Horizontally, vertically, you name it.*

But there was something satisfying in hearing she hadn't imagined that sweetness. Despite his crackling personality and the half foot in height he had on her, there was a vulnerability in him, a haunting gentleness that was the thing she loved most and made her want to protect him.

She'd written to Mac once or twice during those years, in between the summers. He'd gone to a private boarding school. He was a pretty bad correspondent. Now she thought she knew why.

Avalon suddenly felt the need to defend the girl she once was. "He thought pretty damn highly of himself."

"He did turn into rather an insufferable teenager practically overnight," her mom agreed, equably. She was looking at the washing machine dubiously now. "The way he drove that Audi of his through town! A kid's first car should be at least ten years older than the kid and smell like generations of his family members inside."

Avalon's first car had been a Plymouth Duster that smelled like her grandfather's cigarettes and her brothers' feet. The back seat had been chewed through by her uncle's Boxer, Maxine, and even though they'd stretched a cover over it, at high speeds pieces of fluff would escape and circulate in the car cabin.

The very last time she'd seen Mac Coltrane in Hellcat Canyon he'd been a collection of glints: the shiny Audi his parents had given him for his sixteenth birthday, the flash of his sunglasses, the gleam of the blond hair of the girl next to him. His arm had been slung around her. He'd been eighteen.

She'd made sure he hadn't seen her that day. Part of that was shame and shock over what he'd said. But another wiser, crueler part of her knew the best way to punish him was to take herself away from him.

Her mom pulled open a long narrow cupboard and they found inside a cunning little ironing board. "Avalon, would you look at this!" her mom said. "Isn't this cute?"

"Almost makes me want to wear clothes I have to iron."

Her mom snorted.

They went upstairs, and discovered the fourth stair groaned like a dying person. They found her dad studying a charming little flight of stairs suspended on a set of chains, leading to what looked like an attic door.

Avalon could see at once that his earlier tension had dissolved into a sort of smug satisfaction. "Boy, they don't make them like this anymore," he said. "This place is a beaut. You're going to need to replace at least one of those window frames down here, though, and that's an ugly job. Grout in the bathrooms needs redoing. I'll get Doug out here to check the foundation and have a look at the roof tonight, but seems okay to me. You can get this done by the first of the year, easy, if you plan it right. Maybe sooner."

That was a little over a month away.

"Thanks, Pop. And I promise I won't bug you guys about it."

He just shot her a wry look.

"*Marco!*" Her sister Eden's voice rose up from downstairs.

"POLO!" Avalon bellowed.

They all thundered downstairs to greet her.

She'd sent Eden a quick text with the gist of what had gone down with both the house and Corbin. Eden had sent back an emoji of the scream face, followed by a house, some celebratory confetti, and a question mark. Which about summed everything up.

"Hey! So happy you're here, oy, except for, you know, the *circumstances.*" Eden lowered her voice on the last word as they moved in to give each other a hug.

"Hey, what shampoo is that?" She and Eden were forever sniffing each other.

"I grabbed it because it was on sale at CVS near the register when I was in a rush. It's pale pink, that's about all I know." Eden was busy as hell. A single mom with her own business. The nearest Sephora was hours away.

A colty-legged blur hurtled into Avalon and wrapped her arms around her in a big hug. Annelise had added a pink streak to her hair that made her look like a wild little fairy. She was ten, going on eleven. "Auntie Ava!"

"Baby girl! Good God, Leesy, did you grow five inches since the last time I saw you?" She and Annelise Skyped and FaceTimed, but not as often lately. She just worked so much. She and Annelise got the biggest kick out of each other.

"I'm going to be taller than Mom."

"I'd say that's a safe bet." Eden was long and lean, while Avalon was short and curvy, like her mom. Whoever Annelise's dad was (and Eden wasn't telling) clearly wasn't petite, either. And her sister Eden's continued silence on the subject of who Annelise's father was bothered her parents more than they would ever say out loud. And there was very little her mother wasn't willing to say out loud.

Annelise slipped her hand into Avalon's. "I saw your blue car parked in the driveway, Auntie Ava. It's soooo pretty."

"Thanks, sweetie. I like it, too."

"It's called a douchemobile, right?"

Avalon nearly choked.

"ANNELISE HARWOOD!"

It was an astounded chorus. Four jaws swung open and hung there.

Avalon almost laughed. Boy, when it rained ignominy, it poured.

Eden found her voice and wow, she sure sounded like their own mom. "Annelise Emily Harwood. What in the . . . *where* in the . . . *what* in God's name did you just say?"

"What? What's a douchemobile? What's wrong with saying douchemobile?" Annelise was both genuinely surprised and a little thrilled to have caused such an uproar, and clearly rather savored saying that word again, because she likely had a hunch this would be the last time she'd get to say it.

And now Avalon's parents weren't precisely *glaring* at Eden, but their expressions of mingled hilarity, severity, and alarm did rather demand answers.

"Oh, God, Ava, Mom, Dad . . . I swear I have no idea where . . ." Eden looked wretched. "The internet?" she hazarded weakly. The source of all unknowns.

Pity for Eden surged through Avalon. Her sister always felt as though she was damned if she did, damned if she didn't. "See?" she'd imagine people saying. "Without the bulwark of a complete set of parents, a word like *douche* is bound to creep into a child's vocabulary."

"Hey, Leesy?" Avalon draped an arm around her and scooped her into her side, so Annelise would know she wasn't mad. "My car is actually called a BMW, and it's an awesome car because it's built very well and it can go very fast, so it's fun to drive. But a lot of people who aren't very considerate drive *much* too fast and recklessly in them, which is dangerous and bad. And those people are sometimes called douches, which is another way of saying 'jerk.' But it's not a nice thing to say to *anyone*. You only say it to hurt someone's feelings or if you're being naughty on purpose. So we'll give you this one, but you can't say it again. Deal?"

"Deal." Annelise beamed up at her worshipfully.

Avalon felt a bittersweet pang. The last few years had whipped by in such a blur of work. How had she forgotten how much she just loved hanging out with kids?

Eden shot Avalon a grateful look. "Annelise, where did you hear that word?"

"Megan's brother Tod. He said BMWs are . . . that mean thing I'm not allowed to say anymore." She was a little subdued. She shot a look at Avalon. She was worried she'd hurt her auntie's feelings.

"Megan is . . ." Avalon prompted.

"From Hummingbirds," Eden said. "Ponytails. Little, wiry, and mouthy."

"Hummingbirds are . . ."

"A sort of scout troop. They do crafts, earn badges, shred my nerves, stuff like that. Apparently they also get ad hoc vocabulary lessons when my back is turned." She fixed her little daughter with a quelling stare.

Ava was missing a *lot* of interesting stuff by being away in San Francisco.

"Gosh, Tod sounds like a charming guy," she said.

"He's a senior in high school. He drives a yellow car that has a gray door," Annelise volunteered. "He has a fuzzy mustache." She put her finger beneath her nose.

"Well, that explains a lot," Ava said. "He's probably just a little bitter. Growing a mustache as splendid as your grandpa's takes years. So does owning great cars. Well, usually."

She thought of Mac and the Audi and she wondered what became of that car. If it had been taken from him, too.

"We're sorry if we hurt your feelings, Avalon," Eden said firmly. "Aren't we, Annelise?"

Annelise nodded, big eyes limpid with sympathy. Her hands knit together worriedly. "I really am sorry, Auntie Ava."

"Oh, ha ha, don't be silly. No worries, you guys," Avalon managed gamely. "C'mon! You know me. You'd have to do a lot worse to offend me. Like maybe shtup my inter . . ."

Crap.

Eden closed her eyes and shook her head slowly to and fro.

"What's *shtup*?" Annelise of course missed nothing, including the abrupt loaded little silence.

"I meant to say *stuff*, baby, but I'm so tired my tongue tripped over itself."

Avalon's dad sighed. "I'm going to go outside and poke around a bit. We have to get going but we'll be back with some furniture tonight, eh?" He smooched her on the cheek, and so did her mom.

"We have to roll, too," Eden said. "Annelise has a project on the Greeks due tomorrow and we have to get poster board. Maybe we'll get the full tour later this week?"

"If you can get away, that would be awesome."

Eden squeezed Avalon in a hard hug on her way out and low-voiced her good-byes. "I'll visualize

Corbin doubled over from a groin injury. Maybe I can have the Hummingbirds make voodoo dolls and stick pins in him."

"I'm on board with that. Every little girl needs a merit badge for Revenge."

Eden laughed.

And then everyone was gone.

The quiet in the house was so *complete*. It was like she was a bug captured in a jar. Only the apocalypse would visit that kind of silence upon San Francisco.

She knew if she remained still long enough, the country's ambient sounds would reveal themselves to her. The house would creak and pop and settle with wind and temperature; outside she'd tune into the birds and squirrels, the rustles in the grass and trees.

She opened the sash window in the living room and stood by, listened.

She thought she heard the low hum of a riding lawnmower off in the distance. The bleating of goats.

Her heart gave an involuntary little jolt.

Like a bird pecking its way out of an egg.

She drove downtown and stopped in at the hardware store to buy a slew of cleaning and scraping things, brooms and mops and buckets and sponges and the like, and took home about a ream of those paper paint samples. She stopped in at the grocery store to get some tea and food that could be noshed from a box or heated in the oven. By the time she got back Truck Donegal and Giorgio and her parents had arrived with the rec room couch, the squashy old bean bag chair, a short fridge, her twin bed, a card table, and a couple of chairs. She paid them in beer and pizza.

When they were gone, Avalon threw her yoga pants and T-shirt in the washing machine and found an old T-shirt and leggings her mom had stuffed into her gym bag. She pored over paint samples as if they were the Rosetta stone that would crack the code on all of her life issues, sorting into stacks she considered "probablies," "love but have no use for," and "afternoon light."

By the time the very first star winked on in the purple sky, she was ready to crawl into the twin bed in her turret and sleep like the dead.

The sheets her mom donated were regular old white spares Avalon recognized from the family linen closet, which meant her mom must have upgraded her condition from "suffering" to "doing okay and probably going to survive." She was amused by that subtle vote of confidence.

She slept fitfully, though. It was one thing to be under her parents' roof with the two of them snoring away a few rooms over; here, she was profoundly conscious of being alone in the bed, almost as if she were perched on the end of the world and was in danger of tipping off because Corbin's hot skinny body wasn't next to her to stop her.

She dreamed that it was her job to assign unique color names to everything in the world. Furniture

and bathroom tile and clothes and hair dye and lip-
sticks and animal fur. Her deadline was tomorrow
morning because all of her deadlines were always
tomorrow, forever, and it was already midnight.
Corbin was there, pacing manically to and fro, to
and fro, nervously pulling his fingers up through
the front of his hair in that way he had, over and
over, that she'd once thought endearing and she now
realized was why the sink in their bathroom was
always clogged, and his fingernails were painted
a sparkly orange. And Mac was there, too, in the
background, shooting pool shirtless, because it was
her dream after all. She'd never even seen him shoot
pool, which was kind of odd. Boy, had her subconscious given him a fabulous set of abs. Her squirrel, Trixie, was sitting on his shoulder, and her heart
nearly broke open with happiness when she saw the
two of them together. But with every step she took
toward them, the carpet spread wider and wider, like
an oil stain, and they got farther and farther away.
She stopped trying, remembering her deadline, and
had just decided she'd call the sweater Corbin was
wearing Bastard Orange when she woke up with a
start, heart pounding.

The sunlight squeezing in between the slats of the
blinds (homely ones with chipped edges; she'd want
to replace them) was benign and lemony.

A split second later she remembered Mac Coltrane
was nearby.

And in that undefended moment just after waking,

where her reason was too sleepy yet to corral her heart, it was like an entire sun rising in her chest.

It was telling that Corbin was her third thought.

Funny that her job was after that. Her entire life was enmeshed in something she'd created but patently wasn't missing at the moment.

CHAPTER 8

If she'd had to guess, she'd say it was about eight in the morning, a little later than she normally slept in, on the days when she did indeed sleep in, which had been . . . four years ago, maybe? Life had been pretty much a solid wall of work.

She stretched, flinging out all of her limbs like a starfish, and hesitated before reaching for her phone. She was loath to surrender that fresh, innocent, just-woke-up feeling to reality. And the possibility of a text from Corbin.

She had a few texts; none from Corbin.

Relief lifted her mood again.

From Rachel:

> I'll see you in a couple of hours today! I can't wait to see the place!

Hurrah! She'd be able to replenish her savings sooner rather than later, if her luck held. With credit cards and another scoop into her savings, she could drop about ten thousand on improvements.

From Eden—a photo of that bottle of pink shampoo. Avalon laughed. From Annelise: a photo of her cat, Peace and Love, upside down in the sun. One from her mom: Let us know if you need anything!

Both excellent ways to start her day.

She texted all of them *X*'s and *O*'s and a quick pic of the view from her turret window.

Then she went downstairs, made some tea, ate one of her store-bought muffins, curled up on the giant old sofa in the sunny room with her laptop, fielded a few GradYouAte emails (she'd sent the cheerleader avatar art back to the drawing board, with a sardonic, "Surely not all cheerleaders are blond?") clicked "like" on a friend's Facebook photo of her baby with cake smeared on its face, then got sucked into a YouTube video about pangolins. All the while she was aware of a very potent urge hovering on the periphery of her awareness like a teenager outside a 7-Eleven waiting to hit up a grownup to buy beer.

She finally caved to it: she typed "Mac Coltrane" into the search window.

As she'd done at least a half dozen or so times before in her life.

And as with every time she'd done it, her heartbeat picked up speed.

Nothing new was revealed. There was the Mack Coltrane in Nebraska, a smiling professor who was a Sylvia Plath expert. "Maximilian" also yielded exactly nothing beyond the odd mention in old articles about his dad. *Lots* of those.

His life was pretty inscrutable.

And then a lightbulb pinged on over her head, and she typed in Devil's Leap, doing the deeper search she ought to have done the other night. She learned that the last known sale price of the parcel at Devil's Leap was ninety-eight thousand dollars, sold to Graybill Sutherland LLC.

Ah. Mac must have bought it through Graybill. Doubtless he'd had enough publicity to last anyone a lifetime.

She turned toward the window she'd struggled earlier to open a few inches; through it came a grassy-scented breeze and the unmistakable sound of a mail truck trundling down the road. It was about eleven. She decided to go down to the mailbox to see if Enrique had overnighted her anything interesting.

She could feel the house looming behind her as she followed the flagstones down the walk and across the lawn. Maybe not so much looming as . . . peering. In a companionable fashion. Like a loving partner trying to help with the crossword clues over her shoulder, not like some thug hovering behind her at the ATM trying to steal her password.

She slowed her pace when she reached the gate that had clonked her head.

Then stopped.

A man was sauntering up the dirt road parallel to hers, toward Devil's Leap swimming hole.

Even from a distance she knew instantly it wasn't Mac. One encounter with him yesterday had reminded her that his presence disturbed the air around her the way bubbles disturbed champagne.

As he drew closer, she saw that this guy was wearing hiking boots with white socks poking out of the tops and a blue baseball cap that said NPR.

And nothing else.

"Morning," he said cheerily, and touched the brim of his cap. "Nice day for it, huh?"

He sauntered on, whistling something that sounded like that song by The Baby Owls, the one about going around and around in the forest. There was a little spring in his step, a little white cooler in one hand, and a furled striped umbrella and what looked like a rolled towel tucked into his armpit.

She rotated slowly, slowly, slowly, to watch him go.

He had broad shoulders, a big, comfortable hairy stomach that provided a modest awning for his penis, which was nevertheless present and accounted for, unassuming, perfectly ordinary of size and proportion, and minding its own business.

"Morning," she parroted finally. Faintly.

Though he was already making his jaunty way around the bend in the road and there was no way he could have heard her.

She'd lived in San Francisco a good decade or so, and during that time there wasn't much she hadn't seen there. And though it was hardly an everyday occurrence, she was no stranger to naked people cropping up where you didn't expect to find them. It didn't really make it any less startling. I mean, you always knew the jack-in-the-box clown was going to eventually pop out of the box when you spun the crank, but didn't everyone still jump a little each time it did?

But no one blinked at anything crazy in San Francisco. And you did get a sense for when something had veered outside the usual tolerable weirdness into the realm of threatening.

This guy hadn't felt the least threatening.

Frowning thoughtfully, she pivoted back to the mailbox.

And froze.

Two more naked-save-for-hats—his the baseball variety, hers a vast, navy straw-and-polka-dot confection she could have worn to the Kentucky Derby—people were advancing up the road, each carrying a beach tote and a cooler and a rolled-up towel. The woman was wearing those expensive, highly engineered–looking sandals favored by women who had said "up yours!" to the tyranny of fashion in favor of comfort, which made Avalon decide they were about her parents' age.

"Morning," they sang out happily.

"Hi!" The effort to sound nonchalant sent Avalon's voice out about three octaves higher. "Where are you off to on this beautiful day?"

She should have anticipated they would stop.

Dear God, where did she park her eyes? On their eyes.

On their naked, naked eyes.

"Devil's Leap, dear." The woman gestured. "That's where the party is today."

"Party?"

Behind them, a half dozen or so more naked people

had appeared, smiling, chattering, and wearing sensible shoes, sun protection for their heads, and nada in the middle. A quick glance told her that no one had subjected their body hair to the kind of rigorous shaping Casey at the Truth and Beauty, for instance, would have applied. No triangles or hearts or landing strips. It was a free-for-all. The same applied to the bodies.

"But . . . isn't Devil's Leap Mac Coltrane's property?"

"Oh, Mac called me yesterday and said we could hold our clothing-optional weekend at the Devil's Leap swimming hole. Morty's been asking him for ages," the woman in the navy hat told her.

Suddenly it *aaalllll* made sense.

And like a wishbone she was yanked between feeling *incensed* and thinking it was the funniest, most original damn thing.

Sauntering in the middle of the nude people was a clothed guy who, by virtue of the glorious way the olive-green long-sleeved T-shirt stretched across his chest and the way a pair of soft, old jeans hugged his hips, seemed more naked than all of them.

"Good morning, new neighbor," Mac said to Avalon. "I see you've met Morton and Helen Horton."

"Not formally." It felt odd to use the word *formal* when nearly everyone in this conversation was naked. "Wait . . . your name is Morton Horton?" She swiveled her head toward him.

"It's a great name, isn't it?" he said happily.

"It really is." There was no denying that, at least.

"Mac here is an old national guard buddy." Morty jabbed a thumb in Mac's direction.

Avalon pivoted. "*You* were in the national guard?"

Mac briefly looked cornered.

Morty answered for him. "Heck yeah. Mac was an engineer. You name it, he can build it, fix it, plan it, finesse it, coax it."

"I can't build an imaginary school for grownups to play in on their phones or anything," Mac said modestly. "Just bridges, engines, buildings . . . things like that."

She narrowed her eyes at him. Unsurprising, perhaps, to know that Mac had spent a little time on Google and was probably up to speed on Avalon and GradYouAte.

"What happened, Mac? Did you lose a bet? Get drunk and enlist? Flee a paternity claim?"

"Is all of the above an option?" he suggested.

She didn't answer that, because more naked people were filing down the road.

Avalon cleared her throat. "Okay, now, while I'm not remotely a prude . . ." she began brightly.

Morty's and Helen's smiles evolved into something indulgent and sympathetic, a touch cynical. Which was when Avalon realized nothing made a person sound more like a prude than saying "I'm not a prude."

"Pretty uninhibited, are you?" Mac said idly, flipping through his mail as though he was looking for something in particular.

They all waited politely and with apparent benign interest for her answer.

Mac finally looked up, raising his eyebrows coaxingly. His face was solemn but his eyes were full of wicked, insufferable glints.

She cleared her throat. "I think I'm pretty open-minded and accepting. I mean, I went to the Folsom Street Fair in San Francisco and I saw a guy leading around another guy who was wearing a leather harness, like a pony. No biggie."

Now they were *all* studying her a little skeptically, as if Avalon might be an actual perv. Skeptically, and a little pityingly.

"Oh, honey," Helen said warmly, "that sort of thing is a little outside of our experience. We just take our clothes off. It's not much more complicated than that. We don't put on leather harnesses or anything that might go up our heinies or in our mouths and the like. I imagine they would chafe quite a bit." Helen rotated her shoulder, apparently imagining it. "We're not crazy about chafing, as you can imagine, which is one of the points of going clothing optional. But to each his own," she added magnanimously, laying a gently placating hand briefly on Avalon's shoulder.

Avalon wasn't crazy about chafing, either. And her nerves were chafing big-time right now. These naked people were very nice. Even though their presence could spell disaster for her plans to sell the house to Rachel.

"Once the renovations on the house are completed,

corporate retreats will be held here, and visiting executives may find nude strollers and swimmers a little startling. Perhaps a bit counter to the image they'd like to be cultivating," she explained, with as much diplomacy as she could manage.

"I imagine you'll work something out with Mac about that sort of thing. You seem like a bright, competent young woman."

Helen was probably a retired schoolteacher. She clearly had an "accentuate the positive" approach to life.

"That's kind of you to say," was all Avalon could manage for now. She studiously did not meet Mac's eyes. She didn't need to. She could practically feel the rays of his wickedly amused triumph from where she stood.

"I wish Mac would join us. He's always good for a laugh," Morty volunteered.

"Me, I'm a little shy," Mac said. "I'm not uninhibited like Avalon here."

Avalon shot him a look that by rights ought to have singed his hair.

He gazed back at her with limpid hazel eyes.

Morty gave Mac a little back thump. "Someday you'll be my age and you won't give a crap about what anyone thinks you look like. And that, my dear boy, is called being comfortable in your own skin. Maybe it's why our skin gets looser as we age. It's metaphorical. It gets roomier outside because we all feel roomier inside."

And with that philosophical gem he winked at

Avalon and gave Mac another chummy back thump and trundled unconcernedly on down the path, Helen alongside him. She called, "Lovely to meet you, Avalon," over her shoulder, and Avalon was pretty sure she meant it.

"See you at the meeting, Mac!" Morty called.

What meeting? Smartasses Anonymous?

Avalon watched them until they disappeared around the bend in the road that led to the rock.

Morty's butt was broad and perfectly square, like the cushions on her parents' living room sofa, and traced by curly hair all around, like Christmas tinsel around a window. It was a sort of Almond Sunrise. Or Winter Blossom. Helen's butt was reminiscent of a pair of empty, medium-sized handbags hung side-by-side. Morning Latte, she'd call the color. Or maybe Misty Mocha.

They looped their arms around each other and Helen tipped her head against his shoulder and she laughed at something Morty murmured.

Dozens of conflicting emotions assailed Avalon then. Oddly, the most piercing was envy. And if envy was a stab, then yearning was a pull. She knew she was witnessing happiness and comfort and abiding love and two people clearly meant for each other.

And as she watched them stroll off, she was 100 percent certain she'd never known that kind of love as an adult.

She drew in a breath and tore her eyes away from them.

Right up into Mac's hazel gaze.

She'd startled him in the midst of some fascinating indecipherable expression.

He hadn't been watching Morty and Helen.

He'd been watching her.

"Don't think I don't know what you're up to," she said, finally, conversationally. The nonchalance she delivered that with was a supreme effort.

He tipped his head quizzically. "Up to?"

"I mean, I've *seen* naked people before."

"Yeah?" He dropped his gaze again and feigned abstraction as he leafed through his mail, flyers and periodicals and bills, from the looks of things, and he paused to frown at a manila envelope. "Have you now? In quantity? Good heavens, Avalon Harwood, what kind of company have you been keeping?"

He kept his face lower, but she didn't miss his little smile.

"Well, you know how San Francisco is."

He looked up at her then, and something about the shift in his stance told her he was about to deliver a coup de grace. "I happen to know there are no hippies left in San Francisco. They were priced out. They have to import the weirdos and eccentrics and free spirits now, and they go home to other cities during the day. Everyone's a workaholic and no one thinks about sex. The Summer of Love it ain't."

Damn. So he did know how San Francisco was. Jefferson Airplane and the Grateful Dead and all those guys wouldn't recognize the place today.

"Which is why I'm sure your corporate millionaires and other geeks on retreat here in Hellcat Canyon would find an unpredictable parade of middle-aged nudists . . . refreshing," he continued.

Mac met her eyes, *kapow*, the better to savor her reaction. "It might make them nostalgic, even, for that time of free love . . . and so forth."

This was so brilliantly played she was arrested by admiration. She had every faith it would give way to anger in a second or two.

Because the moment he said "sex" that's all she was thinking about, and yet she couldn't quite remember the last time she'd had any of that, the same way she couldn't remember the last time, say, she'd had a piece of toast, though surely it wasn't that long ago.

She honestly couldn't think of a single tech worker she knew who could say the word "hippies" without snorting. Or who would willingly whip off their hoodies to reveal their skinny bodies, untouched by the sun in eons thanks to San Francisco weather and all that work. Let alone whip off their *undies* in front of their coworkers. It would take an awful lot of alcohol or some truly splendid Burning Man–caliber drugs.

Rachel was pretty cool, but she was a businesswoman after all. She wasn't going to want a property adjacent to a part-time nudist colony.

Avalon was going to have to keep her from coming out here today. She fidgeted with her phone, clutched in her fist.

Mac's eyebrows went up, urging her to say something.

"You don't know what you're up against, Mac," she said idly.

"Don't I?" he said softly, sympathetically.

She didn't like that. It reminded her of the times she'd been up against him. And how it clearly hadn't meant much to him.

"How's your head, Harwood?"

"Harder and cooler than ever," she said tersely.

"You have a little bruise. Blue's not a bad color for you, though."

"Such a relief to hear I'm not an eyesore."

It was like a thousand new suns were born in her chest when he smiled slowly at that.

She fought the feeling as if she was actually being sucked into an orbit. She realized that at no point had Corbin ever made her feel as though she could lose herself in him and not even notice. Her boundaries had never been compromised.

"I hear . . . do I hear chickens?" she said suddenly. That muffled, contented little *bock bock* sound was almost as good as a cat's purr.

"Those would be my chickens."

"You have *chickens,* too?"

"Yep."

She was silent, and he studied her face as if she herself were the results of a Google search. "You want to pet them, don't you? You want to pet them and give them names."

"No," she lied, swiftly.

This made the corner of his mouth dent.

Though she did wonder why they didn't have names. Maybe because he ate them.

She was suffused with a million questions, but equally determined to continue proving she did not give a crap about him. But *why* had he joined the national guard? She was pretty sure that was at least an eight-year commitment, including active and reserve duty.

Her stomach reflexively contracted at the notion that someone might have shot at him, the same way she'd been panicked at the idea of someone taking away his P-29. She couldn't help it.

"So how's your brother? Is he a 'farmer,' too?" She air-quoted *farmer*.

It seemed safer to ask about somebody else first, to go at it obliquely. He might slip up and reveal more about himself. He and Ty had been so close.

"I don't know," he said shortly.

"*What*?" She hadn't meant to sound surprised.

"I. Don't. Know," he repeated evenly, slowly, patiently.

But a chilliness had crept into the words.

"But . . ."

He waited.

He didn't issue the usual "but what?" as a prompt.

She had a feeling they'd be standing here like this until California broke off into the sea if she didn't speak. The man was nothing if not stubborn.

So she spoke.

"I'll give you a hundred thousand for your Devil's Leap land."

His eyes flared in surprise. And then something very like bald admiration flickered and heated them. They locked gazes. His became a trifle lazy.

"Silly girl," he said fondly, finally.

WOW.

It was the *perfect* response. Because it made her want to deck him, and he knew it.

And he knew *she* knew why he'd said it.

Which is why his smile got a shade more wicked. Daring her to react. Inviting a response he could parry.

Damn, but he was a competitor, in ways both subtle and overt. He always had been, of course. Perversely, it was as invigorating as walking into a blast of cold air whipping off the sea.

It made her doubly determined to win. *I'm no hick from the sticks, Mac. I beat you before and I'll do it again.*

A little rustle made her turn toward the bushes. The brown-and-white cat emerged and sat down next to Mac like a spaniel called to heel.

It was all Avalon could do not to drop to her knees and coo at it. She yearned to pet it.

"Hey, cat," Mac said nonchalantly to it. It was ridiculous, but in that moment it felt like he was actually rubbing in the fact that he had a pet, even if he couldn't be bothered to give it a name.

"Well, guess I'll see you around the grounds, neighbor." Mac turned around.

The cat did, too.

"Oh . . . I meant to tell you. Whatever you do, don't go up in the attic."

And with that enigmatic little warning, he strolled off, whistling a little tune.

It sounded like the Jefferson Airplane's "Somebody to Love."

Hey Rach! Can we do a raincheck on lunch today? Sorry! Something came up.

She sent the text immediately. Then she took her laptop out onto the upper story deck to answer GradYouAte-related emails. They wanted her to approve the revised art for the cheerleader module—which was her idea in the first place, just like GradYouAte. She referred them to Corbin.

But all afternoon pale butts twinkled and flashed in her peripheral vision as bathers scaled Devil's Leap and leaped merrily into the swimming hole, their peens and boobs cheerfully flapping as they sailed down. KERSPLASH! Laughter swelled and ebbed and echoed, voices cheerfully shouted to each other. All those naked people out there were having the time of their lives. Being who they were. Doing what they loved. Absolutely unashamed.

And here she sat, feeling so hollowed out with vague yearning and restlessness it was a wonder a wandering breeze didn't coax a note from her, as if she were a didjeridoo.

Finally, she gave up, propped her hand on her chin and glumly watched the frolickers. She scratched beneath her bra strap.

All at once it felt like a little lace-and-wire jail.

She scrabbled underneath her T-shirt and unhooked it as if it were an octopus that had her in its death grip. Then with a series of shrugs she wriggled from the straps and yanked it out of her shirt sleeve, no mean feat, and hurled it in a fit of pique across the deck.

Whereupon it disappeared over the side.

Surprise, surprise. She'd overshot the mark.

CHAPTER 9

She abandoned the email answering a few minutes later and, on the theory that a little exercise might burn off her restless mood, began washing the walls in preparation for painting them.

And then she saw them: the Bluetooth speakers she'd hauled in from her trunk, the ones she was supposed to give to Corbin. They were a dazzling bit of technology that could make your house sound like Coachella was trapped inside.

Or . . . outside.

She abandoned the wall washing.

And set to work with the cool-headed purpose of an assassin assembling a bomb.

She was just ahead of him, so close her hair flew out behind her and lashed his face. His lungs burned with the effort to keep up.

She scrambled up Devil's Leap as nimbly as a mountain goat, and he was just about to reach out, to drag his fingertips along her shoulder blades in a tag, to make her turn around so he could pull her into his arms. Something seized him by both arms and yanked him back so hard his head snapped; he looked down upon the strong hands of his father, that old gold wedding ring, the hairy forearms, the tendons straining as they gripped him fast. And as he fought to free himself, Avalon stopped and looked at him then, her eyes radiating warmth. She stretched out her hand and uncurled her fingers; in her palm was the little stone heart he'd found for Trixie the Squirrel's grave. Then she spun around and hurled it far, far out into the water. It sank below.

She leaped in after it. She sank. And didn't come up.

"Avalon!" he screamed, his feet scrabbling in place like Fred Flintstone in his little car. And finally his father's hands were gone. Instead, one of his favorite goats, Baaa Baaaa O'Riley, was standing up there with him.

"You win some, you lose some," the goat said.

Which struck Mac as a pretty cavalier thing for a talking goat to say. "That's not very nice," he said, quite stung.

And then the goat opened its mouth and screamed and screamed and screamed.

Holy fucking—!

Mac jackknifed out of deep sleep into a sitting position, his heart pounding like a floor tom, his arms helicoptering around his head reflexively to ward off an attack.

He was panting as if he'd actually made that run all the way up to the rock.

That was it: *no* more pizza before bedtime.

His lungs were still heaving. Which was why it took him another millisecond to become aware that it wasn't a goat scream that had terrified him out of sleep. Rather an *actual*, keening, tormented cry had sliced right through his dreams like an icy cutlass.

Gooseflesh raced over his body. All the hairs on his skin leaped erect.

What the fucking *hell* was that?

A . . . siren? An air raid?

No. No siren could sound so sort of . . . *personally* anguished.

The sound was definitely human.

In a single fluid motion he scrambled nudely up out of bed, seized his twelve-gage shotgun, shoved the window up, and cocked the gun.

The sound rose and fell. Dirgelike.

It was actually another second or two before his violated senses and assaulted nerves could reassemble and work together to draw a conclusion. And when he did he slammed the window shut again and stared at it blankly.

Oh, yeah. It was human, all right.

A very particular human: Melissa Manchester.

More specifically, it was the Melissa Manchester song "Don't Cry Out Loud."

From the sound of things, broadcast through speakers the size of boxcars.

Every wailed note and histrionic piano chord was delivered with pristine clarity.

He moved gingerly, slowly, pensively, locked his gun and hung it back up on the wall.

He tentatively opened the front door. He was tempted to hold his breath, as if he was plunging into noxious gas. He stepped outside.

Holy *shit*.

However it was accomplished—God knows they made teeny speakers these days that could produce just about the same amount of noise—the sound *felt* loud enough to crumble the walls of Jericho, or to be mistaken for the kind of fracking that could cause earthquakes three states away.

He was held motionless in a veritable net of sound. It was like the trees, the hills, the very ground and air were singing.

Singing the worst, the *worst* song in the whole world.

The execution of this fiendish plot had been diabolically skillful.

He stood, still naked, in that storm of sound, buffeted by a full dozen more emotions, which was about double the number that had even twinged him in the last few years.

But he was shocked by the impression he decided to nourish.

It was: *she remembered.*

Avalon remembered I hate *that song.*

He'd mentioned it to her maybe once in his entire life, and there was a very good reason why he'd never mentioned it again.

But she'd remembered.

He imagined a shrink would have a *field* day with

the fact that, in the middle of his righteous and quite justified outrage, a perverse little pilot light of joy glowed.

Because if she'd remembered a stupid little thing like that, he had a hunch she remembered every-thing. Because that's what you did when someone meant something to you. You hoarded every little detail you could.

How long had it been since he'd felt truly known? Something in him that he hadn't known was tense shifted a little. Like he'd been given just a skosh more leg room on a flight.

He stood there until the song ended, as if to make sure an attacking army really was in retreat.

He sucked in a long, long breath, as if the air was finally clean again.

Well. Points to Avalon. It was a *helluva* way to wake up.

He turned and went back into the house, hefted a bag of kibble and poured some into The Cat's bowl.

The Cat, unoffended by being jounced out of bed unceremoniously by Mac's sudden leap out of it and who had in fact hopped back in and stolen his warm spot, jumped down, did a sort of nonchalant down-ward dog stretch and headed for his bowl. The Cat always rebounded swiftly from the many vicissitudes of humans, and never seemed to hold any grudges. In this way he and Mac were probably a little different.

Mac stepped outside again and stretched his arms luxuriously upward into the chilly morning. He'd been contemplating planting about a quarter acre with winter crops, and he needed to clean up the rest of the hydrangeas he'd trimmed behind the Devil's Leap house and get as much work out of the way as possible during this warm spell, including trimming branches near the roof and cutting back the oleander.

He started the coffee, pulled on some clothes, and dozily communed with six deer moseying down the road, who all turned big limpid brown eyes on him, eyes which reminded him of the very person who was torturing him with Melissa Manchester.

The Cat came to sit next to him and wash his face. Mac always talked to The Cat. "Looks like it's going to be a beautif—"

DUN dun DUN dun DUN dun . . .

He froze, blank with a sort of dark amazement as the sound hammered his nerves like they were piano strings.

The motherfucking song was starting *all over again*.

Well.

Now he knew how it would go down.

It was horrible. And original and impish and *fiendish*. Precisely the sort of thing he'd expect from the girl who'd once turned the top of Devil's Leap into a tap dancing stage, who had once put acorns into an Easy-Bake Oven recipe and had then needed to go to the hospital for a stomach ache, who had suggested they all pretend to be mummies and walk off the edge with their arms outstretched. What if she did this every day?

Now the game really was on.

Later, when he stalked down to get his mail, Avalon was standing at the mailboxes, shuffling through hers like a Vegas gambler who knows she has the winning hand. He had a hunch she'd been waiting there for him to show up.

"Oh, hey, Mac."

"Kicking out the jams today, are we, Avalon?"

She looked up, her velvety eyes innocent and questioning. "Don't you like my taste in music?"

"IT'S NOT MUSIC AND IT'S NOT TASTE."

Her eyes widened very slightly.

He took a subtle breath.

"Gosh, I didn't mean to *upset* you, Mac," she said very, very mildly. A little furrow crumpled the smooth tawny skin between her brows.

"I'm not upset," he modulated, perhaps a little too much. Because now he sounded like an announcer on NPR. He'd tried to work with earplugs in. It hadn't quite done the trick.

"Well, it's just that you raised your voice just now," she pointed out, reasonably, and still so, so sympathetically.

"Well, it's just that I thought I needed to because I thought you might be losing your hearing in your old age. Given the volume of your chosen 'music.'" He bent his fingers in air quotes around that last word.

"Ohhhhh, *that*. I just wanted to be able to hear it wherever I went in the house. And it's a big house. As you know. Cavernous. So roomy and so comfortable and so very, very . . . mine."

A bird oblivious to the gravity of their showdown trilled like it was Beverly Sills and this was *La Traviata*.

"Don't you think the birds and the squirrels and deer mind the noise?" Mac suggested.

"Don't they mind the *music*, you mean?" she corrected, her nose wrinkled fetchingly in faux confusion.

"I meant the noise," he repeated evenly.

She shrugged indolently with one shoulder. "Animals often love music, Mac. I'm sure they'll get used to it. It's just that I sometimes get in the mood for an inspirational, motivational ballad. And I never know when the mood might strike. Sometimes it strikes very, very late at night. Sometimes it doesn't ease up until morning."

"Is that so, Avalon? Get lonely and bored late at night, do you, these days? Need to burn off a little angst?"

He detected a blip in her aplomb. A hesitation.

That was interesting. What was up with the boyfriend?

"Why *do* you hate that song so much?" she asked suddenly.

"I hate the belabored circus metaphor, what with the clowns and tightropes and whatnot. I hate that she's advising people to keep all the feelings inside, which, my God, strikes me as *terrible* advice. And that she's actually yelling about *not* crying out loud, which, I mean—how does that make any *sense*? I don't like advice yelled at me from a song."

"I think Miss Manchester would characterize it as singing," she said finally. Sounding subdued. But she looked dazzled. Her eyes were lit with hilarity.

"Miss Manchester would be deluded."

"She has some good songs. 'Midnight Blue.' Pretty good song." Now she was messing with him.

He waved this opinion away with an impatient chop of his hand.

"I like songs like . . . like that Baby Owls song. About being lost in the forest and going around and around and around. Perfectly adequate lyrics. Keep it simple. Lost in the forest, going round and around and around. Happens to someone every day, right? Not this sentimental histrionic dreck."

"Yeah, but that Baby Owls song is kind of existential, when you think about it. The round and around is meant to symbolize the circle of—"

Mac clapped his hands over his ears. "LALALA-LALALA."

She smiled.

He smiled, too.

"You used to like Roxy Music," he ventured quietly, into the delicate, soft little silence.

"Maybe my tastes have changed."

"Maybe you're lying."

She didn't disagree with this. But she was restless now; her eyes had gone guarded and cool.

"I think the only stupid thing about that song is

that the singer gets back up on that tightrope over and over even though she falls off and gets hurt over and over again. Every time."

That sure sounded like a message. Maybe a warning.

He didn't much care for innuendo. Some instinct of self-preservation prevented him from poking at it.

"Hey, Avalon?" Mac said suddenly. "You know what else the deer and squirrels might not appreciate?"

He reached into his back pocket and withdrew the thing he'd found while he was trimming back some oleander. He gave a little flick of his wrist.

Her blue bra unfurled and fluttered in the breeze, twisting and dancing gaily from his fingers.

"Littering," he said.

She stared at it. Hilarity and outrage mingling in her face; her cheeks went pink. It was about as adorable as it gets.

Then she snatched it from his fist. "I was wondering where that got to," she said.

She was smiling when she returned to the house. Despite herself. It was just that Mac's explanation for why he didn't like that song was so at the ready, so idiosyncratic, so *him*, that everything in her leaped with pleasure at its force and originality. She remembered that Mac had kind of felt, in fact, like a song you could really dance to. Or the kind like, say, "Stairway to Heaven," with soft parts and loud parts and crescendos.

And she was happy to get her bra back.

And she understood something else clearly in that moment: Corbin's ethos of rejecting anything commonplace did not in and of itself constitute taste. Or a personality. It was what he did because he didn't know himself; it was what he did because he feared, and probably rightly, that he just wasn't terribly interesting.

It was quite an epiphany.

And Mac had remembered about Roxy Music.

Something soft, something perilously teenage, something that felt like hope, turned her insides tingly until she ruthlessly squelched it. After all, he'd soundly mocked her fantasy about slow dancing out there on Devil's Leap. And he was still that guy who had no patience for spectacle.

So she kept "Don't Cry Out Loud" going at whimsical intervals all day while she washed her walls. Just to show him she meant business, until about nine thirty at night.

Which was when the fuse blew

Instant blackness was accompanied by a sort of groaning sigh that spelled the expiration of all lights and appliances.

She froze where she stood, a Hot Pocket with one bite out of it clutched in one fist and a Jellystone Park glass full of iced tea in the other.

"Huh."

The living room had become a cavern. The corners she'd swept so thoroughly were suddenly dense with shadowy mystery. Out the big windows the dark was that kind of thick-textured, velvety purple dark that you only get in the country. Trees speared up into it.

She used a slanting stripe of moonlight as a road to get to the couch, which was where, serendipitously, she'd propped her lantern. She settled her Hot Pocket and her tea down on the overturned box reincarnated as a coffee table, curled up on the sofa that smelled like her family's rec room and therefore her family, and pressed a number on her cell phone.

"Hey, pumpkin."

"Hey, Dad. When you were prowling around outside, did you happen to notice where the breaker box was? Asking for a friend."

A little silence, during which he probably stifled an "I told you so."

"So are you sitting there in the pitch dark?" He sounded amused.

Her dad was smart.

"I have my lantern. And the glow of my cell phone. And the moonlight is rather picturesque on these hardwood floors. It's illuminating all the scratches." She aimed the lantern beam at the back wall and made a shadow dog with her hand. That was a mistake. In this light it looked more like the Loch Ness monster than a dog and there were enough unidentifiable shadows as it was.

"That house has a fuse box, not a breaker box. It's outside behind that little round door. You got any fuses handy?"

"Sure, Dad, I got a whole box full of fuses right here."

"You *do*?" Her dad sounded so touched and thrilled she was instantly filled with remorse.

"Sorry, Dad. I shouldn't tease you like that. Do fuses even *come* in boxes? Can you order them with an app?"

He snorted. "Do you have lights in the other parts of the house?"

Ava cast her gaze up the stairs. The entire flight was so dark she couldn't distinguish one step from another from where she sat. The light switch at the top might as well be down a deep, dark well. Moonlight threw shivering shadows of pine boughs against the wall, thanks to the big windows.

"Mmm, yeah," she said vaguely. "I think so."

"What were you doing when you blew the fuse?"

"Um . . . listening to music and heating something up in the microwave." It wasn't a total lie, but she crossed her fingers. "I think the refrigerator is on that fuse, too, though I don't have too much stuff in there that can go bad."

"You know how to get into the basement?"

She hesitated.

"Yep."

"You can do it, pumpkin. Maybe the groundskeeper has a fuse."

"Thanks, Dad."

She might be a grown woman, but "you can do it pumpkin" would never lose its motivating power, and that's why she'd called him instead of Googling.

She hooked the lantern over her arm and headed out the door into the deep dark, down the flagstone path.

Five feet away from Mac's front door a cloud shifted and Avalon stopped cold and tilted her head back. The half moon hung up there like a neon sign over the door of a heavenly speakeasy. Behind it, a million stars pinned the blue velvet sky up in place.

It was preposterously beautiful and so *strange* when you really thought about it, that enormous radiant shape in the sky.

Honestly, it was so dumbfoundingly gorgeous in the country all at once it felt like insanity to live anywhere else.

She took in a long, long breath for courage. To attempt to settle her hammering heart.

Exhaled.

She raised her hand to rap on the door.

It flew open before her knuckles even brushed it. She was treated to a backlit glimpse of pillow-rumpled hair, a lamplight-burnished torso partitioned in muscles as satiny and distinct as quadrants on a Hershey bar, low-clinging red boxers, and a jaw shadowed in stubble.

The impact was a bit like taking a mallet to the head. Her ears literally rang from the sheer sensory input.

"Hold out your hand, Ava." His voice was gruff from sleep.

Her hand, much to her chagrin, was already kind

of out. What in God's name was she going to do with it? Strum her hand down those muscles like she was playing a xylophone solo? Reflexively touch each quadrant, like a child learning to count?

He slapped a fuse into her hand.

And when it seemed she wouldn't move he slowly, gently curled her fingers closed over it.

And *bang*.

Shut the door again.

Shot the bolt.

And killed the lights.

She stood motionless. From just that little touch, her entire self seemed to be humming like a plucked string. How about that? Her subconscious had known he had amazing abs.

The first step she took away from the door was a little unsteady.

The next one was more certain.

Because she'd lay odds he was still watching. And she'd be damned if she'd let on that he'd rattled her.

For some reason, the notion that he was looking out for her was as disturbing and comforting and oddly beautiful as the moon.

It was cold and he didn't heat the house at night, but Mac stood in his bare feet and boxers and tweezed open his blinds with two fingers to watch Avalon move through the dark, find the basement door, fumble with the keys, then vanish inside.

And despite the fact that she richly deserved a

foray into the spidery basement in the deepest dark of night, he was rooting for her.

Because with some logic he barely understood but which was having its way with him now, because his mind was sleepy, it seemed like the world itself wouldn't be safe unless she was.

And so when the lights blazed on again in the house he smiled.

And a few minutes later, when the lights went back out again, he decided to go back to bed.

He folded his arms around the back of his head and smiled.

Because she was safe, sure. Because of the look on her face when she'd gotten a look at him in those boxers.

But also because of what he had in store for her tomorrow.

CHAPTER 10

Sleep was dreamless and morning dawned a little chilly, something she realized the moment she put a foot down on the wood floors in the turret. She fished about in her gym bag to see if her mom had donated any warm things. She found woolly rainbow-colored socks, the sweatshirt featuring the giant disembodied face of Annelise's cat, Peace and Love, that Annelise had given her grandpa for Christmas, and a pair of slippers with cocker spaniels on the toes. She put all of them on. The sweatshirt hung down almost to her knees.

She fumbled for her phone; it was only seven in the morning. How about that: the gently increasing light in her room had been her alarm clock. She decided to give herself a reprieve from looking at emails and texts until at least eight. Instead, she reflexively moved to open a window to let in birdsong and country air.

She stopped a few inches from the window.

And frowned.

And sniffed a little.

What the hell was *that* smell?

Heart pounding in dread now, she flung open a window, then slammed it down like a guillotine and scrambled backward. "Oh Jesus. Oh sweet Jesus!"

Only a thousand cows cooperatively farting in unison would create a smell like that.

She lunged for the hand cream in her purse, whipped the top off and snorted the vanilla-sandalwood blend like she was Al Pacino in *Scarface*, then bolted down the stairs, her hand sliding along the silky wood of the banister.

"Please . . . not . . . the . . . septic. Please. Not. The. Septic."

That was her prayer, one word per stair, like they were rosary beads, all the way down.

She froze in the foyer. Through the door she could hear a muffled *BEEP . . . BEEP . . . BEEP . . .*

It sounded for all the world like a big truck was backing up outside.

And all at once a hundred nightmare scenarios flitted through her mind like bats released from a cave, all of them involving Mac and revenge.

She flung the door open. Nobody was out front. That was a bit of a relief.

She followed the sound, bolted down the path and out onto the drive and up the flagstone path as fast as her spaniel slippers could carry her.

She came to an abrupt halt at the fork in the road, just before the gate, and stared.

Mac was standing out there, hands planted on his hips, a few feet apart, looking like a happy pirate on the deck of his ship.

In front of him was a huge red truck, the movements of which he appeared to be directing.

"Good morning, Mac," she called. "What fresh hell have we today?" Ava said it as brightly as a kindergarten teacher.

"Fresh *manure*," he corrected with cheery self-satisfaction. "Not fresh hell."

The manure in question was heaped in the back of said bright red truck, which was driven by a big guy wearing a white undershirt and a San Francisco Giants baseball hat. One tan arm bulging with muscle was propped on the open window.

The guy shouted merrily down to her over the sound of his idling engine. "Mac doesn't cheap out when it comes to his crops. This is some good shit. Top notch! About time Mac decided to do some winter planting. You been out here, what, three years now, Mackie?"

Avalon turned very, very slowly to Mac. "Your *crops*?"

"My *winter* crops," Mac reiterated in a tone that reminded her of a Buddhist monk she'd once met, who had clearly successfully meditated away every shred of anxiety, past and future. There was, however, a faint and very wicked hint of "duh" in his voice. "Fresh Loads is my go-to guy."

At first Ava thought Fresh Loads was one of those

terrible nicknames men give each other instead of demonstrating affection, like Bumpy or Skid Mark (two guys she'd actually gone to school with), but Mac gestured with his chin and she looked. "Fresh Loads" was indeed lettered on the side of the truck, in an ornate old-timey font embellished with feathery stalks of corn and lusciously blooming flowers.

Mac glanced over at her, and the glance became a comical double take. He whisked her from the top of her sloppy ponytail to the spaniels on the toes of her slippers, and, depending upon how sharp his vision was, in between might have noticed she hadn't shaved her shins in a few days, and now little bristles sparkled in the direct sunlight.

"You sure you got that fuse in okay last night? You kinda look like you got dressed in the dark. You *did* look a little dazed when you walked away from my place." His brow was furrowed in mock concern.

He was a wicked, wicked man.

"This is what I wear to work every day," she informed him loftily.

He grinned at this as if she was a slot machine that had just paid off.

The driver cut the engine. The truck shuddered like a big animal. "Is there a problem, ma'am?"

"No, no. I just thought I might have a septic emergency."

"Understandable," he said solemnly. "Pretty pungent. The good stuff always is."

"Don't worry, Avalon," Mac soothed. "It'll only

smell like this when the temperature gets into the high seventies or eighties. Which it will be for . . . oh, the next few weeks. We're looking at a warm spell. Or when a breeze sends it up toward the house. Which is usually only during the day. It's a little more pungent in the summer though. When I plant my summer crops."

All of which of course meant she had to cancel with Rachel indefinitely.

He was a stone-cold evil genius.

"I kind of like the smell," she lied coolly.

"Smells like prosperity, doesn't it?" said the philosopher in the truck, in all seriousness, listening to this exchange. He sucked in a long breath and sighed it out with pleasure bordering on a purr. "Farm-to-table vegetables! Nothing like it! Knowing who grew your food and where it grew and in what it grew. It's how food *should* be. Mac is great at it."

Despite Mac and the Stench (now there was a band name if she ever heard one), Avalon was charmed. She supposed she was glad there were people in the world who took pride in doing things like scrubbing crime scenes or cutting linoleum with those terrifying knives shaped like little scimitars or formulating gourmet poop, things she was ill-equipped to do.

But something about it made her wistful and restless again. It was pretty clear that even the gourmet poop guy was more fulfilled than she was currently.

Fresh Loads gave his truck door a friendly pat. "Well, if everything's okay here, I'm going to go drop this load off. You comin', Mac?"

"Right behind you, Randy."

Randy fired up the engine again and steered his fragrant load off to wherever Mac would be planting his winter crops.

Mac turned to her. "So what's the deal, Harwood? Are you on sabbatical? Are you going to be here indefinitely?"

"Why? Trying to suss out how fast I need to sell this place so you can plan another skirmish? How stupid do you think I am?"

"Not even a little bit stupid. Now, if you'd asked me about your *judgment* . . ."

Her temper was ramping. "If I'd angled the ramp just a little farther back, I would have made that jump across Whiskey Creek."

"Hindsight is a wonderful thing. So is physics. Funny thing is, now I could easily calculate the right angle for a ramp that might get you across. If the mood strikes you."

"And now you're trying to kill me?"

"Why? You tempted to make that jump?"

The word *tempted*, with all its soft plump consonants, hung there, throbbing with dimensions of meaning.

For a moment neither of them spoke.

"I notice you haven't made me a new *financial* offer for the house yet," she countered.

His expression didn't change in the least. It was like he hadn't even heard her. She was positive he had.

"The giant cat on your shirt is staring at me and

you're wearing dogs on your feet. Don't you think you're overcompensating for not having a pet?"

"My mom donated this stuff to me."

She realized that raised a lot more questions than it answered, so she hurriedly added, "How's *your* mom, Mac? What does she think of your farming and groundskeeping career?"

"Who knows?" He shrugged with one shoulder, indolently.

But then he looked away from her.

The indifference threw her. He didn't talk to his brother and he didn't talk to his mom. He could have good reasons. But she had no vocabulary, she realized, with which to discuss someone who seemed to have severed himself from his family.

He turned back toward her again, and he suddenly looked weary.

"For crying out loud, Harwood," he said gently, almost exasperated. "Get a pet. It's pretty isolated out here. You should get a dog. A really big one. The kind that barks loudly at predators and prowlers and fetches the sheriff when you do things like fall down wells."

Just the very notion of a pet made her go silent against a swoop of yearning.

He reached into his mailbox then and retrieved a flyer he must have missed yesterday.

"I'm not going to fall down a well," she said finally. Sounding nine years old.

"I won't hold my breath," he said absently. He

ducked his head to read the flyer, then he turned to walk away without saying another word.

She turned away, too, and sighed heavily, and the next intake of breath was richly redolent of manure.

Maybe she'd get used to it.

Damn, but it was practically a coup de grace. It was brilliant. And she ought not to admire it, but she was nothing if not fair.

And she was nothing if not a competitor.

Her trip back to the house was a little more leisurely than her initial bolt from it. Suddenly her phone erupted into The Plimsouls' "A Million Miles Away." Her sister. It was kind of nice that she wasn't actually a million miles away now. She was just about twenty minutes away.

"Hey, Edie. What's shakin'?"

"Avalon, I have to hit you up for a favor, and it's a big one."

Ah, siblings. Formalities like "how are you?" went right out the window in favor of expediency.

"Well, you know me. Go big or go home. Or go buy a big home. Ha ha. Ha."

"Yeah. Ha! I'm so sorry to dump this on you, but I can't believe I forgot it was my turn to host the Hummingbird meeting at my house today! We're supposed to make friendship bracelets and plant seedlings in egg cartons or some such shit, because they need their gardening badges and I have to feed them lunch. I have all the egg cartons and the dirt. But a big order for a Saturday funeral came into the shop and my supplier sent me daisies instead of lilies and do you have any idea how ridiculous it will be to cover the scion of an old Sacramento family in Gerbera *daisies*? And now I have to scramble to find the right flowers and drive to Black Oak to beg Cheryl at 'Coming up Roses' for her supply of flowers or I could lose the funeral business and I can't let this *happen*. Do you think you can fill in for me for at least an hour? I can get them all set up for you and I'll be back as fast as I can. Probably inside an hour."

Eden made it sound as though she'd forgotten to lock the lion cages at the zoo.

But Eden was burdened with perfectionism. The prospect of failure was probably torture, not to mention letting people down. Avalon wanted to save her, because she really hated it when Eden suffered.

Also, she knew she could bank the favor. Because that was the law in the world of siblings.

"Wait—the Hummingbirds are Annelise's scout troop, right?"

"Yes. About eight little girls. Smart ones. Darling girls. So sweet and good and just a *dream*."

Eden oversold it. Avalon was suspicious now. "Didn't you tell me one of them is mouthy? The one who has a brother with a sad mustache and a skeevy vocabulary?"

"Yeah. *You* should get along great with her."

Avalon snorted.

She could only imagine what the others were like. She *loved* kids. She was, by nature, whimsical and energetic and prone to non-sequiturs even as an adult, and she wasn't particularly daunted by the prospect of wrangling a whole passel of little girls. It sounded like a blast.

In that little pause she could hear goats bleating.

And the metallic, rhythmic clang of some kind, reminiscent of weekend mornings and her dad attempting to whack their old lawn mower back into life.

And just like that, an evil little lightbulb pinged on above her head.

"Hey, Eden—you know what? You should bring them up here! We'll drag a picnic table out front and do the crafts there. Plenty of room for them to run around and have a good time and tire themselves out."

"That's a fantastic idea!"

"And hey, do you think you might have any old clothes you can spare that might fit me?"

"I'll look. And I swear I'll only be gone and leave you with the girls for an hour or so. You're the best!"

"I am," Avalon agreed placidly, turning around and looking in the direction of Mac's cottage, as if she was addressing him. "I am indeed."

CHAPTER 11

A gorgeous heap of manure was mingling with the turned earth in his garden now, and Mac was feeling cheerful. He liked the beginnings of things. And he'd grown to love doing things from the very beginning to the very end. It had been his salvation, pretty much.

He'd kind of lost his knack, if he'd ever possessed one, for fielding ambiguity. Or for addressing an onslaught of equal but incompatible feelings, like lust and hilarity, or affection and fury, like yearning and a sense of brutal competitiveness, like admiration and impatience. Avalon Harwood was a whole freaking noisy symphony of those things.

Taking refuge under a tractor that needed fixing seemed like a restful way to spend the next few hours.

He crawled beneath, happily tinkering, not thinking about much, until he slid partially out from beneath the tractor to reach for a different wrench.

A pair of little blue eyes were peering right down into his.

He jerked in shock and banged his head on the metal so hard it rang.

"Ow! Shit! Sorry!"

The eyes belonged to a little girl, wearing a green beret. She took a step back.

"Hi!" whoever this sprite was said brightly.

"Uh, hi yourself. Sorry about the swearing. You startled me. Whoever the he . . . whoever you are." He rubbed his poor head.

"That's okay. My grandpa swears a lot. He puts a nickel in the jar every time. My grandma says they almost have enough in that jar for an above-ground pool."

Realization dawned. "Ah, you must be Avalon's niece." He knew Eden Harwood owned the flower shop downtown.

"Yep. My Auntie Avalon owns this big house here. I'm Eden's daughter, and Glenn and Sherrie's granddaughter, and Jude's niece and Jesse's niece, too."

"That's quite a family you got there."

"I know!"

He couldn't help but smile at her unfiltered delight in her good fortune to be loved by a lot of people. Even if his head was still ringing like one of John Bonham's cymbals.

She bent down to peer under the tractor with a frown. "What seems to be the trouble?"

"Know a lot about tractor motors, do you?" He gave the lug nut a good twist.

"Nope, I just like to know stuff."

"That sounds a lot like your Auntie Avalon. She thinks she knows eeeeverything." He gave a bolt a ferocious twist with a wrench.

"Auntie Ava is really smart. She's got a head for business."

"Don't I know it," he said grimly.

"I can play guitar. I can play G, C, and D now."

Children and their non-sequiturs.

"I bet you can make a lot of songs with those three chords."

Why was he making conversation? He gave the nut another ferocious twist.

"You wouldn't believe how many! What's your name? I'll make up a song about you."

"Mac," he said. He knew it was a mistake but was frankly curious about what would happen next.

"Mac took a snack out of the shack and he told all the girls they betta jump back! *Holla*!"

He laughed. She was quick. He slid all the way out from under the tractor and pushed himself to his feet. "Not bad, Annelise. Hey, um, sweetheart, I'm kinda busy right now, so . . ."

He turned around.

And froze.

"*What* the . . ."

He was surrounded.

He counted eight little girls in green dresses, knee socks, sashes, and little green berets. Sixteen bright eyes, ten sets of braids, two ponytails extending vertically from her head, like handlebars on a tricycle, one shining bob, one woven with a festival of colorful beads.

They might as well be Martians. Because he knew exactly as much about little girls as he did about little green men, and was just as pleased to see them. Absurdly, he was tempted to turn around and run exactly as if they were aliens. ("There were eight of them, officer, with these little beady eyes . . .")

They stared back at him with that combination of unblinking, uncensored fascination and lack of self-consciousness particular to children.

"It smells like poop out here," Annelise noted, matter-of-factly.

"Yep," Mac agreed. "It's for my garden."

"Do worms poop?" a skinny one sporting brown knee socks and short horizontal ponytails asked. She had mischievous little brown eyes.

"Everything poops," he said irritably.

They all giggled. He definitely hadn't been going for a laugh, but he was flattered anyway. Unless they were laughing *at* him.

"Cows poop?" she persisted.

"Oh, yeah. Big time."

"Horses?"

"You bet."

"My dad?"

"Hopefully."

This answer was apparently better than they ever dared dream. They erupted into squeals of hilarity and buckled over.

"Do *angels* poop?" a little blond one asked slyly. A creative thinker, that one.

"I'm not prepared to answer ecumenical questions, ladies."

At which point he took off at a brisk pace toward the main house.

"Avalon!" he bellowed.

She was nowhere in sight.

"What does eckmechanical mean?" This was Annelise, scurrying along on his heels, demanding the answer in the manner of a prosecutor.

"It, uh, means questions about angels," Mac said, hoping if he lengthened his stride he could outrun them.

"How do you spell it?"

Uh-oh.

"*I-T*," he hedged.

"I meant the other one!" Apparently she'd heard that joke before.

"Er . . . *E-C-U-M-E-N-I-C-A-L*. Um, Annelise, I need to talk to your aunt. Do you know where she is? AVALON!"

He heard his voice echo: ". . . *valon valon valon*."

There was no way Avalon would have let these little girls wander about unsupervised. He was certain she was lurking somewhere, hovering like a mad scientist observing an experiment.

He walked faster. They seemed to have imprinted on him like ducklings and they were fast as hell. He picked up the pace; they scurried behind. He stopped abruptly and they collided with each other and nearly crashed into him, too. He'd stopped because he saw a flash of pink and gleaming chestnut hair: Avalon on the upper deck. She waved gaily, like she was on a cruise ship leaving shore.

And disappeared rapidly inside.

"I think you're dodging the question," said Horizontal Ponytails, clearly a future lawyer. "I asked, do angels—"

"Angels poop feathers," he said definitively.

"They do *NOT*!" she crowed as if she'd laid that trap particularly for him.

"See? *Told* you I didn't know."

For some reason this made them fall all over themselves in giggles again.

He'd never dreamed he was this amusing.

He picked up his pace, heading around the patio beneath the balcony so he could peer in at Avalon through the French doors.

They all broke into trots.

"AVALON!" he hollered again. Like Stanley Kowalski in *A Streetcar Named Desire*. Only more incensed than panicked.

Oops. There she was!

Craning her head to see him from the *opposite* window. He caught a glimpse of her mouth wide open in laughter.

"Listen, girls, I need to get a lot of work done today, so . . . AVALON! *AVALON*!" He waved both arms at her like a man on a desert island spotting a lone biplane.

She ducked back into the house like a gopher into a hole.

Oh, she was a she-devil. A crafty, crafty she-devil.

"Hey, Mac. Auntie Ava said she had a hunch you would show us what you're planting and how you plant it and stuff. We need it for our badges."

"I'll just bet she had a hunch. Wait, what do you mean, badges? Are you sheriffs?"

How about that. He had to admit to himself that he was deliberately going for laughs.

They obliged him by erupting into those now familiar giggles. Apparently being a child was not much different from being a drunk. Life was intoxicating.

"Nooooooo!" most of them crowed.

"We're *Hummingbirds*," Annelise corrected him, mopping her eyes of laughter tears.

"There's a surprise," he said grimly. Hummingbirds were cranky, tireless, demanding little things that never stopped moving. Nevertheless, he kept two hummingbird feeders going because they were, in a word, enchanting. "Is that like a scout troop?"

"Yep," Annelise said firmly. "And we need to earn badges for gardening. Because Tiffany's gang in Black Oak Hummingbirds already has them and we *need* to beat them. They keep beating us! It's embarrassing! Appalling, really."

He blinked a little at her vocabulary. "Tiffany's gang? You have *factions* inside the Hummingbirds?"

His own reflexive sense of competition reared up.

"What are factions? Like three fourths, one half, like that?" Annelise wanted to know.

"Well, um . . . sort of."

"Because one half of the Hummingbirds have one half of their badges and *I* never get behind so I need my gardening badge. We always win."

Boy, did she sound like Avalon right then. Which only made it harder to resist her.

"Pleeease help us." She implored with folded hands, all limpid blue eyes. Arrayed all around her, all of the eyes, all those shades of blue and brown and hazel and long fluffy eyelashes, beseeched him.

He craned his head toward the balcony again.

No Avalon.

He looked back toward the Hummingbirds.

He was made of something like stone. But how did *any* human resist those faces?

He heaved a sigh so exasperated it ought to have fluttered their ponytails.

"Well, this is what I'm doing today, girls. I need to check my tomato plants for worms that can hurt the tomatoes. And then I need to pluck them off when I find them. And they're so gross. I mean, grosser than poop. Really icky. They're fat, and green, and they kind of have little diamonds on their sides, and horns."

"Real diamonds?" One of them was skeptical.

"Real horns?" Another sounded hopeful.

"It's not nice to call something fat." This was from a stern-faced little girl sporting the shining, symmetrical bob.

"Diamond the shape"—he outlined this in the air

with his fingers—"not the diamonds that you can wear in your ears or in tennis bracelets." Too late it occurred to him that they might have no idea what a tennis bracelet was, as they weren't old enough to date spoiled rich boys yet. "It has really *little* horns." He demonstrated by propping two fingers atop his head. "And it's squishy and plump and doesn't mind being called fat, because it's an accurate description and because it's a worm."

They absorbed this, assessing whether they wanted to be involved, perhaps.

"Because that's what I'm doing. Today is all about worms. I'm pulling worms off the tomato plants."

He said all of this almost desperately. Hoping for at least a token "*ewwwwww!*"

But they were all eyeing him with fascination.

They were silent, he realized too late, because they could not believe their luck.

"We can help you do it!" Annelise announced. "We can help you in your garden! We need to learn about worms and gardens for our badges. It'll be perfect! Oh please oh please oh please."

And now they were pogo-ing around him with excitement.

He closed his eyes briefly and tipped his head back as if beseeching a heartless God.

How had *this* happened to his morning?

Avalon freaking Harwood. *Damn*, she was good. And it was yet another thing she'd remembered: he'd claimed to loathe children, way back then.

"What do you do with them when we find the worms?" Annelise was worried. "You don't hurt them, do you?"

"I . . . um . . . put them in a coffee can. And then I send them to live on a different farm where they have plenty of room to roam." He crossed his fingers.

"That's what my dad did with our dog Rufus when he got old!" the bright-eyed Hummingbird named Emily told him.

Poor old Rufus, Mac thought. "You don't say."

"But aren't other worms good to have around?" Annelise demanded.

"Excellent! They certainly are. Just like people, different kinds of worms have different kinds of jobs. Earthworms help the soil. They eat stuff and poop it out and the soil becomes richer and more fertile and your vegetables become more delicious."

"So does that mean when we eat tomatoes and lettuce and stuff we're kind of eating worm poop?" Annelise asked.

He hesitated only a second. "Abso*lute*ly," he intoned solemnly.

If she never ate a salad again, that was his revenge on Avalon.

"Awesome!" she breathed.

They didn't make little girls like they used to. Or maybe they did, and they just felt less obliged to be sissies for little boys, which was probably a good thing.

Avalon, for that matter, had never felt obliged to be a sissy of any kind.

He found coffee cans for them to drop the worms into, if and when they found them, and set them loose in his garden, about a quarter acre of tomatoes and peppers, and he kept an eye on them, because he simply couldn't help it because they were just so *little*, and how did parents not panic when they set these reckless, energetic, gleeful little creatures loose in the world?

He did his own worm hunting. He found only one.

He could see the house from this field, and out of the corner of his eyes, he saw Avalon peering out at them from the balcony. With binoculars. Even from where he stood he could imagine her grinning.

He didn't have time to be incensed because he felt obliged by his sheer size and adultness to watch over his charges as surely as if he were a sheepdog. He was a slave to some sort of atavistic protective instinct.

They never stopped talking. Never. It was like being trapped in an aviary. *Peep peep peep peep peep peep* in their little high-pitched voices. A ceaseless bombardment of often startling incisive questions, sprung from minds so alarmingly quick and sparklingly new it made him feel like a dullard, like every bit of his thirty-two years. They shrieked in triumph when one of them found a worm, and they plucked with surgically delicate fingers, and showed him every single one.

He had to admit, they were better at this stuff than he was.

An hour had gone by in an eye blink, and yet it felt like he'd been sprinting that entire time.

And they'd found ten tomato worms.

That was a damn good hour's work.

He gave each of them a beautiful ripe tomato. As solemnly as if he were bestowing badges. And as it turned out, he kind of was.

They accepted them with touching awe and great care into their cupped hands.

"Girls!" Avalon had her hands cupped to her mouth like a mini-megaphone and was now shouting through them. "Snack time!"

He pivoted and marched toward Avalon. Unbeknownst to him, he looked like a general leading a miniature parade. They followed him at top scurrying speed toward Avalon.

Avalon had set up a long picnic table neatly arrayed with shiny craft supplies, the kind that crows would just love to steal. A golden heap of hot dog buns and bowls of plastic-wrapped something or other and a cooler with juice and sodas poking up out of the ice were at the other end.

Off in the distance near the driveway, willowy Eden Harwood was moving at a brisk mom-jog, one of those giant ubiquitous mom bags slung over her shoulder, heading straight for the picnic table.

The girls broke ranks and swarmed upon all the food and shininess with their typical gusto.

"Hang on, ladies," Avalon commanded. "We're going

to do this politely. Remember how you need to earn your good manners badge? Say good-bye to Mac."

They paused to wave. "Bye, Mac! Thank you, Mac! Bye! Bye! Bye!"

He waved, charmed by the thank yous and the utter cluelessness to the chaos they had imposed upon his world. They took for granted that their needs would be accommodated. Happy little tyrants.

He smiled, despite himself. Albeit tautly.

Because he was not well pleased at how Avalon Harwood had engineered the disruption of his day.

"Hey, Mac. You kind of looked like a mama duck there with your little posse. You seemed to be having such a great time I hesitated to interrupt."

"Avalon," he said pleasantly. And casually transformed his waving hand into a single upraised middle finger and rubbed his forehead with it.

Avalon noticed. But she just grinned at that as if she'd won an Olympic medal.

"We're going to make friendship bracelets out here on the tables. And then have a sing-along. And games. Involving mallets and balls. Care to join us for hot dogs and fruit smiles?"

He could vividly imagine a day's worth of shrieking. Croquet balls hurtling through his windows. Little feet trampling the well-tended landscaping. Unannounced visits while he tried to work on his tractor or the lawn mower.

"No. Thank you. I'm good."

Her hair was piled in a ponytail on top of her head,

and it fluttered in the breeze like the tail on a fox. She was wearing a perfectly ordinary dark pink T-shirt and a perfectly ordinary pair of faded jeans, rolled up a little at the bottom, but the way they smoothed so perfectly over her curves made her look more edible than a "fruit smile," whatever the hell that was. He imagined resting his hands in those sweet notches of her waist, and he would bury his face in that little hollow beneath her ear and whisper dirty things and explicit compliments . . . and . . . and . . . lick her.

She tipped her head and studied him. "You look more like you'd like to drink a fifth of Jack for lunch."

He said absolutely nothing. Because he couldn't yet. Thanks to the previous unbidden reverie, his head was as light as if he'd sustained another blow to the head by a tractor bumper.

"Next week we thought we'd have a campout. Games and songs and activities. All. Day. Long. We'll maybe do it once or twice a week. Maybe even *forever*." She whispered that last word like a Marvel Comic villain.

He was silent.

And grim.

Honestly, lickable or not, there really was only so much a man could take.

"You really want to do this, Avalon?" he asked idly. His tone said: *bring it.*

"I'm sure I don't know what you're talking about." She laid her hand delicately across her sternum, as if that's where an invisible rope of pearls was draped.

He fought the impulse to look below the hand at the boobs.

"Those girls found ten horn worms on my tomatoes. Pretty useful. Best thing that could have happened to me today."

"Huh." He could tell it took a good deal of self-restraint for her not to ask what had become of the worms, even though the Harwoods of course had a garden when she was growing up and hornworms had likely met a similar demise back then. He saw the flicker of worry anyway, and he knew a shocking surge of tenderness and impatience that made him curl his fingers into his palms and dig his nails in a little.

"They can be quite a . . . handful . . . don't you think?"

The question had begun as a sardonic little test; oddly, it ended on a different note. She was asking a genuine question.

And all at once he understood something: part of why she seemed so attractive now was that she was literally *glowing*. When he'd found her flat on her back outside the gate a few days ago, she'd been tense and pale and nervy; he knew now it was because something had made the light go out of her. Some element of joy she'd always radiated had been missing. But it was back now.

How did she veer so far off course?

How did the two of them veer so far away from each other?

Had she seen something in *him* that warned her of disaster, or heartbreak?

"They didn't bother me in the *least*." He gave it an ironic lilt. To make it sound like a lie.

But there was a peculiar, surprising ache in his chest.

They locked gazes. Something in her eyes told him that she knew he wasn't entirely lying.

"Avalon . . . why aren't you a teacher?"

She blinked. Her eyes widened in surprise.

She looked back toward the table, at all the little girls, the tomatoes, the friendship bracelets in progress.

"GradYouAte is kind of a school," she said vaguely, finally.

He didn't know quite what to say. "Right. Sure. Of course."

She didn't turn around to look at him again.

So he just said, "I'll see you around, Avalon."

She smiled faintly. "You very likely will."

She'd noticed then that Eden was watching this little tableau from about twenty feet away at the picnic table, where everyone was busily making friendship bracelets. A shiny red orb glowed at each place setting. A tomato.

He'd been great with the kids, even though he'd once claimed to loathe them.

In all likelihood, what he didn't like was being responsible for the feelings of another being.

She moved over to her sister. She actually kind of wanted to make a friendship bracelet, too.

Annelise was giving Eden a rapid-fire recap of the afternoon. "Mom! We totally caught tomato worms!" Annelise informed her.

"Oh no! You caught tomato worms! What are the symptoms? Do they make you . . . ticklish?"

Annelise doubled over with gales of laughter as her mom went in for a good tickle, then ran off to join her friend.

Eden pulled Avalon toward her by looping her arm through hers.

"If that guy looks as good from the front as he does from the back, then I have no idea what you're doing hanging out with the Hummingbirds and me, Avalon."

Avalon dodged that. "How's the Sacramento scion? Was he sent off with appropriate flowers?"

"A wreath of gladiolas and ivy shaped like a dollar sign."

"You're kidding me, right?"

"It's 'what he would have wanted.'" Eden made air quotes. "And I provided it. They were happy. At the very last minute. Which means I'm happy."

"Good on ya."

"So who's the guy?" Eden gestured.

"That's the groundskeeper."

"Whoa. Are you *kidding* me? Does he have a name?"

Avalon hesitated. "His name is Mac."

Eden frowned faintly; the name was clearly tickling the memory banks.

And then she seized Avalon's arm as if she were about to fall off a cliff. "SHUT. UP. Mac *Coltrane*?"

Avalon sighed. Then nodded, resignedly.

Eden was silent and frozen, clearly mulling the ramifications of this. She maintained a grip on Avalon's arm.

"You were going to let him touch your *boob*," she finally said on a hush.

They both stifled an eruption of giggles.

She had indeed confided this to Eden one breathless summer night, and they had discussed it with all the seriousness of a peace treaty negotiation. Eden was all for it, though she'd rather superciliously admonished at the time, "You should be careful because you tend to get carried away, you know."

That was funny. Eden could be such a *priss* back then.

When you store up all your wildness and don't release it a little at a time, you are bound to accidentally let it all out at once the first time a truly hot guy comes around and get mysteriously knocked up.

"I think he still wants to touch your boob," Eden said sagely. "He had that look about him."

"Shut up! You only saw the back of him." The back of her neck was hot now.

"I saw the way he turned around just then. All huffy and . . . sexy."

"*What*? How the hell does anyone turn around 'sexy,' Eden?"

Eden ignored this question. "And macho. And your heads were practically touching when you were talking."

"Were not." Were they?

Edie was grinning. "I'm teasing. But boy did you ever take the bait."

Avalon snorted. "We were arguing. It wasn't anything sexy at all." Which actually felt like a lie, because, let's face it, she told herself, everything he did felt sexy. "He's an arrogant—" She recalled she was around a passel of ten-year-olds and refrained from saying "SOB" aloud. "He's arrogant. And he wants to buy this house. He apparently tried to buy it at auction. He's not well-pleased that I bought it."

"You're not gonna let him, right?" Eden knew her sister.

"Of course not. But he owns Devil's Leap. The part with the swimming hole. Turns out these are two different parcels."

Eden took this in and wisely didn't editorialize. "Did you know that going in?" She attempted to be neutral but there was the faintest whiff of schoolmarm about that question. "Wait. Don't answer. You'll get that land from him somehow." Being a mom had edited Eden's schoolmarmy impulses a little. "You talk to Corbin yet?"

"Nope. Texted him once and told him to stop texting me. I bought myself at least this week of time away from the office. He's going to just have to keep handling things."

Eden could gauge her mood. She wisely didn't pursue that line of questioning.

Avalon lowered her voice. "So what's up with *you*, Edie? Going to let anyone touch your boob?"

"Sure. I think I have ten minutes next Wednesday between the time I pick Annelise up from school and her guitar lesson for some stranger to cop a feel. Maybe we should send out a press release."

Eden didn't date. She claimed she didn't want to. It was pretty clear she didn't have time to, given her work and her devotion to Annelise. Avalon was pretty certain guys went out of their way to order flowers and buy various gewgaws from her shop just for a chance to talk to her. Eden probably didn't notice.

"I've almost forgotten the point of men." Eden shrugged. "I'm getting it done, aren't I? The momming, the shop, everything? With a little help from my friends?"

Two cars pulled in one after the other to pick up the Hummingbirds.

More moms would be on the way soon.

"Sure," Avalon said, after a second, because now was not the time to advance her theory that Eden was kidding herself, at least about the man part.

Although that could, of course, make two of them.

About twenty minutes later, all the little Hummingbirds had gone home with a mom or a dad, and that included Eden and Annelise.

"Bye, Auntie Avalon! Bye! Bye!" Annelise walked backward blowing kisses at her. Little goofball.

Damn, but she was alone. Not that she wasn't before, but the sudden influx of light and joy made everything seem a trifle fuller in contrast. They all seemed to have taken just a little bit of her with them when they left. Surely that was an illusion.

She sat down at the picnic table, which could stay right where it was for now, and rested her chin in her hands.

She'd been buzzing from the pleasure of bedeviling him and from being around her family and the kids. But Mac's question bothered her. It burrowed right in and felt almost like an accusation, an existential quiz. *Why aren't you a teacher?*

He'd sounded genuinely troubled.

She plucked up the friendship bracelet Annelise had made for her and twiddled it in her fingers.

She gasped when a squirrel hopped up on the table.

Her heart gave a happy skip. They really were characters, sparkly little individual souls, with their smooth gray coats and plump white tummies, their curving tail plumes. She'd rescued and nursed a squirrel back to health. Trixie had lived with Avalon for almost a year, and Avalon had loved her with her whole heart. She'd passed away in her sleep in her cage for mysterious squirrel reasons, and to this day the memory was an ache. Funny how something so small could take a divot right out of your heart.

Avalon found a scrap of hot dog bun on the bench next to her and held it out. The squirrel leaned delicately forward, snatched it and ran off with it in its mouth.

And she was alone again.

Get a grip, Avalon, she told herself. *This maudlin ruminating is ridiculous.*

She knew exactly how she intended to spend the next couple of hours.

CHAPTER 12

When Mac headed out to the mailbox one afternoon, Avalon was there. She was holding what looked like mail in one hand; in the other arm she was holding what appeared to be a large, dusty cotton ball.

A bathroom rug? An exotic lampshade?

"Hey, neighbor . . ."

"Yikes!"

The fluffy thing had stirred in her arms. It turned what was apparently its head to look at him. It had the happiest eyes he'd ever seen. Little glittering brown beads of joy shining from a nest of fluff trimmed away from its eyes.

Good God above.

Whatever it was, it was almost upsettingly cute.

"What. The hell. Is that," he said by way of greeting.

He was alarmed by the compulsion to lean over and snorgle his face into its blond fluff.

And he didn't know what "snorgle" even meant but words adorable enough to discuss this creature hadn't yet been invented. On some level his brain knew this and was making them up.

"*She's* a dog. I got a dog!"

Two pairs of brown eyes were sparkling at him now.

He pressed his lips together and studied it a moment longer.

"Are you . . . are you sure?" His voice creaked a little.

"Quite sure," she confirmed.

There was a little silence.

"That's not a dog." He said it firmly, as if he could make it true with adamancy. "A baby chicken, maybe. A baby chicken and . . . and . . . something took a startling turn in its DNA."

"I got *her* at the animal shelter," Ava said. The dog tipped its head back and looked up at her adoringly, as if she was a movie star. "Her name is Chick Pea. Go on. Pet her."

He sighed so gustily the fluff around the dog's eyes shimmied. He pressed a tentative fingertip to the plush place between its eyes. His finger vanished into fluff. The dog's little tongue darted out to taste him. *Lap lap.*

He retracted his hand before his heart caved in like an overripe apricot, permanently, dangerously softened.

"Chick Pea is like one bite for a coyote," he assessed gruffly.

"I prefer not to think of her in terms of bites."

"Bite," he repeated. "Singular."

Ava studied him for a wordless moment. "Are you worried about Chick Pea?"

"No. I'm frowning because I've never seen a bunny dog before and it's upended my view of the world."

This was a lie. He was actually worried about both of them. Because the day they'd buried her squirrel had been a bit like falling down a well in the dark. That sort of helplessness was a first for Mac Coltrane. He'd wanted something that he couldn't have, which was for Avalon's heart not to break. And to know what to say to take her pain away. He could only provide a velvet shroud, a heart-shaped rock, and his aching silence. It was all he'd known to do.

And here she was with an animal that was bound to break her heart sooner rather than later.

"So you went inside the animal shelter, and you said, 'I'm looking for a hairy garbanzo bean,' and they said, 'Wait right here, we have just the thing in the back'?"

"She was wandering dirty and lonely and matted around town and they washed her up and she's been there almost a year. No one else wanted her because she's getting old. She's nine years old, I'm told."

There was a silence.

"Maybe I should have been more specific. I meant Rottweiler or Doberman or that dog that the guy at the feed store has, that big black super hairy thing, when I said you should get a dog. Not something that probably craps little pellets. Like a bunny."

He could feel her temper and tension winding.

"I could only get one dog. So I got this one."

He could have said, "That dog may not last out the year."

He could have said, "Boy, they saw you coming."

She knew all that, too. And even though she probably despaired at the knowledge, she would love it anyway.

He didn't know whether this was madness or bravery.

She put Chick Pea gently on the ground. She wasn't even as high as the top of Mac's boot.

He looked down at the dog, frowning. Inwardly, he knew that same peculiar reflex to protect.

Chick Pea radiated joyous simplicity up at him. And switched her fluffy backside a little.

"Does she at least bark?" he tried. His voice was tense, too.

Chick Pea turned an excited circle and made a sound. It sounded more like a soft beeping sound than a yap.

He closed his eyes and shook his head. "Dear God. A fifteen-year-old asthmatic collie would still do a better job of guarding you and your house than . . ." He gestured at the fluff-ball.

"Her name is *Chick Pea*. Chick Pea! Just because you can't be bothered to name your cat because that would imply you cared about it and caring about things is for suckers, right, Mac?"

He froze, astounded.

"He *has* a name." He was absurdly, badly stung.

"'The Cat' is not a name," she retorted. "It's a . . .

a . . . setting on a See 'n Say toy." She mimed pulling a string and cocked her head and nastily mimicked, "'The Cat says meo—'"

His voice rose. "That's his *name*. His name is The Cat. Initial caps on both words. Like The Hulk, or The Green Lantern, or The Dude. He's called The Cat because he clearly is the *best* cat, so obviously there could be no other name, THE CAT. When we go to the vet, that's what they call out. The Cat."

He was aware that while he wasn't shouting, he also wasn't *not* shouting.

Chick Pea made one of those beeping bark sounds, so she was doing her part to be a guard dog.

He knew the conversation wasn't really about the dog. It was about all the swirling amorphous emotions Avalon had brought right back into his life, and the net result was a ramping anger.

Did she *really* think that was who he was?

Shouldn't it be goddamn obvious that he cared beyond *reason*?

Chick Pea was sniffing his boot now, which made him want to snatch her up and tuck her under his arm. Jesus, a coyote would nosh on this dog in seconds. A stiff wind would blow it into the next county.

And then he saw the rolled-up trade magazine in Avalon's hand. She was gripping it pretty tightly, as if she wanted to swat flies with it. Or maybe strangle it.

It was some sort of gaming organization supplement, a free-with-membership trade magazine type of thing.

It was impossible not to see who was on the cover. The curly dark hair, the wide smile, the calculatedly dorky glasses, the slightly too-big nose. The boyfriend.

He had a hunch some of her mood had something to do with his tension, too.

"You subscribe to *Tools Monthly*, eh, Avalon?"

"Ha," she said blackly. For a second, amusement flickered.

"Isn't that your boyfriend, Corncob, on the cover?"

She hesitated, as if deciding how to answer this. "His name's Corbin," she said tautly.

"Honestly, is Corbin really a *better* name than Corncob, or just more accurate?"

"They're both ridiculous. Much *less* ridiculous to be named after a Roman emperor, huh, Mac? Maximilian is much more memorable. It's just a shame that 'a million' part of your name doesn't apply anymore."

He froze as if she'd literally run him through. So thoroughly shocked by the attack it was almost funny.

Because just like that, she'd hurdled a few days' worth of passive-aggressive gamesmanship and landed right smack in the heart of an ugly hurt. He hadn't even realized he had a spot left unprotected.

He was Achilles, though.

And now it was clear she was targeting that undipped heel.

Damn, she played dirty. But even as he half admired it, he could feel his own face pale with a low-simmering fury.

She knew he was angry, but met his eyes anyway.

"Some people seem to have found it easy to forget," he just said, evenly. Almost dispassionately.

She blinked. Surprised.

And then he nodded as if he was bored.

He didn't know it was a gesture he'd gotten from his dad, a gesture that implied that whomever he was acknowledging was in fact not really worth acknowledging, as dismissive as a gesture could get.

Mac was on his third beer, an uncharacteristic overindulgence, but then, he was in an uncharacteristic mood.

Usually a meeting with the local veterans helped put things in perspective for him, but he was distracted and edgy and so blackly silent throughout, they all told him he should go get a beer. Which was pretty funny. He was clearly lowering the overall mood and they were trying to show him mercy by getting rid of him for the afternoon. He didn't take offense. He was suitable for his own company only, and frankly, that's pretty much all he wanted.

He looked up from his battered wood table at the back of the Misty Cat as Gabe walked in.

"Hey, Coltrane."

"They let just anyone in the Misty Cat these days, don't they?" Mac said dourly.

"I wish there was more than one respectable drinking establishment in town so I wouldn't have to look at your ugly mug," Gabe said in reply.

Affectionate greetings out of the way, Mac and Gabe argued over who would get to buy the beer, which Mac won. He felt like he needed a win.

He held up two fingers and Glenn Harwood—Avalon's father, of all people—brought them over. They were between waitresses here at the Misty Cat since Glory Greenleaf's fortunes had changed so dramatically, which also meant the caliber of open mic talent had rather plummeted. Glenn didn't show any signs of recognizing Mac as the kid who had run around Devil's Leap with his own kids about a thousand years ago, though he did nod politely to him and to Gabe. Who, as the school principal, was often at Glenn's granddaughter's various pageants and softball games. Mac had been busy over the past year planting and caretaking. He wasn't precisely a fixture in anyone's life in town.

"Good meeting tonight?" Gabe asked.

The meeting of local vets was pretty informal; guys from all branches of service from the various small towns nearby convened in a meeting room at the Adult Learning Center, and Mac and Gabe were both in a position to help in a lot of ways. Sometimes Mac made repairs to wheelchairs or gave advice on home repairs; they swapped farming stories and tips; he taught guys how to build and repair their own stuff, too. They all swapped financial advice and war stories.

"Yeah. Randy, Morty . . . pretty much everyone made it this week." Except Mike, he didn't say, but Gabe would have guessed that. "Why'd you miss it?"

"Basketball game at school. I'm pinch-hitting as coach."

"Kind of mixing your metaphors there, aren't you, Gabe? Not a lot of hitting in basketball."

"You should watch kindergarteners play it. Pinching *and* hitting. Also, sitting down in the middle of the court to cry, and wandering off because they saw something shiny."

Mac grinned at this.

"Mike pay you back yet?" Gabe asked shortly.

"Nope."

Mike Wade was a friend who'd had his leg blown off in Iraq. Mac had loaned ten grand to help him keep his house, which was underwater. Mike had sworn he'd had a line on a job and he could pay Mac back in full pretty soon, but he hadn't been to any of the meetings for weeks. And before he'd even offered the money, Mac had promised himself that he would never hound the guy with calls or visits. His credo was: don't give or loan anything you can't afford to lose.

He wondered if that applied to his own stony little heart, too.

Which was smarting right now, with righteous indignation. Almost as though it wasn't made of stone. He knew better, though.

"Sorry, man." Gabe knew what Mac could have done with that ten thousand dollars.

Mac just shrugged. "I wouldn't have done it differently, but the timing kinda blows."

Quite an understatement. It was a large part of why he wasn't offering Avalon actual dough for the house. Which was why he was left working whimsical strategies that were effective in the short-term but doomed to fail, because her head was as hard as a rock. Lucky for her.

As hard as her heart was soft.

And her lips. Her lips were soft. He remembered that all too well.

And her eyes.

"So . . . I heard through the grapevine that Avalon Harwood bought that house at Devil's Leap."

"Oh, but she did indeed," Mac said darkly. "That she did."

Gabe regarded him wonderingly. "What's with the 'indeed'? Are you Irish, suddenly?"

"Drunkish," Mac corrected. And took another sip.

"Sorry, man. Really sorry. About the house. If I could I would have—"

"You're a freaking elementary school principal. And a veteran. You can't afford it. But that, as far as I'm concerned, is about as heroic as it gets. After the day *I* had the other day, not sure which one you deserve more medals for."

"Oh yeah. I actually heard all about your tomato garden and the worms and your goats. A few girls can't stop talking about it."

"Yeah?" Mac was oddly flattered by this.

"Yeah. Seems they were playing 'Tomato Worms' at recess. They put their fingers like horns over their heads and tried to ram each other with them. Two of them got in a fight over it and one got poked in the eye and they both wound up in the office for hair pulling."

This was actually pretty funny. "I did make the worms sound pretty dangerous and badass. At least they learned something."

"They all, and I quote, 'totally want to do it again.'"

"Huh." Despite himself, this was rather gratifying. "I put them to work finding tomato worms. Their little sharp beady eyes and their teeny little fingers came in surprisingly handy. Child labor laws are so yesterday."

Gabe snorted. "Apparently you taught them a lot about worms and dirt and the growing cycles of tomatoes and I got a lecture on all of that from Annelise Harwood. They are *into* it. How the hell did that even come about? Apart from the fact that you like to tell people what you know and boss people around."

"Let's just say there was an unexpected Hummingbird invasion on my property. I was ambushed. They took me hostage. How do you say no to all those little pleading eyes? I'm seriously asking. Seriously. That Annelise Harwood at the head of the pack."

"That little girl is going to be president one day."

"I think she wants to be a rock star."

"Well, it's really only a matter of time before a rock star is elected president, so."

Mac understood, fully, perhaps for the first time,

what it might be like to root for a kid. To savor the moment-by-moment gleeful chaos and actually relish helping them turn out to be whoever they wanted to be. His own dad had been an aggressive chiseler in more ways than one. He'd done his damnedest to turn Mac and Ty into chips off the old block. It had worked with Ty, pretty much.

Mac wasn't made of anything so malleable as rock.

Maybe that's what Avalon was seeing. A guy who was downright petrified. Like a Jurassic tree.

He took another hit of beer.

"Well, kudos," Gabe said. "You really are quite the farmer these days, Mac. And maybe even an artist— that goat brie you made is the bomb. And here I thought kids gave you the heebie-jeebies."

"They do," he said mildly, mostly because he knew it was expected of him. "It's just that it was . . ." He took a sip of his beer then put it down on the table, and lowered his voice. ". . . it was fun. I had fun."

Gabe put the beer bottle down hard. "SHUT the front door."

"Fun in the way those *American Ninja Warrior* obstacle courses on TV look fun. Really dangerous and kind of slapstick and exhilarating if you make it to the end. And don't dislocate something or knock out your front teeth or have a nervous breakdown. Fun requiring ingenuity and on-the-spot thinking. Like a freaking military exercise."

He was, of course, exaggerating for effect.

"Yeah, kids are great," Gabe said mildly, with

typical understatement, though he was clearly wildly amused. He was a freaking elementary school principal, after all. He'd also been a navy SEAL, which, as far as Mac was concerned, should be a prerequisite for any kind of job in a school system.

"Okay," Mac allowed carefully. "If you say so. But do they have to *scream* their enthusiasm?"

"Yes. Yes, they do. You didn't have any sisters, huh?"

"I have seven goats. A half dozen chickens. Thinking of getting a donkey."

"Why the hell would you get a donkey?"

Mac glared at him with defiant incredulity. "Because . . . they're . . . *cute*."

It occurred to him he might be a little drunker than he'd originally thought.

"Especially the baby ones," Gabe agreed benignly. "Hey, did you see that video of the baby donkey in the hammock?"

"*Cute*," Mac confirmed triumphantly. And they tapped their beer bottles together.

Seemed Gabe was on his way to getting a little drunk, too.

Mac definitely had the head start, though. He was thinking about that poor damn dog Avalon had adopted, old and alone until she went in and picked it out.

He had begun to wonder if Avalon had seen something wounded in him, too, that needed rescuing way back then.

Too late, Avalon, he thought.

She literally thought he didn't care about a damn thing. It still threw him.

It was so profoundly the opposite of how he'd always viewed her that he'd known a moment of vertigo when she'd said those words.

They were quiet while Mikey McShane tuned his guitar up on stage.

"Might get a horse, too," Mac said suddenly. "A sad deaf horse that needs some love, maybe. And maybe an eagle that can't fly because it hurt its wing. And a dog and an owl who are best friends."

Gabe took this in, staring at Mac, his brow furrowed deeply. And then his expression cleared.

"Are you by any chance having woman problems?"

Mac thunked his beer down a little more adamantly than he might have otherwise. "Why else would I be drinking like a fool and spouting nonsense if I didn't have woman problems? You've known me long enough. I don't get careless. About anything."

"No. You sure don't."

They watched the kid on stage. He sported dyed jet-black hair and a little loop through his nose.

Avalon had been like a . . . window. His life had been so rigid and prescribed for all its excesses, and being with her had opened up this other dimension. Not because kissing her was a freaking erotic miracle for a teenager like him. The way she saw things. Animals, for instance. Once upon a time he'd seen squirrels as just scenery, everywhere, all the same, not as distinct little beings with their own little cultures and ways of relating. It was like the invention of a new color. He'd been as pulled toward her romantic view of the world as he was suspicious, even disdainful of it.

Funny to think how, in some ways, she was responsible for the life he was living now. He was a fucking goatherd! It was pretty funny.

"I don't think you've ever cared enough about a woman to get drunk about her," Gabe said idly.

"What a tribute, eh?" Mac lifted his bottle in a sardonic toast. "But I *don't* care about her. Not. At. All. She's just a thorn in my side."

"Sure, sure."

"And she has these . . . these *eyes*." Mac pointed to his own with two fingers. "Big brown ones. And you just want to kind of sink into them like . . . like a fur rug or a warm bath or I don't know."

"Sounds way cuter than a donkey."

"Word," Mac said, grimly, and took another sip. "She can be mean, though."

"Yeah. And you're a delicate little flower."

This made Mac grin. His grin faded. "It's just that some people can say things to me and they roll right off, but when she says the same damn thing . . ." He swept a hand back through his hair. "She sees things, you know?"

"I get it." He couldn't possibly, because Mac was hardly being a beacon of clarity, but the sympathy and brotherhood were a balm.

"I just don't like *anyone* getting the better of me."

"Yeah. That must be what's bothering you."

Mac shot him a black look.

"So who is it?" Gabe demanded.

"Don't wanna say."

"I bet I know."

Mac fixed him with a look that dared Gabe to keep guessing at his own peril. That was going to be the end of the subject.

And as if his friend had actually issued a command, Gabe raised his hands in mock surrender and lowered them again.

They drank in comradely silence for a time, and watched Mikey McShane struggle with his guitar. Mac found himself hoping poor, frustrated young Mikey McShane made it out of this town. A lot of people lived in this region because they couldn't afford to be anywhere else. And Mac knew you needed to leave before you really understood whether you belonged in the first place.

"I've been looking into grants for at-risk kids," Gabe mused, as if he was reading his thoughts. "We just don't have enough programs for after school. I wish there was a place for them to go to learn actual life skills. To build some self-esteem and confidence when their home lives are just shit, or outright battlegrounds."

"Yeah, otherwise they might end up singing Goth folk songs at open mics."

Gabe laughed.

But the wheels of Mac's Sierra Nevada–moistened brain began to spin. "They have grants for that sort of thing, huh?" he said idly.

Gabe left it at that. But a seed had been planted. You didn't poke at a seed after you planted it. You had to give it a chance to grow.

"This song is called 'Rainforest,'" Mikey McShane finally said. He cleared his throat again and dragged the mic stand toward him, and the mic squealed so aggressively everyone's head contracted into their bodies like the audience was comprised of so many turtles.

"Gosh, what do you think the song is going to be about, Gabe?" Mac asked his friend.

"I'm going to go out on a limb and say it's about the rainforest, Mac."

"I hope so. I really hope so."

Open mic nights at the Misty Cat were sporadically attended and unfailingly entertaining in a variety of ways for the person willing to see them multi-dimensionally.

"The woman I can't stop thinking about hardly knows I'm alive."

Mac turned toward his friend slowly.

Gabe had issued this so wryly, out of the blue, that it cut right through Mac's four Sierra Nevadas. But Gabe wasn't looking at him.

Given that Gabe was six feet four and usually knee-deep in PTA moms and even a few dads who all but performed acrobatics in order to get his attention, Gabe was the proverbial catch. He didn't really seem to know it.

"Given that you're a conspicuous bastard, Gabe, I doubt that."

"Takes one to know one," Gabe said, easily.

"Rainforest . . . disappearing like your love for me," Mikey sang and strummed. "*Rainfooooorest . . .*"

Somehow the song proved to be much more moving than either Mac or Gabe had anticipated. So they just listened.

CHAPTER 13

Avalon had read up on all the best methods for removing wallpaper, all of which involved spraying and steaming and so forth. She'd dutifully watched a number of achingly tedious videos about the process, keeping her promise not to bug her parents.

And she'd given it her best shot. But none of the methods were foolproof. Only once or twice did that hideous black-and-gold wallpaper neatly peel away from the wall in little satisfying sheets, like a sunburn. The rest of it seemed to have become one with the wall.

She wound up doing a *lot* of scraping. It was brutally hard work but jabbing a metal implement at a wall was both punishment and reward.

The reward part was burning off a little angst.

The punishment part was because she felt like a shit for being mean to Mac.

She jabbed at the wall a little harder.

Chick Pea was happily dozing in the sun in her

doggie bed downstairs, after gnawing for a while on a toy with what teeth she had left. Avalon was fully aware that she could have a heap of vet bills in her future. It hadn't mattered a damn once she saw Chick Pea. The house felt like it actually had a soul now, a furry one. And truthfully, having a pet felt like exhaling a breath she didn't know she'd been holding.

Mac had known that. But he also knew of her inclination to fall in love with creatures whose lives tended to be startlingly finite.

Funny that he'd been able to identify Corbin's face even when it was rolled into a tube. Mac had clearly done some Googling, which on the one hand was normal and rather gratifying. On the other hand, there wasn't much she could do to find out about him.

Apart from take jabs to see where it hurt.

There had been zero satisfaction in watching him go still when she hit her mark, though. She might as well have jabbed herself.

She had to hand it to him, though: *Tools Monthly* was actually pretty damn funny. Funny because it was true.

And Mac had said "we." When "we" go to the vet. He included his cat as a little partner in that sentence, and this struck her as almost unendurably poignant and cute.

As she worked, she'd attached her phone to one of her Bluetooth speakers and set it to shuffle. That was a mistake, because some of the songs were songs Corbin insisted she listen to, by bands so obscure that he might actually have been the only person to have ever heard of them.

She kind of just wanted to hear Erasure's greatest hits right now.

But then, suddenly, up popped a song by one of those Corbin-curated bands she actually loved: The Antlers. "Stairs to the Attic." It began urgently but quietly, barreling toward an anthemic climax. It was all about the unbearable lure of closed doors, about the wonder and pain of them. And how when the singer made it to the top of the stairs, all he found was a whole universe of stairs.

"Whatever you do, don't go in the attic," Mac had said to her.

Damned if that wasn't a metaphor for Mac in general.

Right then and there it seemed important to drop everything and go up into the attic.

The narrow flight of stairs—good dark wood mounted on a system of heavy chain pulleys—was down the hall in a modest-sized room probably used as an office over the years. She'd dumped the bean bag chair her parents had brought along in that room.

She experimentally put all of her weight on the bottom step.

No groaning or ominous creaking ensued; the chains held her.

So she took another step. Jounced a little. Again: no ominous creaking or groaning suggested she might not want to continue.

So she scaled the next and the next and the next.

When she was near the top she stood on her toes and looped her hand around one of the handles on the square door in the ceiling and pulled.

Nothing happened. It simply didn't give at all.

So far the Mac metaphor appeared to be holding.

She peered up at it. It was likely sealed stubbornly by a decade of old paint and dust.

She scaled another step for leverage, then looped both of her hands around the door handle and yanked. Hard. A grinding crunch almost toppled her from her perch, but she caught her balance just in time. This time her yank had yielded an intriguing wedge of darkness. Her heart gave an exultant little leap.

She scaled the final step to give herself more leverage. Took a breath. And pulled at the door with all her strength.

The door banged wide open in a cloud of agitated dust.

When she leaned eagerly toward the opening, the stairs lurched and swayed as if they'd just hit an iceberg. She gasped and flung her torso forward, arms flailing, scrabbling for a handhold inside the attic. She'd managed to sling one leg up there, in a frog-like splay just as, with a hideous, metallic shrieking groan, the chain gave way.

She screamed, threw her entire body forward, and crouched in a fetal position.

BAM.

The door snapped shut again behind her with a

thunderous Armageddon-like crash and thud which shook the house.

"Holy shit!" she said out loud after a blankly terrified, stunned fifteen seconds or so of sitting in the pitch dark of the attic.

Her heart was pounding so hard for a moment she could hear nothing over the whine of blood in her ears. That easily could have been her toppling ten feet to the floor instead of the stairs.

That had certainly happened quickly.

But then she supposed none of the disasters of her life had happened at a leisurely pace.

How the fuck was she supposed to get out of here?

She remained motionless, allowing her breathing to settle, willing her eyes to adjust to the dark. She hesitated to let her hands crawl blindly lest they encounter something else out crawling with more purpose. The attic was festooned with cobwebs; they tickled her face. Her fingertips sank into velvety dust when she touched the floor. Shadowy outlines of boxes came into view. But there wasn't much stuff, on the whole. Some random crap leaning in the corner, the typical flotsam of everyday life that wound up in the attic: an umbrella, what looked like a music stand, a pair of what might be barbecue tongs or those things you use to pinch stuff off high shelves, a solid-looking Ebenezer Scrooge–style cane.

A few patience-testing seconds later, she could just make out the outline of the door handle. She tugged. Hard.

It wouldn't effing budge.

She tried pushing.

That didn't do the trick, either.

She tried kicking it, thumping her feet against it like a trapped rabbit.

Nothing.

She yanked back hard, gripping it in her hands and letting the rest of her body act as a lever and pulled. "*GnnnNNNNNNNNNARGH!*" She staggered backward and landed hard on her butt. She drew her hand tentatively along the contours of the door, investigating a suspicion: yep. It was wedged at an angle. One of the hinges had likely broken.

Along with the stairs.

And so.

It occurred to her that this very well might be the reason Mac had told her not to go in the attic.

She scanned the space carefully and then . . . yes! Hallelujah! A sliver of light, behind stacked boxes. A window. She took two enthusiastic steps toward it.

Just as something rustled about three feet away from her.

She froze. Her stomach literally iced over and all the hair on her body stood up.

So she had company. Something bigger than a rat, from the sound of its scrabbly little feet. As much as she loved animals, it was difficult to be crazy about the ones she couldn't see.

The box in front of the window shifted easily enough, but when she reached for the latch, it wouldn't budge. The damn thing was painted shut.

Failing Chick Pea leaping free of the house somehow and running out to fetch Mac, barking a message ("What is it, girl? Did Avalon do something
stupid again? Lead the way!"), she was going to need
to break the glass. She had a hunch Chick Pea was a
little deaf.

She seized hold of that old cane, made a fortress of
the boxes, huddled behind them, pulled her T-shirt
up over her head to protect against flying shards of
glass, and then jammed the cane into the glass.

Nothing happened, except for a vibration that shot
up her arm and into her teeth.

Now she was good and pissed.

She hauled back and whaled on the window like
the building was on fire until finally, with a crunch
and a tinkle, the glass gave way. She kept smacking
until most of the glass was clear of the frame. Then
stood on her toes and hollered through it. "Help!
HELP! HEELLLP!"

Maybe she ought to yell "Get the paddles!" instead. She entertained a fleeting fantasy of her family
convening upon Devil's Leap, their Spidey senses
a-tingle.

"Mac!" she bellowed. "*Maaaaaaaaac!*"

She suspected that even if he heard her, he might
mistake her for one of his goats.

"HAPPY BIRTHDAY TO YOU! HAPPY BIRTH-
DAY TO YOU! HAPPY BIRTHDAY HAPPY
BIRTHDAY HAPPY BIRTHDAY TO YOU!"

Now, who wouldn't get curious about the birthday
song emerging from the middle of nowhere?

Still nothing.

She really was in the middle of freaking nowhere. And to think, only a day or so ago she'd been pondering why anyone would live anywhere other than in the country.

"YOP!" she tried finally. "Yop!"

That's how the Whos got Horton's attention, after all.

"Avalon? Is that you?"

Mac's voice was right underneath the window. She nearly crumpled with relief. "Yes!"

A little silence. "Did you . . . did you just say *yop*?"

She hesitated. "I said a lot of other things before you showed up," she hedged.

"I thought for a minute one of my goats had gotten out and a coyote had him. That must have been you."

"Probably."

"Are you . . . *stuck* up in the attic, by any chance?"

"Yes."

There was more silence. "I'm guessing you kind of understand why I told you not to go up there."

He was really going to make her work for it. The sheer effort of holding in his laughter was probably building yet another quadrant of muscle on his abdomen.

"Also?" she added. "There's . . . something up here with me. Something that . . . moves."

"Oh, you've met our ghost?"

"There's a fucking *ghost*?" Her voice went up an octave.

"Don't you guys have a ghost at the Misty Cat?"

"It's less the *idea* of ghost than the context in which the ghost is currently occurring."

"I see," he said, gravely as an academic. "So if you passed the ghost in the hall on the way to the bathroom you'd high-five it. But it's the dark . . . close . . . stuffy . . . cobwebby . . . attic that gives you pause?"

There was a beat of silence.

"It's a her?"

"One of them is."

The motherfucker was really enjoying himself.

"Um, Mac. Do you think you—oh God oh God oh God it *moved again*."

She could see the shadow rearing up against the wall.

"That's what she said." His voice was trembling with laughter now.

The shadow shifted; she thought she saw a needle-like nose.

"Oh, I think it's just a possum." She was somewhat relieved. "Wow, that thing is big. And *not* cute. At least it's not moving fast."

"Those things can be mean. And they'll eat just about anything. It's probably hungry. Maybe even rabid, if it's moving slow."

"You really are a dick, Mac."

"I really am," he agreed with purely evil placidity.

He fell silent again.

"Mac?" She hated that her voice was a trifle querulous.

He was instantly as brisk as a sergeant. "Okay, honey, let's get you out of there."

Did he just call her *honey*? Exactly as if he'd done

it dozens of times before? Funny how instantly comforting the word was.

She had no idea how he planned to get into the house, but apparently that was no challenge. She heard footsteps thundering right below her within about a minute.

"Avalon, can you hear me?" he shouted up.

"Yes!"

"I'm going to ram that door open and then we'll just lower you down on my shoulders. I can handle it. Should be nice and cushy."

"*Cushy?*"

Though ramming something sounded hopelessly macho. The very word gave her a little thrill.

"Good cushy. Like a peach. Your butt will feel like one of those neck pillows you carry onto airplanes."

She closed her eyes and growled a lament that tapered into a colorful string of muttered curses. "I'm glad I can entertain you, Mac."

"It's just different, is all." She heard the laughter in his voice. "I was outside fixing the sprinklers on my property. I've done that at least a dozen times before. I've never done *this* before. Stand well back from the door. Way back. I'm going to count to three and go in for the punch."

"Standing back now."

The pointy-nosed possum ducked back into the shadows, as if it was listening to the whole conversation. Or maybe it was simply achieving a better position from which to pounce.

"One . . . two . . . *THREE.*"

BAM!

The door rocketed open in a cloud of dust and Mac's head poked up into the darkness, dust sifting down all around him like he'd just been conjured.

"Hi," he said. His smile might as well have been a lantern in the dim light. "Scooch forward and dangle your legs down through the opening. I'll turn around and we'll get you down on my shoulders."

He vanished again.

She scooched as ordered and perched on the edge and peered down into Mac's up-tilted face.

"I can see right into your nostrils," she said.

"Don't get hypnotized by their depths. You're going to need to have your wits about you. Okay, I'm going to turn around now and we're just going to eeeaaaase you down onto my shoulders. How's your upper body strength? You're going to need some. Mine is stupendous."

"I'm good, thanks."

She wasn't going to mention that her upper body, every bit of it, was stiff from scraping wallpaper from the wall. But she didn't have it in her to admit to a weakness in front of Mac.

She scooted forward, pressing her palms down on the dusty attic floor behind her to brace herself, and he maneuvered beneath her just as her foot swung down and brushed his face.

She saw his nose bend a little to the left.

"Ow! Watch the shoes! That's my nose!"

"Sorry, sorry!" Oh, God. This was already mortifying and she wasn't even on top of his shoulders yet, like some drunk twenty-something at Coachella right before she ripped her top off and waved it around her head.

Mac gripped her ankles loosely but firmly. His hands slid up a little farther, maybe to gain purchase, maybe to savor a bit, but there was no way he didn't encounter a little razor stubble. This was easily the least sexy thing she'd ever done with a man as an adult. Nevertheless, a current that could only be described as lust shot from his hand right into her privates.

When his hands began gliding up her calves to clamp on top of her thighs, her head felt light as a balloon.

Of all the ways she had imagined touching Mac Coltrane again, none of them involved him guiding her on down like he was a foreman on the Golden Gate Bridge supervising a girder into place.

But her poor stiff arms wobbled as she lowered herself down and she landed a little too hard on board that shelf of shoulders, which made her arms windmill wildly, which sent him into a staggering lunge to the left to avoid the stair wreckage. She compensated by flexing her thighs to stay on top.

"Avalon, don't *squeeze* with your thighs, for the love of God! That's my carotid artery! I'll black out."

"Sorry. Sorry." She relaxed her thigh grip but she didn't know where to put her hands unless it was to thrust them out parallel to the ground, à la an airplane, or grip his ears like handlebars. He hoisted his knee and took one Frankenstein-esque step forward. Which tipped her hard to the left.

She squeaked and reflexively seized handfuls of his hair and yanked back hard, like a rodeo queen ten seconds away from clinching the championship.

He gave a muffled squawk of pain, pivoted abruptly, staggered in a semicircle like a dreidel losing steam, barreled at a forward run toward the beanbag chair, shouted, "Look out!" and dumped her into it.

She bounced once and lay still.

It seemed unduly silent after that.

It was safe to say it was a stunned sort of silence.

She slowly, slowly turned her eyes up to his.

They stared at each other in something like mortified, almost impressed, slightly accusatory amazement. As if neither one of them had realized such *thorough* mutual indignity was even possible as adults.

His face was scarlet, either with exertion or pain or mortification—and his hair was standing up in little peaks all over like whitecaps whipped up on a bay.

She was pretty sure she was the same color. Judging from her temperature.

"Maybe we should have gotten a ladder," she offered. Subdued.

"Maybe," he said shortly.

More silence. He was still staring at her with an expression that suggested he thought she might be as possessed as the possum up there in the attic.

She cleared her throat. "Thank you. And . . . I'm sorry."

Her parents had always taught her those were the go-to words when a situation was untenable.

He could take them however he wished.

He just shook his head to and fro, to and fro, slowly and wonderingly. Then rotated his neck experimentally.

She didn't hear any grinding noises.

She was desperately glad she hadn't broken him.

And then he frowned faintly. "Wait. You're sorry about going up in the *attic* or about . . ."

"I'm sorry about needing to be rescued," she said firmly. "I'm very sorry I inconvenienced you. I'm . . . sorry I squeezed your neck and pulled your hair."

Why did their conversations always devolve into something that sounded like an exchange between two kids on the playground?

"It's very soft," she added. Lamely. "Your hair."

His expression teetered somewhere between hilarity and censure.

"I think your cheek says 'Skechers,'" she said, quietly, when he didn't seem inclined to speak.

He swiped at his cheek absently. He missed the "S" completely. She didn't say anything. He'd get around to noticing it eventually. If she was a guy who looked like him she'd be looking in the mirror all the time.

"I'm a little stiff from working on the wallpaper. Otherwise my balance would have been a little better."

"Yeah?" he said abstractedly.

She nodded silently. Like a shy three-year-old.

"Hey, where's your guard dog?" he asked.

"Chick Pea," Avalon called. Then louder, "CHICK PEA!"

A few seconds later, they heard the *click-click-click* of tiny nails progressing sedately through the hall. Chick Pea trotted merrily into the room, smiling a doggie smile and went straight to Avalon, the very picture of blissful obliviousness.

She bent down to scratch her head. "I think she might be a little deaf."

She glanced up at Mac. Judging from his silence and his expression, he was expending significant internal effort to refrain from saying something. "I told you so." Or something in that vein.

She kept her face down. The silence elongated.

"Simon Le Bon. John Bonham. Janis Joplin. Sarah Vaughan. Robert Plant. Bob Marley. Baba O'Riley."

She levered her head slowly up in amazement.

He'd recited these names almost defiantly. It sounded like he was reading a list of war dead.

"What . . ." She wondered if she'd damaged her hearing or her brain in the stair crash.

"Those are the *names* of my goats."

She stared at him. A flush painted her to her hairline.

"Say them in a goat voice in your head," he urged.

Simon Le Baaaan, John Baaaanham, Janis Jaaaaaplin, Sarah Vaaaaughan, Raaabert Plant, Baaaaab Marley . . . Baaa Baaa O'Riley.

Wow, that was *hilarious*. And touching. Vivid and so . . . so him.

Shame made her face go even hotter. She'd accused him of not caring about anything. It was a fairly terrible thing to say to anyone. It had been calculated to hurt him, to jar him into some sort of truth or revelation.

It had worked, though. If she were being scrupulously honest with herself, she wasn't entirely sorry.

"They're very good names," she said, quietly.

His eyes widened again. For a moment there his face was luminous with some complicated emotion.

"My chickens have names, too."

"Okay," she said softly.

He went quiet again.

"Avalon . . . why did you go up in the attic?" he asked finally. The tone wasn't entirely gentle.

She didn't think she could pull off "because you told me not to." The mood of the moment somehow didn't support glibness.

She just looked up at him wordlessly, and widened her eyes in rueful apology.

He just shook his head, slowly. "Avalon . . . I just . . ." He sighed. As if he was about to deliver a truth he was weary of repeating. "All I want is for you to be safe."

And she realized that it was, in fact, true.

Inherent in Mac was a quality of caring that informed his actions.

Even if the words coming out of his mouth implied something else altogether.

She folded her hands together in her lap and looked down at them. Chastened and subdued and suddenly rather confused.

Neither of them spoke for a moment or two. Chick Pea panted quietly next to her.

Finally she lifted her eyes to his.

The corner of his mouth dented a little.

"Hey," he said suddenly, softly. "You've brought a cobweb down with you."

He bent a little in front of her. She could see in his eyes as though they were crystal balls. What she saw was a rapt girl, frozen as if he were a wizard casting a spell.

His hand reached out slowly toward her hair and he delicately freed the strand.

He handed it to her as if it were forensic evidence, or a strand of rare silk.

She watched herself, as if from above, take that damned cobweb like he was handing her his letterman jacket.

Their fingertips brushed when the transfer was made. And just that little brush turned her thoughts to white noise. *Sssssss.* Like lightning had taken out the cable.

He had had his hands on her ankles and pretty close to the seat of all *desire*, there, at the crook of her legs.

But somehow it was this tender intimacy that undid her.

She could all but feel herself unravel, as if she herself were made of something as fine as cobwebs.

She couldn't look up at him because she was afraid he'd see the pulse thumping in her throat.

In that moment, a moment that lasted forever and just a few seconds, everything she considered herself to be, all of her achievements to date, finally, figuratively, softly collapsed like a house of cards. Inside crouched the teenage girl she once was: lustful and confused and madly, recklessly in love, heartbroken and not good enough for him.

She realized in a blinding flash that her entire life to date, from GradYouAte to overeducated Corbin, might very well be an I-told-you-so born of that long-ago moment: Mac had blown her off course.

She looked up at him and prayed that nothing of what she'd just realized was in her face.

She discovered that his face was still. He seemed a little tense about the mouth.

He finally straightened and drew in a long sharp breath.

"Well, then. Guess I can chalk this little episode up to be careful what you wish for."

He said this mostly to himself. And with that ironic, cryptic little statement, he turned around and headed down the stairs.

But she didn't hear that fourth step groan.

He must know that he needed to skip it.

Mac had in fact gotten into the house by shoving a window in the living room open wide enough to squeeze through. It hadn't been easy, though. *That* particular window frame was going to need scraping and sanding and repainting, if she was serious about getting the place ship-shape before she sold it. He wondered if Avalon intended to attempt to undertake that particularly nasty job all on her own. It was nothing but methodical, relentless grunt work, all dust and splinters.

But then, scraping layers off things was never painless.

It was every bit as beautiful as he remembered.

"Hey, Cat," he said to The Cat, who appeared and fell into a long-legged stride alongside him, as if they were a couple of rogue detectives out on a case.

But he was, in fact, feeling a little subdued.

He just . . . found it less and less easy to leave her every time he was in her presence. Even when he couldn't get away fast enough.

Even though every encounter seemed to flay a fine layer from *him*.

He knew how that kind of work could be a very effective form of purging and self-flagellation. But he could tell she was already stiff from it. She wasn't a common farmer like he was, used to laboring away.

He smiled crookedly at himself. He *liked* being who he was.

Didn't he?

But there had to be some other reason she was here all by herself, going at that huge house.

When he got home, he followed a hunch and

whipped open his laptop and navigated to SilliPutty, scrolling through items.

There was a little jab in the area of his heart when he saw it.

> Sources tell us that Corbin Bergson is flailing at the helm of GradYouAte in the wake of CEO Avalon Harwood's sudden mysterious leave of absence. Could the abrupt departure of a certain intern be related?

Mac leaned back against the chair and blew out a breath.

Well, well, well.

He was both grateful and irritated on Avalon's behalf that someone on her staff was loose-lipped or bribable. The notion that she might be hurting, and not just thanks to wallpaper scraping, bothered him a lot, though.

He mulled.

He knew what he *really* wanted to do right now. And wasn't he a guy who got what he wanted?

And yet he couldn't remember his pulse going like this the last time he went after something he wanted.

Maybe the stakes just hadn't been high enough before.

CHAPTER 14

Avalon answered the doorbell a half hour later to find Mac standing there, still wearing what he'd been wearing when he'd maneuvered her out of the attic.

"Do you have a bathing suit?" he said without preamble. "Oh, hello, Chick Pea. Down, girl. Whoa, easy there."

Chick Pea was sitting sedately next to Avalon, smiling politely up at him, eyes agleam with bonhomie, fluffy tail switching a little.

"Why do I need a bathing suit? Do you know something about the plumbing that I don't?"

"I know approximately a million things about this house that you don't. But no, that's not why."

"*You* need to borrow one? Because yours is in the wash?"

"I usually go without one when I go swimming around here, since there's no one around to care," he said affably.

Dear God. What was he trying to do to her? Her knees went buttery.

He cleared his throat. "Listen, didn't you say you were a little stiff from scraping wallpaper?"

"I did say that."

"There's an old natural hot springs about a fifteen-minute hike or so from here. Gets dark fast out there and we'll want to be back before then. We've got about an hour and a half, maybe two, before sunset. You in?"

Delight pierced so abruptly it stole her breath.

It immediately warred with wariness. Getting half-naked with the very hot man who had broken her heart wasn't quite equivalent to sticking her big toe up the faucet, but no one would have called it a *wise* decision.

But then, no one was holding her to a particular standard of wisdom but herself.

And maybe she just needed to prove to herself that he no longer had the power to shape her life, even if he once had.

Finally, pure curiosity tipped the vote. She wanted to see the damn springs.

"Give me five minutes."

The sunset was going to be a pretty good one. A few of the fluffy oblong clouds overhead were already limned in golden light, and with luck they'd go gold or tangerine or aubergine.

While in San Francisco, she'd desperately missed the surprise and variations of sunsets and sunrises. The light of the computer and phone screens and the neon lights over the takeout places never really varied.

She ducked to her knees, which was none too easy, given how stiff her muscles were, and touched a finger to the water. And watched the ripples waver out. River water warmed by the earth and cycled out again. Ceaselessly fresh. She could see her reflection in it; she could see Mac behind her smiling. Behind him was a tall cluster of old boulders.

"It's about three and a half feet at its deepest. You going in?"

It was the first thing he'd said in about fifteen minutes. He'd clearly been so full of thoughts on the fifteen or so minute walk that he couldn't say any of them. Or maybe he was even nervous. Maybe they both were.

The bathing suit her mom had stuffed into her gym bag was olive green and fashioned of fabric that was probably considered space-age at the time; it featured dramatic darts in the boob area and a flouncy little skirt. If her own willpower collapsed on her, this suit might very well keep Mac Coltrane at arm's length, should he make the proverbial move. Her mom must have kept it out of nostalgic reasons; Avalon thought she recognized it from a few old family photos. It fit like a charm, though. She *did* have her mom's curves.

She shucked her sweatshirt and kicked off her thongs, then hesitated for a moment before setting about peeling off the jeans.

Which gripped onto the exotic fabric of her bath-

ing suit the way her feet gripped the adhesive ducks
in the bathtub in the bathroom she and Eden had
shared growing up. It was a wonder there wasn't a
little suctiony pop when she finally got them loose.

Mac watched this whole little dance in rapt, entertained silence.

She was fit even if her own abs weren't quite drum-
tight. She was comfortably certain his silence was a
tribute to the fact that she was well worth looking at,
suit or no suit.

"Wow, that's some bathing suit, Avalon. Speaking
of tightropes and things you might wear to walk on
them."

His voice was a little bit lulled, though. A man a
little bit drugged by his own hormones.

"It's an heirloom," she said mildly. "Passed down
through my family for generations."

He gave a short laugh.

She touched a toe into the hot springs. And the rest
of her body sort of reflexively oozed in after it as if
she were literally melting.

"Ohhhhhhh . . ." It felt like the best thing that had
ever happened to her.

"Good, huh?"

"Holy Mother," she sighed. She closed her eyes for
a few seconds. She opened her eyes.

He was still standing near the largest stone, motionless, watching with satisfaction, as if her enjoy-
ment was something he'd personally accomplished.

"So is your plan that you are going to guard me

like I'm Cleopatra and you're a centurion? You look like you should be holding a spear."

"Aren't you mixing up your cultures and centuries?"

"Probably," she murmured.

"Do you *mind* if I get in there with you? Hot tubs are pretty seventies and you know what they got up to in the seventies."

"Macramé. Heavy metal. Muscle cars."

"Orgies," he contributed.

She stared at him. The word was very conjuring of writhing bodies, always fairly sexy, but in her mind's eye all the men had seventies mustaches very similar to her dad's, and that, as far as she was concerned, *wasn't* sexy.

"Don't you need a crowd for that sort of thing?" She was way too relaxed to bat that innuendo back or to protest. Maybe that was his plan. She didn't care about that, either.

"I don't know. You're the one who goes to, what was that, bondage farmers' markets and all that stuff. But I can make a few calls."

She gave a somnolent snort. "It was a fair. The Folsom Street Fair. A decadent celebration of . . . a lot of things, let's just say. Not a farmers' market. To tell you the honest-to-God truth, I feel about as sexy as a carrot floating in soup. A really happy carrot."

It was a warning of sorts that if his plan was to seduce her, he had his work cut out for him.

And it was also a relief: the less sexy she felt, the

less inclined she was to attempt to climb him like a tree. Because standing backlit by the sunset right now, no one had ever looked more tempting.

He yanked his boots off and peeled off his shirt. Maybe it was the fact that the world went slo-mo that made him resemble a sculptor unveiling a statue. She watched through slitted eyes. The casual undressing held an unexpected walloping intimacy, and her stomach muscles braced as her senses took the impact. There was no way he didn't know the power of his own nearly bare self, because Mac was the sort who thought of all the angles.

He was brownish everywhere from the sun apart from a hint of paleness at his hipbones. An ordinary pair of red swimming trunks clung lovingly there. The rest of him looked like it had been turned on a lathe or cut by whatever tool they use to facet diamonds. She saw a scar across the lower part of his thigh. That was new.

And then all of that vanished under the water, and only his smooth brown shoulders remained above, like two enticing tropical islands.

She might actually be in dangerous territory here. She was literally in the soup!

All she could do was smile drowsily. The warm water resumed doing its business of soaking all the tension out; maybe it wouldn't let any new tension back in.

"Is it yoga?" he asked, finally.

"Is what yoga?"

"Is that how you got thighs like anacondas? Thighs that can strangle a grown man?"

This was pretty funny. "I've never tested that particular application. But I suppose it could come in handy. Yeah, I do yoga. Not with a good deal of commitment, but I do it. San Francisco hills, you know. Good for the legs."

"Sure, sure."

The water lovingly lapped them and they were quiet.

"Big job, getting that wallpaper off," he said idly.

"Yep."

"That master bedroom's thirty by thirty, I believe."

"The length of a football field, if you ask my scapulas and trapezoids and the rest of the muscle gang."

"Boy, there's like five more rooms that size. And then you're going to what, paint them?" He mimed big up-and-down paint roller motions.

"Yes. I'm going to paint them."

All of those words—*I'm* and *going* and *paint*—made her want to sink deeper and deeper into the water.

"Wow. That'll take you *days*. For just that one room."

He was a sadist.

"Yes."

"Where are you going to start painting?"

"I thought I'd go with the main room, downstairs."

"Have you ever painted a room before all by yourself, Avalon?"

She hesitated. "There's a first time for everything."

That sentence was suddenly fraught.

He seemed to know it.

They both stopped talking.

Still, she had kind of the sense he was working up to something.

"You know that main room? The one you put the giant couch in? My mom used to play the grand piano and sing there."

She widened her eyes. "*Really*?"

She remembered seeing the piano that day she'd been inside. It was pretty hard imagining Mac's mom abandoning herself to song. She was like Mac's dad: beautiful in an otherworldly way. She sounded as rehearsed and elegant as Jackie O giving a tour of the White House whenever she spoke. She seldom joined them out on Devil's Leap, and when she did she was a politely remote figure arranged neatly on a towel, as if someone had brought their favorite doll out for an airing.

"Yeah. She liked the acoustics."

"I remember thinking your mom was so pretty. Her hair was shiny and straight like my Barbie, and no other mothers I ever saw had hair like that. She never seemed like a mo . . ."

She stopped herself in time.

He shrugged with one shoulder; the water moved a little, rippling toward her. "It's okay. You're right, she *wasn't* very mommish. Not like your mom was, with the snacks in her purse and the Band-Aids with Sponge Bob on them and the flip-flops shoved in the car door pocket so there was always a spare pair when someone broke one, and how she was just sort of part of everything you did. Momming really wasn't my mom's thing."

He said it easily enough. But it was hard to hear that he'd been fully aware of what he lacked in the midst of all he had.

Even back then Avalon must have sensed that he'd needed to be loved. And she had loved him.

Even if he cared for things, it was entirely possible he just didn't know how to love back.

"It could have been a lot worse, honestly. Hell, how many kids do you know who got an Audi convertible for their sixteenth birthday?"

He was being glib, but his voice was soft, soft as the water, soft as the muted colors of the sky.

She smiled, but didn't want to. And she didn't ask what had become of that convertible.

She had a hunch that it was among the things auctioned off when his dad had been hauled away to jail.

The loss of everything must have been terrifying; it must have felt like being sucked toward a drain.

She fought the urge to reach out and grip his hand. As if she could pull him out of the rubble the way he'd hoisted her out of the attic. Her heart was an amnesiac; it ached as if it was actually being pulled toward him, even though this guy had once made a fricassee of it.

But maybe . . . maybe he was working toward some

truth, now. Maybe she was about to hear some explanation she'd longed nearly her entire life to hear. Something that explained that chasm between how things had felt when she was with him and the things he'd said.

And hope was like a glittering shard, shortening her breath. Hope . . . and fear.

"Mac . . . I'm—I'm sorry all of that happened to you."

He nodded once. Quirked the corner of his mouth. And sighed.

"Those days at Devil's Leap were the happiest I've ever been." He almost whispered it. Confiding a secret.

Her heart was now pounding so hard it was a wonder it didn't send ripples of water toward him.

"That's why . . ." He gave a muffled little laugh. "That's why I originally wanted to buy the house. If you do sell it to me, you can use the hot springs any time you want."

His eyes were on her. Soft and dark. Mesmeric. Once so beloved.

But something about his last words struck her as just a little . . . odd.

A bolt of suspicion smote her.

She coughed a laugh. "Oh. My. God."

Conviction violently uncoiled in her like a spring and practically shot her out of the water. She grabbed her towel and rubbed almost viciously over herself as if she could strip off whatever remained of her idiocy.

She'd startled him. "Avalon . . . what the . . . are you okay?"

She paused. "This whole . . . *thing* . . ." She gestured to him and the hot springs with a swoop of her hand. ". . . the *abs*, the voice, the hot springs . . . was a ploy, wasn't it? To talk me out of the house?"

She could hear her voice stag-leaping octaves. She was aware her fury was all out of proportion to the circumstances. She was furious at herself for getting sucked in again.

She rammed her jeans on, which required a lot of rapid, dramatic hula-hooping, and jammed her feet into her flip-flops.

"I'M NOT GOING TO SELL YOU THE HOUSE," she said, once dressed.

He was clearly shocked. "I swear to *God*, Avalon, that's not what—"

He lifted himself out of the water.

Oh, that dripping, gleaming, lean muscle.

She would *not* look at it.

And then she did.

Turned and stared at him hard. If there was any luck, he'd turn to stone right there because that was the direction he was heading anyway.

"You . . . you . . . God, you really turned into a Coltrane, didn't you, Mac?"

Mac froze. "Now wait a goddamn minute!"

What the hell had just happened? One moment he was sitting in the warm pool, wading into deeper emotional waters than he'd yet dared. And the next she was running away as though a scorpion had bit her on the ass.

It was almost funny how she knew what the cruelest insult would be. And only someone who really got him would understand how to hurt him that way.

Suddenly she bolted.

Yikes! In seconds she'd be out of view.

"Fuck fuck fuck." He punctuated the grab of each article of clothing with that word. But he didn't have time and he wasn't about to let her head back by herself.

Her hair came down and flew out behind her in damp streamers.

And suddenly they were in his dream. He was chasing her; he couldn't catch up.

He nearly tripped scrambling into his jeans, hopping on one foot and then the other. He swore fervently but there wasn't time to tie himself into his boots. So he just grabbed them and ran barefoot, very inadvisable, but in a few seconds she'd be out of view, and at least this was mostly dirt and flattened scrub and fuck it, he could chance it. He was all but tippy-toeing on the balls of his feet like Wile E. Coyote sneaking up on the Road Runner.

CHAPTER 15

"Avalon. *Avalon*. You have it wrong! I swear to God! Please, talk to me, for God's sake!"

She only picked up the pace. Of course she knew how to run, sort of, in flip-flops. They'd *lived* in flip-flops as kids. Running in them without falling flat on your face was kind of an art.

Between her flippy-flopping and him mincing in his bare feet over the ground, it was the slowest, most ridiculous pursuit ever.

"Avalon! LOOK OUT FOR THAT WELL!"

She stopped so abruptly her arms windmilled. Her head whipped to and fro looking down at the ground.

He caught up triumphantly.

Still hopping. He seized the opportunity to drop a boot and shove a foot in.

She glared at him. Two bright pink spots of temper high in her cheeks.

"There's no well, is there? I should have known the only way you know how to get your way is through *bullshit*."

"No. I wouldn't let you fall down it regardless. But I'm not going to let you walk back to the house by yourself."

She just growled ferally and spun and took off again.

At a flippy-floppy trot.

He had a clear view for at least a few yards so he shoved his other foot into his other boot and stuffed the laces in and ran to catch up to her. He flanked her most of the way but she never turned.

Her temper was a force field that could have repelled *Star Wars*–type lasers and it didn't matter because he was going to see her safely home.

She ignored him all the way to the house, rammed her key into the lock and slammed into the house.

ARRGH.

He clawed his fingers up through his hair.

"Well, fuck *me*," he muttered. It was safe to say that had *not* gone the way he'd hoped it would.

He stood there indecisively, staring at the door.

She reemerged a minute later with the dog in her arms and gave a little yelp. "Jesus, Mac, are you *still* here? Shoo! Go home."

"Not going anywhere until you talk to me."

That was the plan, he decided.

Chick Pea selected the azalea nearest to the porch rail to tinkle on. Then returned and hopped up on the lounge chair.

Mac eyed her dubiously as she did all this. That was definitely a sort of hybrid dog-cat. Not necessarily a bad thing, just an unusual thing.

Avalon finally heaved a sigh. "Fine, Mac. Say what you have to say."

"Can I come up there on the porch? Or do I have to semi-shout it from where I'm standing?"

She actually hesitated. And finally she stood aside. *Well* aside. As if in the absence of the availability of a hazmat suit, distance would have to do.

Two pairs of brown eyes, hers and Chick Pea's, watched as he made his way up the flagstone path to the porch.

He took a deep breath. And then the words came in a rush, as if he was arguing for his life. He kind of was.

"Okay. I want to tell you some things about me. The reason I *really* hate the song 'Don't Cry Out Loud.' My mom used to play it on that grand piano in that room with the chandelier and sing in this very sort of pointed, melodramatic way, just banging away and howling with her eyes closed, and my brother and I knew she was passively-aggressively singing it to my dad and *about* my dad. And oh my GOD I hated it. I wanted to curl up and die. It was farcical. Back then it was torture. Every day was a cavalcade of tension. Of things implied but never said. No one ever talked to each other and my brother and I were both together and alone because I couldn't really talk to him, either."

"Jesus, Mac . . ."

"Not fun to hear, right? I used to go out to the hot springs with my brother to get away from Mom and Dad fighting. Going at it hammer and tongs. Yelling at each other, over each other, about each other. Never, ever solving a damn thing. Sometimes I think they liked big houses because both loved the sound of their own voices, so the echo in a big marble foyer was just an added bonus. I have never told anyone that in my entire life."

The silence almost rang. As if it was the aftermath of a little explosion. Perhaps a stair crash.

Her eyes were on him, softer now. But still wary.

"So you don't talk to your mom at all?" she ventured. Not accusingly. Trying to understand.

"No. Not really. She remarried a plastic surgeon. Her nose changes subtly every year. I get the Christmas card."

She tried and failed not to smile at that. "Maybe you can make a flip book out of them."

It was a relief to laugh at that. She was such a smartass, but it came with such warmth.

They had inched closer to each other, without realizing it.

"What about Ty?" she pressed.

He blew out a breath and swept his hand through his hair. "Ty kind of turned into my dad, if you exclude the bit about felonies and federal prison, and that was exactly what my dad always wanted. He's a venture capitalist. Puts deals together for other companies. Brokers buyouts, that sort of thing. He thought I was an idiot for joining the national guard. He was always sticking up for my dad. We fought. It got ugly. We haven't talked in about eight years."

She was still. He watched her shoulders rise high as she pulled in a long breath.

"Wow. I just . . . Yeah, I can imagine you wouldn't back down."

He couldn't quite read her tone. Soft, just a little ironic. But not without affection. And not without a certain sadness. She did know him, after all.

He was breathing easier, now. "It's just . . . I wanted to be as different from my dad as possible. My dad was a destroyer. So I wanted to build things. My life was chaotic. I wanted order and predictability. I never really learned a damn useful thing, unless you counted getting hair gel just right. I never felt I'd been much good to anyone. I wanted to know what it was like to grow or create something from the very beginning, to know my life had an impact and a *reason*. It felt like if you could plan it, and build it, and see it, and touch it, then no one could rip it right out from under you."

She was silent for a moment, taking this in. "Mac . . . you've always had value. You know that now, right?"

He wished she would say, "You, in fact, meant everything to me."

Because he once could have said those words to her and it would have been true.

"Sure," he said softly. Because she was waiting for reassurance, hurting on his behalf. And he wanted to reassure her.

She'd fallen silent again.

Somehow, like shadows stretching toward each other, they'd moved closer still.

"Anyway. I was good at the work in the guard and I made friends based on what I could do and on my own strengths, not who my dad was or how much money I had. I knew I'd made the right decision for me."

Her big dark eyes were fixed on him, and her mouth was turned up in a sort of rueful way. "I just . . ." She gave up and made a helpless little gesture with her hands, almost supplicating. "That's one of the finest things I've ever heard."

He loved the word *finest*. Elegant and somber, almost ceremonial.

"Yeah, I'm a prince. I didn't actually like the regimentation one bit."

"I was gonna say . . ."

He laughed and so did she.

It felt luxurious to be known. "I'm better at leading, I think. Which I eventually was able to do. And I know how to survive. And so . . . here I am."

There passed a moment of silence interrupted only by Chick Pea making snorkeling noises into her flank as she cleaned.

"I honestly don't know what I would do if my world fell apart like that, Mac."

"Ah, you'd be fine. You're a fighter, Avalon. You'd probably go about it differently, but I have no doubt you'd still buy this house out from under me."

She laughed again, and he knew then, definitively, that it was all right. That whatever had spooked her back there he had fixed for now.

"I swear to you . . . all I wanted to do was show you the damn hot springs because you were sore. That bathing suit with the frill on it was *so* worth it."

She flashed a swift little smile. "I believe you."

The mood was feather-soft, suddenly. "So you like my abs, huh?"

"Nope," she said instantly.

They both knew this was a big lie.

"So since I just told you something pretty awkward, why don't you tell me why you're really here in Hellcat Canyon, Avalon. I read SilliPutty. I have my theories."

"Oh, is that how it works?" She sighed. "I might as well tell you. Corbin cheated on me. To be more specific, I *caught* him cheating on me."

He hissed in a breath. "That sucks, Avalon. I'm sorry."

This won him a bleakish laugh. "Nothing a little retail therapy couldn't help."

She gestured to the house.

His theory had been correct. She *was* kind of doing what he'd done: trying to impose a little order on something in the wake of destruction. Metaphorically reforming something that had fallen into disrepair.

He thought of a dozen things he could say about Corbin and how he was out of his fucking mind to cheat on her. But he didn't want another guy in the conversation any longer than necessary.

"You're through?" he said shortly. "The two of you?"

"Yeah," she confirmed. "Mac . . . can I ask you something?" She sounded tentative.

"Of course."

"Do you think GradYouAte is stupid?"

He was so astonished by the question for a moment he was speechless. "Stupid? Avalon, it's *amazing*."

She pushed a streamer of still-damp hair behind her ear. "It's just . . . some days I feel like I got caught up in the momentum of it before I knew whether it was what I really wanted. I had this idea and we just sort of made it happen. I bought this house because I wanted to make a deliberate choice. To do something from the beginning to the end. Kind of like you did, I guess."

He moved closer, nearly closing completely the remaining distance between them.

"Listen, Avalon . . . I know I've given you a little shit about it. But you created a virtual world, something that had never before existed, from just an *idea*. As far as I'm concerned, you're like Hermione Granger with a wand, conjuring something from the ether. No matter how you feel about it now, I'm convinced you can do anything you want. You're kind of a sorceress."

He was a little embarrassed that he'd pulled out a word like *sorceress*. But her face was turned up toward his, luminous and unguarded, close enough for him to count her freckles. She was listening, softly enthralled, her eyes brilliant, intent, in that way he remembered from when they were so hungry to touch each other.

And just like that it felt like someone was playing racquetball with his heart.

His hand closed around her arm. He tugged her up against him.

Her mouth was there to meet his, all softness and yielding hunger. Everything he knew her to be—the sweetness, the ferocity, the fearless pleasure seeker—was in her kiss, and any plans he had for finessing it were swept under by a greedy panic of want. They kissed as though they'd been starved of each other.

Her fingers curled into his belt loops to pull his hips hard against hers; he slid his hands down to cup the curve of her butt and urge her hard up against his cock. A bolt of pleasure cleaved him; her breath snagged and her head fell back; he claimed her lips with his again, and their tongues met, tangled, teased, in a familiar carnal little dance. The only sound was the saw of breath as their lips met, parted, went back for more, for harder, for deeper.

And now their hips were doing what their lips were doing, finding a rhythm that helped them mine every second of contact for every minute degree of bliss, just like teenagers. His cock was rock hard and he thought his head might fly from his body to join the moon overhead from the rush of pleasure. He was beginning to plan how to get her out of that ridiculous bathing suit when . . . not abruptly . . . gently, but decidedly . . .

She took her lips from his.

She ducked her head.

And went still.

A second after that she placed her hand gently on his chest.

He knew that signal. The one for "Stop."

He looked down.

Her hand was rising and falling with the rapid sway of his breathing, like something tossed into a tide.

He lifted his head.

The world was spiraling.

"Mac . . ." The word was scarcely more than a breath.

He decided he had the sexiest name in the world, if it could be said like that.

"Mmm?"

He had a powerful feeling he wasn't going to like what she said next.

"I can't do this."

At least his intuition was dead on.

"If by 'this' you mean kiss like you invented kissing, I disagree." His voice was a husk.

But that was just him trying to be glib.

To rearrange his armor and pull it back into place. He was just trying to forestall the inevitable.

He was pretty sure he knew what she meant.

She eased out of his arms. He had no choice, really, but to let her. It still felt like a sundering. He literally had vertigo.

"Mac . . . it's . . ." She swept a hand back through her hair. "It's just . . ."

And said nothing more.

She stared at him. Her chest still rising and falling with swift breathing.

"Avalon?"

"Sorry . . . thank you. Good night," she said finally.

She pivoted and headed for the house.

He stared blankly.

Thank you, good night? Like she was Lynyrd Skynyrd, and he was a San Francisco crowd?

Chick Pea jumped down from the lounge chair and clicked along after her, and he watched both butts sway off.

It was a pretty adorable view, even if they were walking away from him.

Click.

She turned the lock.

He realized that he did *not*, however, like watching her disappear, whether it was behind a door or not.

He gave a soft, stunned laugh.

Kissing her for the first time, in the path lined with wild blackberries on the way up to Devil's Leap, to this day remained one of the braver things he'd ever done.

And he'd been here at Devil's Leap for about three years, but now he understood something: touching her again was the real homecoming.

But it was both perilous and as exhilarating as walking a wire strung high over the Hellcat River at snowmelt, when the water is moving most violently over jagged rocks.

The kiss was leaving his body only slowly.

And so that's how he made his way back to his cottage. Slowly, so he could feel every moment of that unique intoxication; and by feel, through the dark, the familiar pale flagstones of the lawn and the moon overhead lighting his way.

MAC COLTRANE KISSED ME!

If she'd been fifteen again, that's what she would have written in her diary that night. She would have surrounded it with little hearts and exclamation points. And maybe some lyrics from that particular Roxy Music song.

And then she would have written "Avalon Coltrane" about a dozen times under that. Just testing it out.

How dangerous it now seemed to be that innocent. To not know that kissing boys had ramifications that could fan out through a lifetime and trip you up when you least expected it and cause all kinds of problems, like those invisible laser security systems in sci-fi movies.

She headed upstairs to the bathroom, Chick Pea clicking daintily behind her. She peeled off her mother's absurd old swimsuit with some effort and got in the shower, turned on the warm water, closed her eyes and aimed her face up at it the way you would if something ached. She did ache. Everything ached. Sweetly and savagely. She felt precisely as if she were being pulled apart, slowly, along some sort of serrated internal edge.

She started to tremble.

It was a surfeit of emotion, but damned if she knew whether it was stress or joy or what on earth to call it. The kiss had been so amazing she wanted to cry from it. Not because of its beauty or anything so precious or any of the romantic words that would have made Mac scoff; just because it was now very clear that nothing, nothing had ever felt that *right* since the last time he'd kissed her. So enormous, so peaceful, so consumingly *hot*. And laughing or crying, those were the things available to humans when emotions needed celebrating or releasing. Maybe the next iteration of human should include the ability to shoot rainbows from their eyes.

It was entirely possible she'd spent too much time looking at animated games.

So: it felt right.

But that didn't mean it *was* right.

She'd learned *that* from him, after all.

But shouldn't things that felt so good and promised to be amazing be good for you and meant for you, and not cause pain instead? What in God's name was the point?

Life. Now with More Irony.

She reached up to turn the water off and the old but handsome hot water handle broke off in her hand. She swore blackly.

And she got into the giant flannel nightgown and roped her hair up into a ponytail and sat down on her bed in the turret and curled her feet up underneath her, and Chick Pea went up her doggie stairs to sit on the bed next to her.

She stared through those old curved windows, ever so slightly warped, at the sky full of icily glinting stars, and thought she understood why the original millionaire had built the house there and why they'd included a turret. Because it was like sitting in a pile of diamonds.

It occurred to her that Mac had been a lot of things to her over the years. Rich Boy and First Crush and First Orgasm and Traitorous Heartbreaker and Flag Bearer for All That Was Perfidious About Men. Above all, a symbol.

Implicit in the word *symbol* was a sort of distance.

And distance was safety.

And as an icon he was manageable.

As a person . . . he was potentially devastating. In every sense of that word.

But until tonight, she realized it was entirely possible she hadn't fully experienced him as . . . a person. With dimensions and complexities and motives and vulnerabilities that in all likelihood didn't have much to do with her, though she would bet a few of them did. Shaped by forces she could have actually analyzed and sussed out if she'd tried, because she was good at that sort of thing. She'd been so focused on her own heartbreak. She'd been the tragic heroine of her own story. One she'd allowed to be dictated by the hero.

The hero's story kept going after that book was over.

She had a hunch Mac, on the other hand, had always really, fully seen her. Maybe better than anyone else had back then. She knew it based on how she felt with him: as though the entire world was dialed cleanly into focus.

She'd thought of herself as enmeshed with Corbin, but it wasn't entirely true. The details of their lives were. But it ought to have hurt more to pull free of him. Really hurt, clean to the bone. And here she was, kissing another guy, as if this was where she actually belonged.

She could only imagine the kind of pain that would lead Mac to just sever ties with his whole family. If something was killing you with pain, wouldn't you want it gone? But cutting off a member of her family seemed to her like hacking off a limb because she'd sprained it.

Whether Mac realized it or not, he had his dad's ruthlessness, too. He saw things in black-and-white.

Avalon had a hunch that inherent in that ruthlessness was fear.

So while Mac kissed like an angel, it wouldn't pay to forget that he was just as hard as he was gentle. Being seduced by one could mean being destroyed by the other. He was not a guy who did things by halves.

She sighed.

When she'd laid her hand against his chest to end that kiss . . . she'd felt his heart thudding against her palm. Racing exactly as it had the very first time he kissed her on the path between wild blackberries.

She turned her palm upright and rested it on her lap like something she'd rescued.

She closed her eyes. Suddenly unutterably weary.

Her bed wanted to suck her in the way the hot springs had.

And in one of those romantic gestures that likely would have made Mac scoff, she raised her palm and pressed her lips gently to it. As if she could comfort him that way.

As if she could comfort herself that way.

She certainly wasn't going to come up with any solutions tonight. All she would do was create more existential shreds. Kind of like she'd done to the wallpaper in the master bedroom.

She gave a start when her phone buzzed in a message.

She looked down at it. Her heart gave a sickening, reflexive lurch.

It was Corbin.

> Avalon, I don't blame you for not wanting to talk to me. But I wish you'd let me know where we stand.

Aw. Corbin didn't "blame" her. Wasn't that magnanimous of him.

Still, she could almost hear the misery in his voice. Her throat knotted.

She never could bear his misery, either. Mostly because that's what she did: she wanted to comfort and she wanted to save.

She needed to comfort and save *herself*.

She did have an answer to one of his questions. She didn't know if he'd find it a relief or not.

There IS no "we" anymore.

She sent it, and then shut the phone off.

She wasn't going to be able to avoid an actual conversation with him, or her life in San Francisco, forever. But unlike Corbin, she didn't just foist the difficult things, the things that hurt, the things she didn't want to do, off onto someone else. She would talk to him. And she would take it like a big girl.

She patted the bed next to her and Chick Pea settled into a circle in the crook of her arm.

She closed her eyes and breathed in and breathed out.

And before sleep took her under, she tucked her palm against her cheek.

And she imagined Mac's heart beating against it.

CHAPTER 16

That night she dreamed the master bedroom was papered again in that black-and-gold wallpaper. Every bit of the part she had scraped off had grown back. Horrified, she desperately lunged at one wall with a scraper; it regrew the minute she'd cleared a teeny patch.

She ran downstairs in a panic only to discover all of the walls were covered in it. Outside, Mac's face was pressed to the window; his mouth was moving but she couldn't hear his words, though she thought she detected the word "honey."

She turned around to see Corbin sitting on the giant brown sofa, completely nude and wanking off. "Nobody else has wallpaper like that," he said happily and smugly. "Nobody!"

She was so horrified she woke up gasping.

Chick Pea gave a little woof.

Sweet Jesus!

She felt a little cheated. She'd had a hot kiss yesterday! You'd think she could have at least used it for dream kindling!

Maybe that's what her subconscious *was* doing.

She'd have to mull that one.

She snuggled with Chick Pea while she waited for full consciousness to settle in and provide a sort of emotional weather report.

The primary sensation was amazed, bursting joy, shot through with trepidation, all tied up in a bittersweet ribbon. Self-preservation suggested she shouldn't kiss Mac Coltrane again.

And in the light of day, it somehow seemed entirely possible to resist him.

It would require not seeing him, of course. She knew that much. She admitted this to herself ironically.

She draped an arm across her fuzzy dog who nuzzled her cheek. So much better than waking up next to Corbin, she realized.

She fumbled for her phone: it was only eight. There were no urgent texts or emails from GradYouAte. There was a request for an interview from a trade blog, but it had a wide-open deadline; she could put that off.

In truth, she felt both determined and a little more fragile today than she did yesterday. As if in exposing a little of the darkness and hurt Mac carried around with him he had somehow exposed her, too. They were a little more real to each other now. But also a little more like two live, increasingly bare wires. And everyone knows what happens when live bare wires touch each other.

Today she intended to finish at least one damn wall of that wallpaper.

It was all she did. Methodically, meditatively. Without swearing very much. Her goal was to wear herself out, but she was still a little buzzy from nerves, contemplation, and lingering lust, so exhaustion didn't quite set in the way she'd hoped.

At about three o'clock she finally stopped, took a shower, threw on a green striped T-shirt dress that Eden had donated, eschewing a bra because why subject herself to a lace-and-wire prison, and checked on the frozen lasagna she'd put in the oven a while ago.

She pivoted and glanced at the stove clock. Maybe she should try to make a sal—

BING BONG zzzt clank!

She about jumped out of her skin and even Chick Pea gave a little woof.

That effing *doorbell*. Funny how back in San Francisco she would barely blink at the sound of two drunks screaming at each other about existentialism in the street, which had in fact happened about a month ago beneath her apartment window. But the quiet here in the country was so complete all of her senses were as new as a wall scraped free of wallpaper. A phenomenon she truly hoped to experience one day.

She craned her head.

She saw the shadow at the door. And knew instantly who it was.

Boom. Boom. Boom. That was her heart.

She smoothed her hands down the front of the dress.

She opened the door.

Mac was wearing jeans and an untucked green plaid flannel shirt, which did remarkable otherworldly things to his hazel eyes. His skin gleamed from what looked like a fresh shave.

"Wow. Smells great in there," he said. She liked his nontraditional greetings.

"It's lasagna."

"From scratch?"

"From Costco. Though someone really ought to name a retail chain 'Scratch.'"

He smiled at that. And then the smile dropped away. "I . . . I brought hummus." He gestured with a little Tupperware container.

"Ah, 'I brought hummus.' That's Hipster for 'I come in peace.'"

For some reason the words *I come* throbbed in the air like some sort of *Sesame Street* graphic and they were momentarily flustered.

A sort of fuzzy heat rushed over the backs of her arms and neck.

"Did you grow the garbanzo beans yourself in gourmet poop?" she recovered.

"Next year, I think I'll give that a shot," he said equably. "I'll probably give making olive oil a shot, too. There are about a half dozen olive trees on my property and room for more. I have room for a little vineyard, too. So I think I might give wine a shot."

He stopped talking and frowned a little, perhaps realizing that he was saying "shot" rather a lot.

"Anyway, my hummus secret is I add a few white beans in with the garbanzos. Gives it a mellower flavor. Goes a little better with crackers that have a little bite to them, like chili or garlic or za'atar. I have a few of those right . . ." He produced a little package from behind his back. ". . . here."

She contemplated these offerings. "You actually have 'culinary secrets'?"

"Most of them are children of necessity. As in once all I had was white beans when I was really jonesing for hummus."

"And here I thought you weren't into children of any kind."

"Ha. Listen to how we banter."

And just like that it went dead quiet and awkward.

He cleared his throat. "Avalon . . . I wanted to apologize for last night."

"Which part of last night?"

He sighed. "You're not going to make this easy, are you?"

She smiled crookedly. "That's a rhetorical question, right?"

"I got caught up in the moment. I mean, that green polyester bathing suit with the little frill on it . . . you siren."

She gave a short laugh. "Come on, Mac. It's not like I fainted or swatted you away. You made a pass, I kissed you back. We've done that before. Together and separately. Not my first time."

"Boy, could I tell."

This statement made her realize that few people were ever this genuinely direct. It belonged in the category of things that required getting used to, like ouzo or sauerkraut, but were ultimately addictive.

"And *then* you dashed off all flustered," he added.

"I wasn't flustered," she lied, smoothly. Sounding flustered.

There was a beat of silence.

"I was," he said simply.

Her heart lurched painfully. Like it wanted to get to him but she'd staked it to the damn ground or something, like a savage guard dog.

Don't do it don't do it don't do it, said the infinitely wise and all-too-familiar little voice in her head, the one that usually preceded her doing things she shouldn't do.

"Um . . . why don't you come in. You can put the hummus right here on the . . . coffee table. Which is the box thing near the couch. I have to go pull the aforementioned lasagna out of the oven."

She walked away from the open door and left him to follow her inside.

She slid the oven mitts on and laid the pan on the counter to cool. She stayed there for about a minute, standing over the bubbling lasagna, which despite its resemblance to lava wasn't nearly as hot or dangerous or tempting as Mac Coltrane. She contemplated keeping the oven mitts on. It would be awfully hard to get his zipper down if she was wearing oven mitts.

"Where on earth did you find this couch, anyway?" he called. "What is it, like twelve feet long?"

"Pretty close to that. It's from my family's rec room."

"It's like a freaking barge!"

He sounded delighted.

She smiled to herself. She plucked one of the dishes her mom had donated out of the cupboard— there were roosters on it.

She turned around, squared her shoulders, then returned and sat down next to him on the absurdly long sofa, at a chaste three feet or so away from him, like they were a pair of courting Amish. She even put her knees together, as if she was afraid they would fly right open like a trap door.

Behind them, Chick Pea clicked over the floor, hopped up and settled into the chair across from them and gazed at them brightly and expectantly, as if she were a couples counselor and they'd come in for a session.

He leaned over and shook the crackers out onto the rooster plate and opened the hummus up.

Even over the lasagna smell, Mac smelled faintly like soap.

Which meant he'd showered before he'd come over.

Funny. It was regular old bar soap, if she had to guess, but one whiff and she was picturing him naked in the shower. Her head swam.

"I like the music volume," Mac said, finally.

"What a very specific thing to compliment."

She realized she was still wearing the oven mitts.

She pulled them off one by one and laid them carefully on the table, like a cowboy disarming before a peace summit.

The oven mitts each sported a rooster.

She would never understand why roosters were such a popular kitchen motif.

"In light of the Melissa Manchester misadventure, I thought I should affirm your choice."

"Affirm?"

"I pick up words here and there," he said, loftily, teasingly.

She smiled. Another little silence fell.

"I have wine," she said suddenly and dubiously, "but I think my mom may have bought it to cook with, so accept it at your own risk."

"I can guarantee I've had worse. I'll take my chances."

She sprang up again and fetched the wine from the fridge door, uncorked it and poured about a half inch into two juice glasses that sported Yogi and Boo-Boo, faded by a few hundred go-rounds in the dishwasher. So classy.

She turned around and discovered she was in the beam of his gaze. He'd been watching her that whole time.

He took a sip of the wine and his eyes got wide. He blinked a few times and then swallowed. "Salud," he said wryly, bolted the rest, and winced.

Something had been bothering her a little. "Mac? Can I ask you something?"

"Yeah?"

"Right after you helped me down from the attic, you said something like . . . 'better put this in the be careful what you wish for category.'"

"Yeah?"

"What did you wish for?"

"Oh," he said easily. "I wished to know what it was like to have your legs wrapped around me."

It was as if she'd just bolted whiskey distilled from Lust.

She would not have trusted herself to stand just then. She would have wobbled like a dreidel.

She cleared her throat.

She gestured to his Yogi Bear glass. "Ah. Can I get you another glass of—"

He leaned over and kissed her.

It was as unhurried yet as deliberate as if she'd just asked him to pass the hummus. And she supposed she'd had time to dodge if she wanted to. His mouth landed unerringly on hers, warm and soft, then warm and firm and a little more demanding. He delicately teased the ever-so-slightly parted seam of her lips with his tongue in a way that relit little fuses all over her body. Ones she never even suspected had gone out. Others she never even suspected she'd possessed. And in seconds it seemed her core temperature had ramped to about a thousand degrees and her bones were well on their way to melting.

It was over in a few seconds.

She opened her eyes a few seconds after that.

Surprised to realize she'd closed them.

Interesting. She was pretty positive the room hadn't been turning around in circles before she'd closed them.

Last night's kiss was child's play compared to what had just happened.

Mac sat back, as if to admire his handiwork.

But not all the way back.

She could feel his breath on her chin. She was hypnotized by the rise and fall of his chest.

They stared at each other, and he looked just as hazy-eyed and astounded as she felt.

"I *had* to," he explained, sounding genuinely befuddled. "It's just . . . you were just . . . and your eyes were . . . and I just . . ."

He kissed her again.

And when he did, her hand rose to guide his face in, and her arm looped around the back of his warm neck and the low moan that had been building escaped. She shifted to fit right up against and underneath him as he levered over her, as synchronized as if they were on *Dancing with the Stars*.

Then again, she supposed she had practiced that move or something like it before, quite a bit: in her mind, with her pillow, in the dark, when she was a teenager.

It was almost funny how take-charge and matter-of-fact he was. His competence and confidence were erotic as all get-out and were somehow so convincing she couldn't come up with a single reason not to reach for Mac Coltrane's zipper while he was sliding his tongue down her neck . . . right down to the little tender place where it joined her shoulders . . . where he nipped so, so softly. Little bolts of lightning shot through her veins, lit her up with pleasure.

He kept one hand cradled around the back of her head and the other slipped beneath her dress and he quite sneakily and deftly hooked a few fingers in the waistband of her underwear. And as smoothly and subtly as he might have slipped a maître d' a fifty for the best table in a fancy restaurant, he slid them all the way down her thighs and calves. She gave her feet a little flick to shed them completely.

It was starting to feel a bit like the equivalent of jumping Whiskey Creek on her bike, or off Devil's Leap for the first time. But she was already midair and *everyone* knew there was no turning back once you got that far.

And as his hand slid casually around to her bare hip and rested there—no doubt he had interesting plans for it and that was just the starting gate—there were still layers and layers of pleasure to be had from this kiss, and dear God the way he kissed—sensual, carnal, with a tenderness underlying the hunger so unexpected, and yet so exactly how she remembered him . . . it about did her in. And then his hand was skimming up and up and up and she took her lips away from his as her head went back hard and her breath hissed in when his fingers slipped between her legs and slid against her, hard. He did it again.

"Mac . . . I want . . ."

And with more of that seamless dexterity he maneuvered her pretty quickly onto his lap. He was an engineer, after all.

He tugged at the top of her dress. Thank God for stretchy clothing.

The word that matched the expression on his face when he had her peeled was: "Hurrah!"

But what he said aloud was something like "*Ungh*," and he closed his hands over her breasts as if he'd found the grail.

He cupped his hands beneath them and as he dragged his fingers she made a sound, some hybrid of sigh and whimper and filthy oath. It might as well have been the first time anyone had ever touched her there. Never had it been quite this electric.

And then it got even better when he closed his lips around her nipple and sucked lightly. She felt that everywhere, all at once, as if it had been a lightning strike. She felt nearly savage with a building want. His arms went around her to brace her as she arced helplessly into the sensation and then she took control.

She looped her arms around his neck and slid along the length of his cock, teasing, both herself and him. He arched his hips up to meet her and she slid just out of the way, but the friction was shredding her control. And finally he gave a short, breathless laugh, nearly a mad one, and took matters, and his cock, into his own hands: he held her fast, and guided himself in.

He looked up at her with wicked triumph: *I've got you now.*

He held on to her hips, and arched up into her, eager, begging, as she came down and rose up again. But she took her time about both. She set the pace. Steady, but slow. She wanted to savor his sawing breath, the taut cords of his neck. Her hair dropped down over her eyes, and she whipped it back. He was flushed now, his mouth a slit through which his breath came in hot short gusts, his eyes burning. She smiled down at him. Torturing both of them deliberately.

Somehow it made sense to do this in broad daylight, in front of the hummus and the dog, with her dress furled both up to her waist and down to her waist, her looking down at him looking up at her. His pupils like mirrored black dimes in which she could see herself riding him, slowly, rising and falling slower than his breath. He bucked up to meet her, urging her on; he swore and begged under his breath; he moaned as the release banked.

And their eyes met. And locked. There flashed across his face something raw and unguarded. Something close to awe, maybe yearning. She closed her eyes, because she was afraid he'd see something like that in her own, times a dozen.

She half suspected she was seeing her own reflection.

"Avalon . . . please . . . have mercy, for fuck's sake." His hands slid to her hips to brace her, to buck his

hips, and she could have tormented him because
something buried deep in the strata of her heart believed he deserved a little torment. But in truth her
control was nearly gone, she wanted what he wanted
and that was the explosive release she could feel hurtling toward her. Even now she could feel it preparing to yank her right out of her body.

"Oh God oh God *yes* . . ." He made it a breathless prayer and a Hosannah as their bodies collided,
harder, and faster, and then the world began to get
blurry around the edges as if she were about to be
launched into space, and her skin was spangling
and she heard her voice as if from light years away.
"Mac . . . I'm . . . *oh God,* I'm . . ."

And then it was like a detonation.

She shattered into what felt like smithereens, all
of those smithereens made of bliss. It whipped backward and shook her and shook her.

Seismic.

She might have keeled over if he hadn't gripped
her and drummed relentlessly toward his own release
as she nearly toppled.

"Avalon . . . Christ . . ."

He went still and with a roar reminiscent of gladi-
ators going at each other with spears, his eyes shut,
his head falling back. His big body quaked and shuddered.

She collapsed against him and he held on to her
as if they'd narrowly missed a building cave-in and
were celebrating life. Lungs heaving. Bodies sheened

in sweat where skin was visible. Heathens that they were, the only article of clothing on the ground was her underwear.

His hair was a shambles.

It had been only around fifteen minutes from the time he rang the doorbell.

She ought to get up now.

"Where's Chick Pea?" he murmured suddenly.

"She must have gotten bored and left. If she'd had a remote she would have changed the channel."

He gave a muffled laugh. He was still breathing warmly against her sternum. And then he placed a whimsical little kiss there, a chaste one, right over where her heart was still thudding hard.

She scanned the room.

Chick Pea was on her dog bed near the big window, ignoring them, having a bath and making snorkeling noises into her flank.

She slid from Mac's lap.

This part was always a little awkward. The return of sanity, the reassembly of clothing.

With a series of tugs she got her dress more or less back to the way it was before she pulled the lasagna out of the oven.

"I'm going to . . ." He gestured toward the bathroom.

"Okay." She glanced around on the floor.

"I think they wound up under the couch," he suggested over his shoulder.

She found her undies and she headed down the hall

in the opposite direction, toward another bathroom, tugging her dress down as she went. She caught a glimpse of herself in the bathroom mirror: her mouth was kiss-swollen and her face was pink and her hair was every which way and there were faint mascara shadows under her eyes. She looked surprisingly luscious and ravished and disreputable. Even in San Francisco, she might have crossed the street if she'd seen herself walking toward her in the wee hours of the morning.

Either that, or high-five herself. Because there really was no question about what she'd just been up to.

"I'd even do me, the way I look now," she said to the mirror.

Her expression regarded her, stunned. How in God's name had she gotten so carried away? One moment she was sitting there all demure, and the next she'd gone full cowgirl.

Possibly it was a couple of decades overdue, and that was all. With this guy.

It was also possible all the stuff with Corbin had derailed her more than she realized. That maybe she ought to explore that avenue for an explanation.

Except that deep in the heart of her she wasn't convinced that was true.

She'd better leave this bathroom before Mac decided she was going to disappear again on him for another decade or so.

CHAPTER 17

She returned to the kitchen to find Mac standing in it, looking about thoughtfully. As if mulling what kinds of repairs it might need.

She walked past him, opened up a drawer, fished out two forks, and handed one to him.

He sat down opposite her at the card table.

They ate the still-warm lasagna from opposite sides of the pan. Silently. He ate with unselfconscious gusto, chewed with his mouth closed, and waited for her to gesture that it was okay to plow through the next third because she didn't want it. She was impressed.

Suddenly he paused and went so alertly still it was as though he was about to say, "Hark!"

"Is that toilet still running?"

She listened. "Yep," she concurred grimly.

"I think it was last replaced around 1950. Valve probably needs replacing."

She sighed. "Naturally."

And that was it for the conversation until he put his fork down about ten minutes later.

He leaned back and regarded her as if she might be the next course.

"That was good."

"The lasagna?"

"Of course the lasagna. The other thing was . . ." He paused, and gazed, ceiling-ward, apparently mulling, then slowly lowered his head again. ". . . Do you have a thesaurus? Because I'm not sure a word has been invented yet for what that was."

Her heart flipped over.

And their gazes locked.

She got up from the table abruptly. She collected the forks and the scraped-clean lasagna pan and put them in the sink. She ran the water for a rather unnecessarily long time over the forks.

And there was a little silence.

"Soooo now that I have you in sexual thrall . . . yooooou will sell me the hoooooouse."

He mimicked a hypnotist's intonation.

It was a foray.

He was trying to gauge her mood.

She snorted. "You're not *that* good." She still didn't have the nerve to turn around yet.

She could practically feel the rays of his smile on the back of her neck like a sunbeam. He was perverse, Mac was, but every time it was like opening up a window and allowing crisp air in.

"If that's just your way of daring me to up my game . . ."

Oh God. Just the *idea* of him upping his game and

how he might demonstrate that made her knees turn to butter.

She drew in a long, deep breath for courage and pivoted.

Yep, he was still as good-looking as three seconds earlier.

He looked a trifle warier.

Mac was smart.

"About that. I just . . . Okay. While it was good . . ."

"No, we established, the lasagna was *good*."

But now he also looked alert. And tense.

"Okay. Yes. I agree. This was . . . what we did was . . . something else. I mean, it was really . . . And it was . . . a surprise."

"Was it?" he said. Ironically amused.

She ignored that. "BUT . . ." She took another long sustaining breath. "I'm sorry, but I shouldn't have. I just . . . the thing with Corbin is so recent and I don't know where my head is at, honestly. Or where I'll be a month from now. I just have no business getting involved in anything like . . . I just don't think the pre-lasagna activity is a good idea. Going forward. Is that okay?"

Wow. Nothing like a little Word Salad to go with the lasagna, Avalon, she told herself. Silently.

Mac had gone still again.

He took this in during a silence that seemed to ring.

"Okay," he said evenly. Finally.

She hadn't the faintest idea what he was thinking. But she recognized that look as one disguising an awful lot of internal mulling.

He didn't ask for clarification. Even though God only knew it was warranted and an argument could be made that he was entitled to it.

She didn't ask him if he had any follow-up questions. She wasn't giving a presentation to the Young Entrepreneurs club.

He was watching her now with a certain curiosity. Trying to read her.

"But . . . I'll admit I can use some general contracting work in the house . . ."

"*Some* general contracting? You don't need a thesaurus. You need a dictionary."

". . . and since you're about as general as a contractor can get, and you're always underfoot anyway, I would appreciate it if you'd undertake some of the work. I want to get it all done by the first of the year."

He smiled slowly at this.

"Same terms as your groundskeeping contract," she added quickly.

"Ha. Nice try. Not if I'm doing more work."

Ava actually loved to negotiate. Mac turned out to be startlingly nimble at it, too. Must be in the genes, she thought. Wasn't that basically what his dad had done? Make deal after deal after deal? Right up until that deal with the prosecutor for a decade less jail time?

They happily bickered for a few minutes and arrived on a deal that was pretty much what she'd intended to pay him all along. If a little more.

"I'll get a contract drawn up by tomorrow morning," she said.

"Okay. Have you made a list of things you think need repairs or updating?"

"Of course."

He smiled at that. "Can you email it to me tonight? I'll add my two cents, then I'll work out budget estimates and a schedule and we can make decisions based on that from there. Shall I stop by around ten a.m.?"

Wow. The efficiency was as breathtaking as his abs and nearly as erotic as what they'd just done on the barge couch.

"Sounds good."

At the rate all of this professionalism was going, next they'd be exchanging business cards and a brisk, pumping handshake. She supposed she was relieved.

There ensued an uncertain little silence.

"You can keep the hummus," he said.

The word *hummus*, Avalon thought, would be evocative from now on. Another of those jolts. A reminder that prior to this conversation, they'd said things to each other like "oh God Oh God" and "Avalon . . . please . . . have mercy, for fuck's sake."

"Thanks," she said simply.

They regarded each other for another odd, indecisive moment.

"Okay then," he said. "Thank you . . . good night."

He gave her a chummy little shoulder punch, for all the world as if she were Morton Horton.

And let himself out.

"Hey, buddy."

The Cat emerged from the shrubbery near

the front door and then fell into a long-legged stride beside him like a Labrador. Funny, he had a cat who acted like a dog, and Ava had a dog who might as well be a cat.

And as he walked back to his house, Mac mulled whether he felt rejected. He kind of did.

Technically he had been, but it was also on the heels of the best sex he could remember having, which was reason alone to celebrate the evening. He had a hunch that the rejection might actually have something to do with him, and not Corbin.

And whatever had gone down all those years ago. Why she'd disappeared.

But he was thoughtful. He *definitely* wanted that to happen again.

What he wanted was for Ava to get what she wanted. And somehow, he knew better than anyone precisely what that was. And it wasn't only a little space.

She wanted a choice. She wanted something to go right in her world. She wanted, in fact, to restore her world to rightness, whether she really understood that or not.

He knew how easy it would be to seduce her again. He in fact was cocky enough to believe that he could go right back in there and do it again; casually loop his arms around her, lay a kiss against her warm, soft neck, and in seconds they'd have a conflagration on their hands. She wanted him; he wanted her. That wasn't going to go away.

But that wasn't how he wanted to do this. Any more than he'd build a bridge over shaky ground.

He'd learned patience, of a sort. He'd learned the value and safety of a step at a time.

And it was remarkable how often just doing the right thing led to getting exactly what you wanted.

And there was just the right amount of risk to keep it interesting: because doing the right thing in no way guaranteed he'd have her in his arms again.

Avalon chucked the just-washed lasagna tin into the recycling bin and dried the forks thoroughly, as if she was wiping away DNA evidence when she actually kind of wanted to frame them: *Our First Lasagna*.

Mainly because she was postponing the thing she needed to do.

She sat down at the table, put her phone in the middle of it, and stared down.

But somehow pressing that one speed-dial button was as emotionally fraught as punching in the nuclear codes.

"Avalon. Oh my God . . . *honey* . . . thank you for calling. Are you okay?"

Honey was a weird word for Corbin. He normally would have dismissed it as very regressive. Corbin was *full* of that sort of exhausting bullshit.

Whereas when Mac had said it to her when she was stuck in the attic, somehow that dumb little word sounded like a promise that everything would be all right in the world.

But Corbin did sound worried and relieved.

"I'm fine." *A little sore between the legs after riding my groundskeeper, otherwise fine.*

There was a little silence. She didn't ask him how he was. She was quiet for long enough for him to realize she wasn't going to ask.

"Corbin, I just called to say I'll be away from the office through the beginning of the year."

That was the first time she'd given herself a hard deadline like that.

He was silent for a moment. Astounded, if she had to guess. "That's—that's—about a month and a half away."

"Very good. And to think there was a time I didn't think you knew how to use a calendar."

From the beginning, he was late to dates with her and sometimes forgot them altogether. She was so starry-eyed back then that she wrote it off as all part of him being a brilliant, absentminded eccentric because he'd gone to Dartmouth. He'd coasted on allowing her to feel that way, too.

But *she* had created something out of nothing. Funny how Mac had called her magical, when it was precisely how she'd once thought of him, too. And her something out of nothing kept an apartment roof over Corbin's head.

Corbin just took all of that for granted.

"You'll be back at work in San Francisco after that?"

"I don't know. Maybe. Probably."

Silence.

She savored the texture of his silence, because she could almost *taste* his frustration.

"But what are you—"

"I bought a house."

Her words were clipped, suddenly, like a German commandant in a movie with subtitles. She didn't know why. Maybe because she didn't want to accord him a particle more time than necessary.

This silence was lengthier.

"Sorry," he said gingerly, like a man expecting to be flicked with a rubber band every time he spoke. "I thought you said you bought a house?"

"Yes. I did say that."

Understandably, news of the purchase of a house amazed San Franciscans, given that even teeny shacks in the city were upward of a million dollars. And people did buy them for that price.

She and Corbin had once talked about saving up for one of those teeny shacks.

"You used your savings?"

"Yes."

He was smart enough to draw conclusions about what all this meant. That's what he was doing in the silences. He also knew they both drew on their savings in cases of emergency budget shortfalls.

"But . . . where . . . I mean . . . does that mean you're never coming . . . it sounds like you *are* planning to leave San Francisco for good!"

His voice had climbed in pitch.

"I'm going to do some renovations on the house

and sell it. And they should be done by the first of the year. I'll keep a light hand on things at GradYouAte via email, but you're going to need to be the boss. Period."

She owned 5 percent more of the company than he did. And the company was Corbin's sole source of income. He could argue if he wanted but that would get him nowhere.

Smart guy that he was, he'd figure this out, too. "What will I tell the staff?"

"Tell them I'm taking a leave of absence for personal reasons."

"They'll think you're in rehab or something. And do you have any idea what that will do to the stock pri—"

"Then tell them I caught you fucking the intern in our bed. We'll see how *that* affects the stock price."

That shut him up cold.

"You're going to have to continue handling everything while I'm gone," she emphasized. Not without a certain sadistic relish.

He inhaled deeply, exhaled.

"Okay. Whatever you need."

Damn straight, whatever she needed.

She said nothing.

And neither did he.

But neither one of them hung up just yet.

"So, Corbin . . . Are you in love with Grace?" It was really just rank curiosity. She needed some context for the destruction of her previous life.

Silence.

"*What*?" He was purely astounded. "Why on earth would . . . Good *God*, NO!"

Suddenly a little red screen of rage appeared before her eyes.

"Silly me, imagining you'd bang someone out of love rather than random impulse and opportunity. You know, the way you always grab a handful of M&Ms off the receptionist desk. Because they're there."

"That's *not* why I . . ." He stopped.

"Then wh . . ."

Did she *really* want to know why? Would it matter at this point? Would it change who he was or who she was or what he'd done?

She couldn't get the word out of her mouth.

She could hear him breathing. She knew that sound well. It was somehow peculiarly comforting in its familiarity, and yet she couldn't help fantasizing about covering his face with a pillow.

"You and I haven't had sex in almost two months," he said carefully. His voice lowered as if they were in danger of being overheard.

She waited for more.

But nope, that was apparently it.

"Wow. Two months? It's a wonder your dick didn't dry up and blow away. Good thing you found some place to stash it before that happened."

"Jesus, Ava!" He said it faintly. Genuinely shocked. Which was funny because that wasn't even remotely representative of how mean she felt or how mean she thought she could be.

But . . . had it really been two months? Somehow she hadn't missed it.

Or . . .

Had she avoided it?

Something that might have been a twinge of guilt pinged inside her.

"I mean . . . you couldn't just discreetly . . . self-pleasure . . . in front of some internet porn, Corbin? Wouldn't that have been simpler?"

She had never participated in a more excruciating conversation. They didn't know how to fight with each other. Because they never really did. They exchanged pissy remarks now and again, sure. And there had been relationship calibration type things when they first moved in together: Corbin needed to learn to put the lid down on the toilet seat. (She'd framed it in the form of a logic question: "It's a lid, Corbin. When things have lids, typically you put them back after you use them, right? You know, like jam and shampoo.") For some reason she never closed cupboards all the way; it maddened him. So she'd learned to do it.

"It's not the same, is it?" Corbin was struggling with words that weren't glib, and that's when she realized the two of them just didn't have a vocabulary for this disaster. "Wanking to porn. We're both so busy. We only ever talk about work lately. I felt like . . . we were growing apart. I was *lonely*."

And that faintly bewildered yet entitled tone in which he issued the word *lonely* . . . that summed Corbin up right there. It was somehow inconceivable to him that any need he had wouldn't be comfortably met.

"*Lonely*? We saw each other every freaking day!"

"But we were both just so busy . . . it was all work. We'd just fall into bed at night and get up and do it again. I was lonely and I have my needs, for God's sake. I just—"

She closed her eyes. "OH MY GOD. Corbin. STOP. Just STOP. STOP. Saying. Stupid. Things. STOP."

The tone made him wary, clearly, because he did shut up for a second or two.

"And by stupid, could you be more spec—"

"Your stupid answer to my question and stupid to use *our* bed and stupid, stupid, *stupid* to do our intern. Stupid and boring and careless—and—and—*lazy*! It's like that time you just stood there in front of the refrigerator and ate three pickles out of the jar because you couldn't be bothered to peel back the plastic on one of the Lean Cuisines and put it in the microwave. She is *literally* the first woman you see every day. After me, of course."

"I was horny and lonely and *she* came on to me, Ava. You should have seen how aggressi—"

"*ARRRRRRRRRRGH!*"

She roared right into the phone. She hoped his eardrum shriveled at that onslaught.

She couldn't bear to hear him blame Grace be-

cause that just made him an even bigger chickenshit.
And what did that say about her and her judgment to
align her fates with such a feckless chickenshit? And
sure, Grace was appallingly feckless, too, natch, but
she was only twenty-two and was clearly about to
learn the hard way about life and men and jobs and
that whole lot. She had a few decades of big mistakes
ahead of her, probably. Avalon did not give one crap
about Grace.

Well, except:

"She wasn't hurt, was she? When she fell off the
bed?"

"No," he said sullenly. "You were right about the
rug pad."

They did have a pretty thick carpet in there.

Stupid, but that little thing right there: the carpet
pad. Romance was all well and good, but lives were
knit together by little things, decisions about whether
to put extra padding under the rugs.

"Corbin, you literally almost *never* stop talking
unless you're sleeping, and you couldn't have said
something, *anything* to me about feeling horny or
unhappy or lonely? Seriously, is that what you're telling me? This is the whole of your rationale? Your
first impulse was to betray me in the biggest, most
cliché way possible, because, and I quote, you were
'*lonely*'?"

The word *betray* felt melodramatic in her mouth.
Formal, almost medieval, like *cuckold*.

Corbin had his Dartmouth degree. But he'd been

a spoiled child and Avalon had always been a better arguer. If you had siblings, especially wily, smart ones like she had, you learned how to fight and fight hard.

Corbin apparently didn't know how to respond. There was just more of that breathing, this time a little halting.

He was trying not to cry.

She had never once witnessed him crying.

Oh, hell. Despite it all, she couldn't bear the idea of making him cry.

"Nothing is the same without you," he said finally. His voice was frayed and hollow.

"DUH."

Somehow it was the perfect word: infantile, mono-syllabic.

But her voice broke.

Corbin misinterpreted the crack as an opening for him.

"I miss you, Ava."

He sounded wholly miserable and lost and . . .

And just a little bit wheedling.

The miserable and lost bit . . . well, that was her wheelhouse, wasn't it? She could bear her own suf-fering, but somehow not the suffering of people she cared about. She had to swat back the traitorous reflex to comfort him. He'd done this to himself.

Did one, albeit horrible, act laser love away com-pletely? Just zap it gone, scorched earth and all that?

Or had she truly, really, *ever* loved him?

She knew one thing for certain: somewhere in the

wheedling was the guy who was still sure he could get his way by somehow charming her into it. And that alone told her he had no clue, no *clue* of the enormity of what he'd done to her.

Mac had been the spoiled son of a billionaire, but she couldn't in a million years picture Mac . . . *whining*. His life had fallen apart, publicly and horribly, and he'd rebuilt it bit by bit, from the ground up, the hard way. There hadn't been a shred of self-pity in what he'd told her about the national guard, but God knows he was entitled to some.

So there were a dozen things she could say to Corbin right now. What she said was, "I don't miss you. We're over. For good."

She pressed the red button and ended the call without another word. And dropped the phone.

She looked out the window. She knew a minute twinge of guilt, because somewhere in there was a sort of acknowledgement: she might well be responsible for the distance between her and Corbin.

She might even have sort of noticed, and . . . she might not have minded.

The hum of Mac's lovemaking hadn't even left her body. Absently, she touched her lips, still tender, and dragged her hand around to the back of her neck.

She was pretty sure that if she hadn't had sex in two months, it wasn't because the two of them were busy.

It could be because she'd stopped wanting it with Corbin.

She yearned for comfort right now and there wasn't a soul she could call about this, but a reflex made her stand up and turn toward the window.

She couldn't see the light on in Mac's house. But that sure wasn't the direction of safety or certainty, either.

She curled up on the bargelike sex sofa, and for the first time in possibly years, she had a good, long, weary, frustrated, sick-of-herself cry, while Chick Pea propped herself on her knees and licked her cheeks.

CHAPTER 18

At ten on the precise dot the next morning:
BING BONG CLANK!
Mac appeared at the door with his laptop. He looked so impersonally brisk it was a wonder he hadn't tucked a pencil behind his ear and clipped a corporate ID and a pen protector to his shirt pocket. Or pump her hand in a handshake and call her "Ma'am."

She served coffee on the coffee table box and sat at a safe distance while he showed her a *breathtakingly* organized spreadsheet incorporating her input and his, including time and cost estimates for every element of the project, person power required to accomplish it all, and names of suggested hired help, including Truck Donegal and a few other guys who were unknown to her. He'd even prepared three different bottom-line totals, with variables factored in (new blinds or refurbish old ones?), and a proposed timeline for the work, from floors to walls to fixtures.

She looked at him for a long, silent moment.

He looked back at her. Arched a single eyebrow. "Well?"

She was tempted to say, "I've never been more turned on in my life."

From his expression—the slow, smug smile, all amused, gratified triumph—he knew exactly what she was thinking.

He crossed his arms behind his head contentedly, heaved his feet up onto the box.

Nothing was more erotic than a big, hot, strong guy armed with a spreadsheet whose object was to make her life easier. Even if she had to pay him.

"I'm very impressed," she settled upon finally. Faint with admiration and, frankly, feeling a little shy, which made her realize that it had been some time since she was in the presence of breathtaking competence unaccompanied by whining.

"Not my first time," he said easily.

They were in innuendo territory again. .

How very, very easy it would be to just . . . crawl into his lap again and bury her face against his brownish neck and breathe in the manly cleanness of him and then maybe stick her tongue in his ear.

She had to look away in case her face became as readable as a billboard.

"Here's our duty roster," he said, and pulled up another spreadsheet.

"Who are these guys?" She pointed to the personnel column.

"Some guys I know pretty well. Vets who could

use the work. They'll do a great job. I meet with them once a week downtown, so I trust them pretty implicitly."

Ah, *that* was the mysterious meeting.

She knew good jobs were hard to come by in Hellcat Canyon and in a lot of the surrounding cities. You either created your own business, or you drove to a bigger city to work for a larger employer. Or you drew welfare.

"I put these three guys on wallpaper duty upstairs—including a complete wash and prep of the walls—we'll have it all finished in a couple of days. Unless you're really dead set on doing that room yourself."

She thought about her dream and almost shuddered. "No, I'm happy to hand that off."

He nodded. "I'll work on replacing and wiring fixtures that need it—I'll do a thorough test, first—do the new toilet innards, tear up the linoleum and lay tile, check doorknobs and hinges, fix that obnoxious doorbell and the fourth step of the stair, stuff like that. We'll get a couple of guys to work on the window frames that are warped, because that's a bitch of a job. For the windows missing blinds we can get good prefab blinds and I can cut them to fit, or you can get fancier, depending upon how much wiggle room you have in the budget. We'll make sure wireless internet works in every room and we'll create a system of surreptitious partitions so that the ballroom can become meeting rooms.

"And we'll arrange all the work so there will always

be a room that you and Chick Pea can migrate to and sleep without breathing in a lot of fumes."

He'd made a little column labeled "Chick Pea." Her job was to "be fluffy and savagely attack intruders."

Which made Avalon laugh out loud.

He'd put Avalon on paint duty downstairs.

She noticed that the two of them would be working in different parts of the house for nearly the entire duration of the project. It was a skillful bit of scheduling, and, she was certain, absolutely deliberate.

And they would likely never be alone in the house.

That couldn't be an accident.

She was touched by his solicitousness.

And, ridiculously, a little disappointed that he'd taken her so very seriously.

"I've planned it so we can get all the noise and fumes over with at roughly the same time. I figure, give or take wildcards, we can get it all done inside of a couple of weeks, but let's give it three weeks on the outside to account for any surprises. I can crack the whip."

She chose the Column B Budget option: more guys on the job, a little more expensive.

The sooner it was done, the sooner she could sell this place, replenish her savings . . . and maybe bail on GradYouAte, if it came to that.

He clapped his laptop closed. "All right, then. Let's go paint and tile shopping."

"Me and you?"

"You're the lady with the checking account . . .

boss." He stood and gave her another little chummy shoulder punch.

Within a day of Mac making phone calls, the house seemed aswarm with big guys, most of them on the diffident side. There were, in truth, only about a half dozen of them at any given time, but they took up a lot of space and they walked with thunderfeet up the stairs and overhead so that their presence filled the whole house. She kind of liked the energy. They greeted her respectfully, received their assignments from Mac. And like a sergeant, he dispatched them upstairs to get to work after they masked the downstairs rooms for painting.

He set her up with a paint tray and a roller—First Date was ironically the name of the paint for the first room, a pale cream with some warmth in it, with the faintest hint of blush pink when the light hit it. It glowed like the cheeks of a girl on her way to the prom.

"Okay, Avalon. You dip it in like so . . . got it?"

She dipped. As instructed.

"And then you stroke it up and down . . . up and down . . . up and down. Up and down."

She watched the muscle play beneath his T-shirt as he moved the roller up and down.

He turned, eyebrows up. "Want me to show you how?"

God, yes.

"Got it. I'm going to stroke it. Up and down. Up and down. Faster or slower? Which do you like better?"

He stared at her, thoughtfully.

"Well . . . eventually, it's always good to go as fast as you can . . . but it's probably best to start out slow. For everyone. Right? Slow, even, constant strokes."

She was faint. But not from paint fumes. She stared at him blankly.

"Got it." Her voice was arid from lust.

"Excellent." He actually performed one of those brisk little hand swipes people do when they check something off a list. As if his own pupils hadn't gotten big and black there for a moment.

"I'll check on things in a little bit. Let me know if you have any questions."

And then he basically left her alone.

To think about up-and-down strokes as she performed satisfying up-and-down strokes of paint.

There passed about a week of bonhomie and progress that was practically choreography. At the end of each work day Mac called a huddle to review progress or to present things for her to approve or revise. She was seldom alone with him. He didn't flirt. He didn't touch her. He didn't make up excuses to linger around the house.

But the banter was easy. It was, in fact, one of the most effortless weeks she'd ever experienced as an adult. Even shopping for fixtures and picking out tile was an exercise in ease. He had opinions, but deferred to her eye, because it was clear she had a good one; he offered input on durability and that sort of thing. He made sure she colored inside the budget lines. He located deals, called in favors.

She realized that having someone you trusted implicitly, someone to whom you could surrender burdens, was practically synonymous with inner peace.

And that not trusting someone could be like riding a roller coaster in a cart missing a wheel.

Also: trusting someone to get work done was undeniably hot.

Which kind of made it, in some ways, one of the most erotically charged weeks she'd ever had. A veritably *tantric* week. And as she worked alone in a room, or with some guy he'd assigned to help her, Mac's non-presence was as potent as his presence.

She wondered if this was his plan all along.

Or if he, too, had seen the wisdom in distance from her.

About four in the afternoon on Friday of that week Mac stopped in to check out the ballroom they'd just finished painting. She'd had some help today from a guy named Doug who didn't talk but tunelessly whistled between his teeth until she'd wanted to paint his mouth closed with the chosen color, which was called Pismo, and was sort of a rich, pale sand moving toward mocha. She didn't, though. Together they'd gotten it done.

Mac patrolled the perimeter of the room. She was actually holding her breath as if she was waiting to hear her SAT scores.

He was disheveled and paint-spattered himself. He looked utterly relaxed.

"You have a great eye, Avalon. I'll hand it to you.

The colors you chose are fantastic. This looks like a completely different room from the one my mother used to passive-aggressively sing in."

She smiled at that. "So . . . I know it's not on the schedule, Mac, and it's sort of a divergence from the original plan, but how awesome would it be if we could get the blinds cut for the windows in these two rooms today? I would just love to see how they look in here."

"*So* awesome," he teased her in Valley-girlesque cadence. "But you know, I *can* get it done. You choose. We can do a mix and match with today's schedule. I'll tear up the linoleum in the small upstairs bathroom or I'll cut the blinds."

"Wow. I'll need to consult my eight ba . . ."

She trailed off.

Because she'd suddenly become aware that Mac's hand was parked lightly, companionably on her butt.

Instantly she could feel him go as tense and motionless as if they were playing Red Light, Green Light. Which was how she knew he'd realized it, too.

There passed a nonplussed moment.

"Mac . . . are you . . . sort of resting your hand on my ass?"

His hand dropped away so fast you would have thought she'd severed it. "God! Ava, I'm sorry. I swear to God, it was a reflex. I wasn't . . . It was just . . . it seemed . . ."

He stopped.

They didn't look at each other. Not head-on. But

her face was hot and when she slipped him a glance she was pretty sure there was high color in his cheeks.

He *had* been trying to give her distance. He wasn't actually making a pass.

Thing was, she knew precisely how he'd meant to end that sentence. Because it was indeed a reflexive, companionable ass-cupping, born of a collegial moment. It had somehow felt perfectly natural, which was why it had taken both of them a moment to realize it was even happening.

Anyone strolling past the doorway would have thought them in thrall to the ugly blinds, because they were determinedly looking at them.

But there were no voices. Because they were, for the first time in a week, utterly alone.

And then Ava heard herself say, in a voice so hoarse she inadvertently sounded as sultry as Bacall:

"I didn't say you had to take it off."

His head did a rapid 180-degree turn and his gaze collided with hers.

Gasoline, meet match.

He slowly looked away again toward the blinds, and so did she.

And after a suspenseful second's worth of hesitation, he stretched his hand out behind her and cautiously, gingerly, delicately arranged it right back on her left cheek. As if it were an antique lace doily on a side table.

And yet the moment was at once absolutely ridiculous and deadly earnest.

Her breath was already sawing.

And she could hear his.

But she could hear her own blood ringing in her ears.

He executed the next few seconds like choreography and she now realized this was just one of Mac's gifts: like Joe Montana had been able to see the pocket on a teeming field of giant humans, Mac saw the field of play and he had a *plan*. He used the hand on her butt to expertly pivot her toward him, scooped both hands beneath her, pulled her up hard against his body, and urged her forward as if they were tangoing. And just like that, with a soft *bam,* they were up against the wall. And each other.

It was actually like being sandwiched between two walls: one only freshly painted, the other made of muscle that she wanted to maybe nibble a little. Her hands were already sliding under his shirt as if to test that his abs were indeed that hard, and made of satiny flesh over steel. The heat of his body was intoxicating and the press of his hardening cock against the join of her legs made her grind like a wanton, seeking out a jolt of pleasure.

Her reward was his sucked-in breath and his murmured, "God, yes. More of that."

Her arms were going around his neck to pull him to her just as his face was lowering and their lips crashed. His mouth was better than molten chocolate and his clever tongue tangled with hers and it was deep, and carnal, and very nearly violent, and somehow she was falling into layer after new layer of pleasure.

His hands burrowed up under her T-shirt and savored a swift glide up her torso, and in a single deft swipe unclicked the center snap on her bra. He muttered a happy, filthy little oath when he filled his hands with her breasts, then dragged his thumbs across her nipples, already so hard they could have used them to trim the blinds.

"Oh, my God. Oh, God. Yes," she breathed.

"Yeah? Like that?" He did it again and blissful lightning strikes fanned through her body and her head thrashed back and how was it that she was already so close to *coming*?

She thought the top of her head might just pop right off from the pleasure of it.

She fumbled with lust-clumsy hands for the buttons on his jeans and thank God the worn buttonholes didn't put up any kind of fight. No grizzly had ever lunged for a trout in a stream more eagerly than she dove into his Calvin Kleins. It was apt, because she felt purely blindly animalistic about getting her needs met. She closed her hand around his cock and stroked him, hard, once. Twice. Again.

"Oh my God, yes. Like that," he all but hissed. He arched into her strokes and his eyes were bright slits staring right into hers and then he closed them and his head tipped back helplessly and he was all but writhing thanks to her stroking hands, and he was hot and thick and hard and she was lightheaded and desperate with lust.

Thank God for stretchy yoga pants. He peeled hers pretty easily, almost before she knew it, and the underwear went with them. He slid his fingers into the wet heat between her legs and did a few subtle but fancy things down there that shot current after current of almost intolerably delicious sensation through her.

She moaned and ordered, "More."

He obliged, until she was begging, until pleasure had ramped to hardly bearable levels, until her every cell felt electrified, charged with pleasure.

There was minimal condom fumbling, thank God, he had that down, too: with a yank of the teeth at the package, a flick of plastic, and a deft rolling on. He looped a hand beneath her knee and pulled her up against him like they were about to tango.

He whispered against her mouth: "This is going to be so. Good."

Then he thrust his tongue inside her mouth on a gasp. And then he moved.

Sensuously, at first. An attempt at pacing. A thrust, a leisurely withdrawal. Another thrust. Teasing her, teasing him. Their breath mingled in short hot bursts. He moved, and she moaned low, officially captive to pleasure. She would be begging in a moment.

And it was almost too intense. Some tacit agreement, almost a dare, kept their eyes locked, so they could watch the power they had over each other, to savor each other's ramping helplessness to pleasure. She didn't care if he saw the whole movie of her life in her eyes, every bit of it, the eleven-year-old Ava writing "Avalon Coltrane" in her diary over and over and over, sobbing until her ribs felt sprained that day he'd all but shattered her absurdly naive heart, that moment some years later when she was a little drunk, home from a lame blind date, and had thought about him and masturbated because she figured she might as well put his memory to some use. Right in that moment she'd surrender all of her secrets as long as the tsunami of an orgasm she felt building finally crashed over her.

"Oh God. *Please, Mac . . . please . . .* I . . . please . . ."

"I got you, sweetheart."

It was the best word in the world the way he said it, it was rescue and surcease and utter confidence. She didn't think much beyond that, because his hips were drumming hard now. And then she all but detonated from the banked pleasure. She heard her own tattered scream from somewhere on another planet, as her body dissolved into what felt like a whole galaxy of stars. She was all but whipped right out of her body. And somewhere from out in space she heard his hoarse cry of release.

She slid down the wall to the floor, liquified, sated, stunned, her body humming like the last note struck by a gong.

He slid down next to her with a soft bump.

She wasn't going to say, or think, or do another thing until she'd savored every last sensation thrumming through her limbs and her nether parts and her kiss-stung lips.

She closed her eyes to be alone with it, her lungs still heaving like a bellows.

She heard Mac's breathing, too. She knew a surge of very primal and feminine satisfaction. She'd worn him out.

When her thoughts reassembled, she spared one for the paint job on the wall. Because otherwise she'd have Pismo all over the back of her and they'd have to do it again.

And when their breathing had settled they still didn't speak.

She opened her eyes. The afternoon light had gone amber, and the refinished floors were glowing serenely golden under it.

"So . . . are you going to give another little speech about how you shouldn't do this?" He said this wryly, though. And still a little breathlessly.

"Nope." She'd fully realized the futility of this.

And so they sat in silent contemplation. Perhaps awe.

This. *This* was sex. The frantic surge of lust, the sweat and roaring breath, the grappling, the apparently infinite variety of ways her nerve endings could be strummed to produce umpteen degrees of pleasure. Nothing else in her life to date compared. Certainly not her polite and pleasant couplings with Corbin. All orgasms were good, of course. But . . . it was the difference between that long, flat, torturously dull drive on I-5 from San Francisco and then—ta da! You were in beautiful Hellcat Canyon, and taking the windy, spectacular scenic coastal road to Big Sur, a road that offered something new and splendid around every turn.

"You know . . . this doesn't need to be a big . . . thing."

He made it sound like an idle remark, but she was pretty sure it was studied. A foray. A man perhaps carefully negotiating for more hot sex in the future. Perhaps creating a safe space for her to agree to something she clearly wanted but thought she shouldn't.

"It can be just a thing we do, like trimming the blinds or rewiring the light in the upstairs bathroom? When the mood takes us?" she mused.

"Yeah. Like a morale-boosting team-building exercise. Like . . . trust falls. Only a lot better."

She gave a short laugh. And then sighed and folded her head onto her arms and propped them on her knees. The peace of the moment was replaced with a tension. Between the idea of more of what had just happened, which made her even now feel weak with anticipation, and the fear that there was no way she wouldn't emerge from this freshly scathed in some horrible new way.

Even if Mac could partake in the whole thing the way he would a good meal or, say, volleyball.

Even if it was bound to end.

She ran through a swift bullet-point list of reasons why this was madness in her head: They didn't want the same things, unless you counted this house. Corbin remained quite the loose end. Her life was still in San Francisco, as was her company.

She kind of had a sense that Mac's breath was held.

"We *are* really good at it," she allowed. Cautiously.

"Yeah. I liked the way we kept affirming each other. 'Yes, oh yes!'" he mimicked.

She gave a quick shout of laughter.

Her heartbeat was ratcheting up again when she looked at him.

She wasn't a masochist. She might be a little impulsive, but the object had never been to court pain.

But maybe this was part of their battle, too: this was something she needed to prove to herself and to him. That her heart was a little more muscular now, thanks to the workout she'd put it through over the years. That she was strong enough to take what she wanted without giving up anything critical.

"Nothing much has changed about what I said before . . ."

He turned to her. Clearly aware that her sentence had ended with an ellipsis, not a full stop.

"Let's say . . . we won't exactly add it to the schedule. But it's not off the table."

He studied her a moment. Then the corner of his mouth tipped ever so slightly. "Understood. Wanna shake on it?"

She hesitated, then gave her hand to him with a bit of an ironic flourish.

He took it.

But once he had it, it was almost as though he'd forgotten why she'd given it to him. He held it a moment; his face clouded slightly. He almost whimsically laced his fingers through hers, and he looked down at where their fingers joined and dragged his thumb lightly over the back of her hand, frowning faintly.

And then he dropped her hand abruptly and pushed himself to his feet.

"Guess I should go get started on the blinds, eh?" He headed for the doorway.

He turned around and walked backward a few feet and added, wickedly, "And go hydrate."

She stared after him. Then back at her hand.

She curled her fingers closed.

Troubled and elated.

Because she could have sworn his expression, that fleeting glimpse of his eyes before he stood, was an awful lot like the one she'd seen when she'd opened her eyes, flat on her back, that day in Whiskey Creek.

CHAPTER 19

Two days later, at around four o'clock in the afternoon, Ávalon paced slowly through what was once the Grand Piano Room, and which she would from now on think of as the Sex Against the Wall Room, into the living room, where the giant bargelike sofa lived.

Damn.

Boy, had obsessively poring over paint samples paid off. That one fever dream about color choices notwithstanding.

She'd noticed how the progress of daylight subtly altered the colors of the white walls in the house throughout the day, from cool shadowy mauve to palest blush to warm gold. She'd chosen paint colors that ever-so-slightly enhanced all those colors, so that walking from room to room was like progressing through a mountain day. And now most of the walls downstairs were done.

Upstairs was homage to the gradual progress of a mountain nightfall, from sunset to twilight. Gray-mauve, terra cotta, gold, blue. All of them very soft, muted, one color per room.

The effect was *spectacular.*

Not only that, the whole project was going to come in under budget and ahead of schedule.

And since they'd had their final progress huddle for the day and all the workmen had tromped out, she clapped her hands over her head in a self-five. Then she held her hand up to Chick Pea, who was sitting on the sofa, and Chick Pea paw-fived her.

"Hey, Avalon! Come up here! I want to show you something."

She gave a start and spun around.

For some reason she'd thought he'd gone, too. But Mac was standing on the landing at the top of the stairs, looking disheveled, sweaty, paint-speckled, and as alluring as any siren who had ever sung sailors to their deaths on a rock, if sirens had ever been male. He'd been working on fixing the attic stairs, she knew, which had entailed a certain amount of swearing and crashing. He'd assured her that absolutely nothing interesting was up there, unless she wanted to include the possum.

But his face was lit up with some suppressed news.

"I totally just saw you high-five yourself, by the way."

She laughed, even as her face went warm. "I deserved it. This place looks *great.*"

He grinned down at her. "It does. I should self-five myself, thank you very much. But I think you should come check this out."

And he ducked back into whatever room he'd emerged from.

Molten sex against the wall hadn't caused so much as a blip in their brisk professionalism and the overall bonhomie. But every single second moment was fraught with portent and promise. The very molecules in every room seemed flammable. Simple exchanges were accompanied by smoldering gazes not usually shared when discussing which hinge one preferred to use for the kitchen door.

Short of backing her butt up into his hand again, she wasn't quite sure how or when that would happen. Only that it would. She had her reasons to be cautious. And so, it seemed, did he.

But here he was beckoning her up the stairs. Damned if she would refuse that invitation. Her heart was already pounding as if she'd just finished running up a flight of them.

"In here!" he called, as she was halfway up.

He was in the master bedroom, the one that had once been his parents'.

She hadn't been in there in almost a week, so relieved was she to not have to deal with the black-and-gold wallpaper.

She slowed, awestruck, as she drifted in.

She prowled the perimeter of the room with ruthless eyes. The hideous paper was gone as if it had never been. The elegant, stately proportions of the room had indeed been freed; it was filled with light and air. The walls were now a pale gold that took on a touch of pinky apricot when the sun shone on it full bore. Which it did late in the afternoon for an hour or so.

Which it was doing right now.

The color she'd chosen was called Nostalgia.

"*Wow*," she exhaled, finally.

Mac watched her as she almost gingerly touched her fingertips to the wall.

"It doesn't look a thing like it used to," she said finally. Just to say something.

Because this was true.

And yet it wasn't quite true.

She drifted over to the French doors and peered out to the deck, toward Devil's Leap, jutting up from the swimming hole.

Something about the direction the room faced, the way the old trees sifted the sunlight through their leaves, the French windows . . .

If she turned around now she wouldn't be surprised to see his parents' big double bed, and a hologram of her and Mac entwined and madly kissing. That very last day she'd seen him before, of course, she'd wound up back here at Devil's Leap.

"It's really . . . it's just beautiful. Thank you."

She said it softly.

And it was true.

But there was an ache in her solar plexus.

The room without the paper didn't feel quite the way she'd thought it would.

Because it wasn't different enough.

Suddenly Mac looped his arms loosely around her from behind. Her body couldn't help itself; she melted back against his warm torso the way water has no choice but to sink into earth. But her mind resisted the easy capitulation. She glanced down at the arms encircling her. The hair on his arms glinted copper, just like it had on that day.

He rested his cheek against the top of her head. A gesture so yearning, so intimate and whimsically tender her breath stopped.

He lifted it only a second later.

Perhaps he had unnerved himself.

Or didn't want to give her the wrong idea.

It was also possible she'd tensed.

His arms fell gently away a second later.

They were quiet a moment.

"Guess I'll get going," he said.

She had a hunch they'd both thought a little wallpaper-vanquishing celebration sex on the drop cloth might have been in order. A little voice in the back of her head urged, *His zipper is right* there. *You hardly even have to stretch out your arm to get it undone.*

But suddenly the air was aswarm with unspoken things and, like wasps at a picnic, they were getting in the way of the impulse to get down, so to speak.

In other words, they weren't going to be doing each other up against Nostalgia.

He flicked her with a glance that neatly undressed and savored her. His eyes met hers, searching for something. His were dark with some emotion. Not only desire. Sort of rueful. Sort of guarded.

She knew, and he knew, that he was still leaving for the day.

Lust was a complicated thing.

"See you tomorrow," she said, just as lightly. "Thanks for all the hard work."

"You bet, Harwood."

He turned to go, then turned around and walked a few backward steps, as if he wanted to see her bathed in that amber light. Just to make sure she was real, and not the ghost of the girl she'd been back then.

She'd desperately wanted that wallpaper gone from the wall of the room. And now she thought she more fully understood why.

But suddenly it was pretty clear a few other layers still needed to be scraped away.

But for some reason that aborted gesture—his head resting atop hers—haunted her. She kept trying to analyze it as if it contained layers of coded meaning, like a dream.

And the moment he left, the beautiful house seemed unnervingly filled with echoes, memories, and questions. So she impulsively invited the least ethereal people she knew, her mom and dad, over for dinner, which they insisted on bringing. Hamburgers and salad and cake. They ate out on the deck. She basked in their pride and praise when they saw the house; they made an appropriate fuss over Chick

Pea the way you would over any new member of the family. She relished the homely conversation about the day-to-day at the Misty Cat.

She didn't mention Mac.

She wore her Peace and Love sweatshirt to eat outside with her parents. The nights were getting chillier even if the days were still full of sunlight. It was hard to shake the sense of something winding to an end. Which it was, naturally; she'd known it would. That had been the plan, to fix and flip this house. But her nerve endings were ever-so-faintly twanging with panic, picking it up like a radio signal from outer space. She wasn't quite certain yet why.

Only that she'd begun to wonder that she was still keeping Mac's presence on the down low, because it was possible the whole thing was going to be, a year from now, a page in her diary.

She knew work would suck her in when she returned to San Francisco. And because that's where the jobs were and she needed an income, that's where she was going, Corbin or no Corbin.

"Knock knock."

A little family of deer strolling by stared at her with limpid unblinking eyes and kept going.

No one answered the door.

"MAC?" she called.

"Avalon? Hey! Out here! Robert Plant has ear mites!"

It was entirely possible it was the first time in history anyone anywhere had uttered that sentence out loud.

She followed the sound of his voice and of bleating and found Mac out in the little goat paddock, getting nuzzled and bumped by his little goat posse. He was stuffing a tube of something back in his jeans. Clearly he'd just been administering to Robert Plant. Raaaaabert Plant.

"I got a text from Eden," she told him. "She was wondering if the Hummingbirds can come here and meet your goats."

He smiled crookedly at her. He hadn't shaved yet, and the stubble was *really* working for him. "Tell the truth. *You* wanted to meet the goats."

She couldn't resist the smile. "Well, yeah, that, too."

And she kind of wanted to see his house, too.

"Come in here." He called to her. "Hold out your hand."

He cupped her hand in his so he could pour, to her astonishment, what looked like Cheez-Its into it. Another gesture, superfluous but tender, an excuse to touch her. A touch that lingered a little, then ended too soon, leaving her glowing like a radiator. And pensive.

The goats swarmed her as she entered their paddock. Their funny sweet faces were so full of character, by turns mischievous, dignified, witty. She divvied up the snacks while they bumped her hands for pats. She peered into their eyes and communed with their little goat souls.

Mac leaned on the fence and narrated.

"Janis has some pipes on her. She's a sweetheart but she'll nip you a little if you don't give her snacks fast enough. She's the one going for your pockets right now. John is dignified. Maybe cuz he's getting older and fatter. He's kind of the boss, if I had to pick one. Simon is Janis and John's baby. I have Alpine, a La-Mancha and one Toggenburg. Bob's the Toggenburg."

"I don't think I ever asked you how you ended up with goats." She scratched Simon's head.

"Morty Horton. I finished my national guard stint and I'd been traveling around Europe, when I had a chat with Morton Horton. He knew the grounds-keeper was leaving this property and he had a couple goats and needed someone to look out for them, and, well, I met the goats, we hit it off, so I got some more and . . . what?"

"*What* what?"

"You're looking at me all . . ." He didn't complete that question.

"I just think it's . . . it's a pretty cool story."

She had an embarrassing hunch about what her expression must be. Because she was frankly rather enchanted. By his unselfconscious, charming easiness. By his whole backstory, frankly. *I always knew animals would be your downfall, Harwood,* he'd said wryly.

He'd be one to talk, she had a hunch.

"Um . . ." He looked away, swiped a hand through his hair. "I have some coffee left. Want some?"

"Sure."

The invitation slightly cautious. Maybe even a tad reluctant. She knew he was a guy who liked to be in control, and giving her an impromptu tour of his bachelor pad hadn't been on his schedule this morning.

But suddenly her heart was beating like a teenager's who'd been invited for a ride in the hot bad boy's muscle car.

He vanished into the door and left it open; she followed him inside.

It was basically a studio, a large main room and a kitchen, maybe a thousand square feet, if that. Cozy, though. And snug. It was lit by a long transom window that ran nearly the length of one side and another window that faced the road.

A truly gigantic bed, a California King, covered with a basic white box-stitched comforter that appeared to be about five inches thick, so fluffy was it, was sandwiched between two walls with only a few inches to spare on either side. About eight pillows clearly punched into softness bulged at the top, divided into two stacks. She actually liked a crapload of pillows, too. It was the crack of dawn but he'd made his bed quite tidily. *That's what the military will do for you,* she thought.

She wondered what he would do if she tipped herself facedown onto the bed. A little rush of lust made her head swim, imagining it.

It was funny, though, what just a few seconds'

worth of hovering in the doorway of someone's house could reveal. And she found herself gathering up these details the way she'd hoarded everything he'd told her about him once before.

The little kitchen was pristine and remained 1930s vintage, which was probably about when this cottage was built. The tiled counters were salmon pink edged in burgundy, the white cupboards edged in scallops, the sink a deep farmhouse variety. A few pots and pans hung from hooks. The fridge was old but handsome, eggshell-colored with rounded corners. She'd be willing to bet it was temperamental.

Along one wall was a bookcase featuring a Kindle, an iPad, and a laptop, all charging, and a series of mysterious little black oblong boxes, all stacked. She didn't see any photos or artwork.

A shotgun was hung over the door.

"Gosh. I like what you've done with the place."

He snorted.

There were only a few actual books on the shelves: *The Big Book of Animal Husbandry* was one of them, and it was indeed pretty big. Propped on cinderblocks it would have made an excellent coffee table.

"So sweet of you to go looking for husbands for all of your animals."

"Ha ha."

He seemed a little tense about her exploration, but he was letting her do it.

"I liked it better when you could see the books people thought they ought to read lined up in their living room, like *Zen and the Art of Motorcycle Maintenance* and *Siddhartha* and stuff like that, and when you get closer to them, the ones they actually read in their bedroom. The Ludlum books and whatnot."

"I have *all* of the those on my Kindle."

"What are all those little boxes?"

"That's my art installation."

"They look like tie boxes."

He sighed. "That's because they're tie boxes."

She looked up at him. "Are . . . ties inside the boxes? Is this a fetish?"

"Why, feeling inspired?" He'd perked up.

She ignored that but gave him a little smile just to give him something to wonder about. "Do you sneak off to a job as a stockbroker when I'm not looking?"

Too late she realized that "stockbroker" was basically the opposite of everything he'd ever wanted to be. But he was tracking her pretty intently with his eyes. As if deciding how well she went with his décor. Or perhaps planning a sly way to get her to sit down on his bed.

He hesitated. "Where do you think I got most of my money?"

She paused before she followed that up with, "Where *do* you get your money?"

"I'm actually a fantastic investor." He said this simply. "Grew it from scratch. Kind of like my crops."

"Seriously?"

"I never joke about money, Harwood. I have absolutely nothing against coming by it honestly."

Well, this was rather interesting. She studied him, freshly intrigued.

He hiked a brow nonchalantly.

"So where do you get the ties?"

There was a funny little beat of silence then.

"My brother sends them to me."

She wasn't certain whether the cautious way he delivered the sentence was because of his decidedly ambivalent relationship with his brother or because he just hadn't wanted to tell her that because it was just too much intimacy for seven thirty in the morning.

Most likely he anticipated that answer would just lead to more questions.

"So, on the subject of goats. Do you mind if the Hummingbirds meet all your goats today and learn about them?"

"No," he said shortly. "Not at all," he added.

She studied him for the truth of that. As far as she could tell, he was perfectly sincere. Despite himself, Mac liked sharing what he knew.

She would wager good money that Mac had actually had a good time with the Hummingbirds the other day.

She could feel a treacherous little glow starting up around her heart at the thought.

"I was thinking after that I can give them lunch at

the picnic table and maybe you could tell them about winter vegetables. What do you think?"

He regarded her pensively for a long, silent moment, as if he were mulling a philosophical conundrum.

"I think . . ." he said thoughtfully, ". . . you should take off your shirt. Right now."

CHAPTER 20

She froze. The breath knocked from her for a millisecond.

Instantly something like invisible lightning zig-zagged between them.

They stood across from each other like a pair of gunslingers.

And then he smiled. Slowly and crookedly.

An implacable smile.

She tipped her head, considering another few seconds.

Then she curled her fingers into the hem of her T-shirt. And leisurely, as if she was just rolling out of bed after a good night's sleep and indulging in that first stretch, she furled it up over her head.

She gathered it into one fist. Dangled it for an instant.

And let it fall into a little pink heap on the floor. As coy as a maiden dropping a hankie.

She was a little chilly without it.

She wouldn't be for long, that much she knew.

"Now," he said thoughtfully, "I think you should take off your bra."

He made it sound like an oh-so-reasonable suggestion. His voice had gone hypnotically soft.

They locked eyes.

He wasn't blinking.

She hesitated.

But only for effect.

Then she reached around behind her. Her hands were already a little clumsy with anticipatory nerves.

And she slipped the clips free, and peeled the straps from her shoulders, and slid it down one arm to drop right on top of the T-shirt.

She stood, nude from the waist up, her nipples already going hard in the chilly air.

She had the pleasure of watching his eyes darken to black.

She half suspected wolves looked like that before they pounced on something delicious.

"Now take off your jeans." He employed the same civilized, reasonable tone. Though it was a trifle tauter now.

The room suddenly seemed as silent as a vacuum. They were the only two people in the world. He stayed in the doorway. A sort of self-imposed distance, she imagined. His way of making it that much hotter for himself.

When she lowered her hand to her waistband, his eyes followed it as if they were on an invisible tether.

She watched him while he watched her hand settle

on the snap. And then she thumbed it open. The tiny *click* was as momentous as a gong sounding.

She dragged the zipper down in a leisurely fashion.

She went at this in a very matter-of-fact way. She wasn't going for burlesque. This somehow didn't feel like a whimsical occasion.

And she pulled at the waistband and freed her jeans from her hips and managed to get them off without needing to hula-hoop them down. Magically, her underwear didn't go along for the ride.

And while they weren't anything Victoria's Secret would put in a storefront window, they were black and featured lace and they didn't say "Tuesday" on them.

She was now naked save for them.

His lips curved very, very slightly.

But the heat in his eyes, the tension in his jaw, was making her lightheaded.

"And now . . ." His voice was husky. "I think you should take off your underwear."

She waited again, a little smile on her own face.

And she heard his breath catch when she finally moved.

She slid them down exactly as if she was about to step into the shower, maybe with a little less speed, and kicked them from her toes to land lightly on top of her jeans and T-shirt and bra.

She had a peculiar sense of floating over her nude self while the fully clothed Mac smiled like King Henry VIII contemplating a feast.

For a good thirty seconds or so.

She'd never felt more naked or more purely like an animal, willing to do just about anything to get what she wanted, and that meant, in this moment, doing everything *he* wanted. And to think she couldn't even get lazy old Corbin to do it in front of a mirror.

"Now . . ." His voice was a hypnotist's voice. Dreamy. "I think you should turn around, put your hands against the wall . . . and close your eyes."

She rotated toward the wall with the casement window and pressed her palms against the cool stucco, like a perp about to get frisked for weapons.

And she closed her eyes.

Nothing happened.

There was no sound.

No movement.

Unless one counted her lungs. Her breath shuddered in and out, swiftly. In and out.

In the dark behind her lids, she imagined she could feel his eyes on her, planning what he intended to do to her. And within seconds imagination and anticipation colluded to fire her nerve endings into a state of a sort of raw eagerness as efficiently as a well-applied tongue or a skillful hand.

And it got even better when she imagined him watching her. His own arousal banking by the second as he filled his senses with the sight of her.

Imagined his hand moving to his zipper, sliding it down.

The silence felt acute. Her hearing was suddenly a superpower. Off in the distance a goat bleated.

And then . . . then there was a faint rustle. She latched on to the sound with a desperate hope.

Suddenly she could smell him, his earthiness and an underlying tang of soap.

Behind her, the inch or so of space between them heated so palpably it was almost as if he was against her skin.

Oh but not quite.

It definitely wasn't quite the same.

And still . . . he made her wait.

Seconds more. And a few more after that.

She shuddered and arced like a snapped power line when his fingertips finally landed lightly on her skin, and when they glided from her shoulder blades to her waist, she groaned raggedly and shamelessly.

His erection pressing against her bare bottom. His chest against her back. He was still wearing a T-shirt, and this somehow was even more erotic.

"I'm going to make you scream louder than Melissa Manchester," he murmured, softly, right into her ear, and she started to laugh but she stopped when he applied his tongue and traced slow curlicues there followed by strategic little hot breaths, and continued in that fashion down her throat, sending zaps of bliss to the far reaches of her body, her scalp, her fingertips, down to the soles of her feet. And he followed this by sliding his hand up to cup her breasts, to nipples that were so rigid it was a wonder sparks didn't shoot from them when he chafed his thumbs across.

"*Jesus* . . . sweet oh sweet Jesus," she moaned, like

someone at a revival meeting. Awestruck by the staggering wonderfulness.

His hand made its way down and slipped with alacrity between her legs and discovered her wet indeed.

"Spread 'em, Harwood," he ordered.

She did.

And he trailed kisses down along her spine, and the kisses were followed by his featherlight fingertips, down, down, down, until he kissed that wildly sensitive little place at the base of her spine, and then managed to maneuver his torso between her legs, which was both comical and graceful as if they were Chinese acrobats, and now he was in front of her looking up. He slid his palms up over her thighs and delicately touched his tongue right *there*.

A bolt of pleasure nearly lifted the top off her head. "*Holy* Mother . . ."

He did it again. And again, and then he performed what amounted to calligraphy with the very tip of his tongue. Oh dear lord, could pleasure blind you? She closed her eyes.

"*Yes.*"

And then he stopped.

Her eyes opened again. "Mac . . . please . . ."

"Am I on the right track?" His voice was a laughing purr. His eyes were full of wicked lights.

"Don't . . . *talk* . . ."

And this time he took orders from her. He set up a rhythm. The sinewy talent of his hot, satiny tongue was a revelation. He took cues from her shredded breathing, her moans, her thrashed-back head and undulating hips, her fingers curling into his hair to urge him on, to hold herself up. A tsunami of pleasure was building, building, building.

And when it hit, as he'd promised, she screamed quite shamelessly.

He caught her in his arms before she could crumple to the floor like a marionette, and danced her backward a few feet and deposited her on his bed, and clambered onto it alongside her, hovering over her like a conqueror. Admiring his handiwork. Sporting a glorious erection curving up his belly.

"Off!" She seized a handful of his T-shirt as if she was a teen who'd gotten hold of Harry Styles. "All of it."

He ripped it off over his head and flung it across the room. He yanked off his jeans all the way.

And she sighed again as she reached up for him, dragged her hands over satin skin stretched over those drum-taut muscles, slid her hands into those delicious hollows of muscle on his butt, perfect for gripping when things got fast and hard. He hissed in a breath with the pleasure of her touch, his stomach contracting. And so she let her hands glide over him, her fingertips tracing those fissures of muscle.

He slid his hands into hers and pressed them flat and she locked her legs around his back.

And she looked up at him, and he looked down into her eyes, and she had a hunch that the realization that this was the first time that they had ever lain together, skin to skin, struck them simultaneously. His expression suddenly went serious and very nearly shy. She touched his face and she didn't know why. As if the unguarded Mac, the sweetness she'd always known, was there and she wanted to protect him, acknowledge him, feel him once more before that boy was gone.

He stroked into her deeply, slowly. At first.

And then faster.

Very like they'd discussed earlier about painting.

"Oh my God. Oh God." His words were really tatters of breath as he moved. "Avalon."

And then they collided hard, over and over, in a perfect, greedy rhythm, until their breath came in shredded gusts, until the cords of his neck drew tight, until he rose up over her, his head thrown back, his eyes closed, and shouted her name.

She held on to him, terrified and joyous all at once, as he eased himself down over her. She could feel his heart beating right against hers.

"Should we high-five each other?" she suggested a few seconds later. Still somewhat breathlessly.

"Low five," he said, and gave her bottom a contented little smack.

She curled into his bent arm and he pulled her into the curve of him, and she rested her head on his shoulder which went up . . . and down. Up . . . and down. As his breathing resumed regular rhythms.

"So you'll sell me the house now, right?" he slurred happily.

She laughed. "What is it you said a few days ago? Over my dead body."

"Funny. For a minute there I thought I might have actually killed you . . . with bliss."

"For a minute there I think you did. I saw a bright light and everything. The only thing that brought me back into my body was the prospect of maybe doing this again."

He smiled. Eyes closed. "Gimme a second or two."

There would very likely be a picture of him next to the word *replete* in the dictionary.

"What do I have to do to get you to sell me Devil's Leap?" she teased.

He breathed in and out, still wearing that faint smile. He appeared to be mulling.

"Fellatio," he suggested sleepily.

Is that *all?* she was tempted to say, like the strumpet she'd clearly become.

Out loud she issued a faux-scandalized, "Mac Coltrane!"

Her head was bumped up and down on his shoulder as he laughed silently to himself.

And then he sighed again.

With her cheek against his chest, his arm looped to hold her against him, their calves twined. Silent minutes went by. That satiety expanded into something that felt horizonless. As though the two of them were floating on a raft on a safe and beautiful sea, a warmth, a peace, heady and at the same time righter than anything.

When she was sixteen, she really knew almost nothing much about the physical part. The mechanics, sure. You could read about those. But not about its variations, and how it could be boring with one person and incendiary with another.

But she'd called this feeling, the one she was feeling right now, love, without questioning it.

She still didn't know if it was a feeling to be trusted when it came to Mac Coltrane. And just that little notion alone crept in and sobered her, crisped up the hazy, blurry edges of postcoital bliss. And again she remembered yesterday's gesture: the casual affection that almost was withdrawn before something like tenderness or surrender—his—could be construed.

She thought about this as his breathing was growing more even.

"Can I . . . ?" She gestured at the tie boxes.

He hesitated. "Knock yourself out."

She leaned over and plucked up the lid on one box. It was navy blue and featured a scattering of mountain goats. The kind you might count if you were trying to get to sleep.

"Goats?"

"Yeah," he said shortly.

"So he knows about the goats?"

He didn't reply.

She closed it carefully. She lifted another lid. Inside was a striped red-and-gold tie and there was a 49er helmet on it.

"You always liked the 49ers."

"Yep. Still do. I'm irrational that way."

The 49ers could not seem to win for losing in recent years.

She opened another box. It was a tie featuring a scattering of mountain bikes.

"You loved that Ritchey P-29," she said.

Mac said nothing for a time. "I told you before, Ty has a very fixed idea of what I should be."

"While you have no fixed ideas about anything."

"Ha," he said. Not sounding amused.

She gingerly, carefully settled the ties back into place, abstractedly fussing with their alignment as if she were an engineer and something critical would topple if they were a hair out of place.

And then she turned to him.

"And yet you keep them. The ties."

This yielded stony silence.

"Where is Ty now?"

"New York."

The short answer made his displeasure at the direction of the conversation known.

"Why the inquisition, Avalon?" he asked, a moment later.

"It's not an inquisition."

This wasn't entirely true.

He closed up. She didn't know whether he was even aware of doing it. It was subtle. He slid his hand out from beneath her head and folded it under his own. He shifted a little so that his hip wasn't touching hers. He now occupied a space on the bed described by himself alone.

"It was probably pretty hard for him, too. The whole thing with your dad. And at least he's trying. It's a gesture. A symbol."

"And we know how you feel about grand gestures, huh, Avalon?"

Damn. Ironic, that sentence. Ironic, heading toward bitter.

"Sometimes it's less about what you want and more about what another person might need, Mac."

That was ironic heading toward bitter, too. She did not like the sound of it in her voice.

Suddenly this wasn't just about his brother or the ties.

"It's just . . . maybe he doesn't know *how* else to connect with you. How are you ever going to know if you don't talk to him?"

He drew in a long breath and sighed it out. "Avalon . . . I don't think you understand what it was like after all of that went down. Everywhere I turned there was swirling chaos, like a tornado. And . . . let's say you captured that tornado that would otherwise destroy you and keep on destroying everything else in its path and stuffed it into a garbage can and clapped on the lid. You have one option after that. You keep the lid on all the way and never open it. Because if you ever open it even a little bit it'll escape and it's destruction all over again."

"But was it really that easy to just cut everyone out?"

"Is *anything* easy? I learned a long time ago certain kinds of ties can turn into a noose."

Her stomach went peculiarly cold. "Boy. Talk about a pickup line."

He didn't laugh.

Which was fine, because she didn't think it was funny, either.

And now she was closing up, too, and she only half realized it. She shifted her arms against her body protectively.

Moved away from him.

"I just wish you—"

"Avalon." The word was startling. Flat and cold. A warning. "Enough."

She did not like that one bit.

He looked into her eyes then.

And she hated the fact that she was carefully holding her expression still. She didn't want him to know what she was thinking, or, God help her, feeling.

But when their eyes met it was still almost a physical thing. Every time she could not believe how lovely his eyes were, but she was smart enough to know that the true impact came from the person looking out of them. And his went softer, and his chest went up, came down in a sigh.

She couldn't smack down that little jolt.

His smile was kind of wistful. But his eyes were darker. Not sad, but thoughtful.

"I remember counting your freckles that day at Whiskey Creek because in that second before you opened your eyes I thought . . . what if I never see her again? I never wanted to forget. She had eyes the color of mahogany and big as lakes, I would have said. And thirteen freckles."

Her heart gave a huge thump. As if it were turning belly-up in supplication, like Chick Pea.

There was a suspicious burning sensation behind her eyes.

It might have been the most romantic thing anyone had said to her. From a man who was studiedly *not* romantic.

And yet she wondered . . . that it might actually be his way of saying good-bye. Memorizing her yet again.

She couldn't keep slamming her entire being up against the metaphorical wall that was Mac Coltrane. Didn't he understand that cutting everything out that could potentially hurt or inconvenience him meant essentially cutting out his heart?

Because what is a heart if not inconvenient? A potential source of grave pain, right?

Maybe he knew. And didn't care.

He *did* care about things—his goats, his cat. She was positive he cared about her. But she knew in her soul that she wouldn't be immune from the kind of ruthless exile to which Mac consigned people who hurt him. He'd do it before she had a chance to hurt him, if he thought there was a possibility of that.

And just like that her heart suddenly started beating swiftly as if it knew it was once again in actual and present danger.

She sat up suddenly.

"I should get going. Eden's going to be here in a few minutes and I wanted to get a few things done before she gets here."

Her tone was bright and friendly. It was her presentation voice. Her put-her-best-foot-forward-everything-is-dandy voice. It had always glossed over what she was thinking or feeling and it had always been persuasive.

Mac noticed. He frowned faintly at her. Puzzled. But probably uncertain as to what question he should ask.

"Yeah," he said finally. "Okay. I'll meet you all later out by the goats."

Avalon got dressed.

And she left.

And in the five minutes in between those two events neither of them said a word.

CHAPTER 21

Something had happened in there, Mac knew. And not just spectacular sex.

It felt very like some kind of decision had been reached that neither of them had voiced.

Or maybe it was an ultimatum.

He did *not* like being pushed. Or maneuvered.

His mood was rather dark and his temper was on a low simmer. His mind traced the confines of the issue but it did not want to dive into the dark heart of it, which might have been a failure of nerve, and the idea that there was something left in the world that scared him, pissed him off, too.

He lost himself in work instead. One of the final tasks remaining on the project spreadsheet was the hideously stuck window frame on the lower level. He absorbed himself in the brutal yet delicate scraping and scraping of old paint to free it into motion, the meticulous sanding, the solvents, the paint.

For the first time in about a decade, hours later, the damn thing moved freely.

And that afternoon, as arranged, Avalon and Eden had brought a dozen little Hummingbirds to meet his goats.

He and Avalon managed to play off each other like a well-rehearsed comedy team, effortlessly. They even did the goat voices, which practically crippled the Hummingbirds with laughter. He explained about how scientists thought goats' funny pupils helped them maintain a wider field of vision so they could stay aware of predators. He told them how it was good for the environment to let goats help keep the grass short. He told them about goat fur and goat cheese; he let them hand out snacks.

He'd learned every damn thing about goats when he acquired those goats, because he wanted to know them from the ground up. And there was something satisfying in imparting the knowledge he'd so carefully gathered, which was, in its way, teaching someone else from the ground up.

But when all the Hummingbirds had gone home, Avalon went back up to the house without saying good night to him.

And if he'd only surmised that something had actually happened in his cottage this morning . . . well, he damn well knew for certain.

He was impatient with ambiguity; too often it felt like dread. Or manipulation. He'd always done what he could to transmute it into manageable parts as fast as he could.

He was tempted to stalk over there to get a conversation going.

It was the prospect of not liking what he learned when he stalked over there that kept him from doing that.

He read *Zen and the Art of Motorcycle Maintenance* instead, in the hopes that it would put him to sleep. Because he did, in fact, have it on his Kindle, and he'd never read it.

But that night, his huge bed, once perfect for him, suddenly felt like a sea that wanted to drown him. Much too vast.

The pillow next to his smelled a little like coconut. And he knew this was because Avalon had rested her hair there. He spent a moment being nonspecifically angry about this.

And then he leaned over, dragged it across his chest and gently folded his arms around it. As if it were both life raft and lover. As if he could smother that uncertain ache in his chest with it.

Then he finally got up to get a drink of water around quarter after two in the morning.

He stood at the sink, thinking of Avalon in her freshly painted turret. Wondering if she'd disappeared all those years ago because even if he *was* the equivalent of a wounded squirrel, he was bound to destroy her heart one of these days. Even if she couldn't articulate that in so many words.

Suddenly a stray beam from what he was certain was a headlight swiped across his window.

He was instantly on alert. They were in the middle of nowhere, even for Hellcat Canyon. Cars just did *not* accidentally make that turn into Devil's Leap.

He flung open the door and craned his head. A car was turning up the long drive to the house. This wasn't New York. It's not like she could get any kind of food delivered at this time of night. But if someone wanted to attempt a home invasion, well . . . it was a long way off for the sheriff.

Good thing Avalon had a half-deaf fluff-ball of a dog to protect her.

He didn't bother getting dressed. He shoved his feet into his shoes, grabbed his shotgun off the rack and jogged up the road, swiftly, on the balls of his feet, matching his breathing to the fall of his feet, heedless of being bare-chested and boxer-shorted.

He ducked low and crept around the side of the house from the back, flattening against the wall, inching toward the front.

He froze when heard the unmistakable sound: a twig cracked.

Crunched with the kind of force only a human foot could apply.

His hackles rose.

Seconds later he saw the man creeping up the flagstone path.

Or . . . maybe not creeping. Striding, actually, as purposefully as any pizza delivery boy. Really tall guy. He was wearing dark skinny jeans and a grayish hoodie pulled up over his head. All of that looked like a burglar costume, or worse.

Apart from the fact that he was apparently using his cellphone as a flashlight. You'd have to be a pretty stupid burglar to do that.

Mac cocked the shotgun. That sound was about as primal as the growl of a wolf.

The guy froze.

"Yeah, whoever you are . . ." Mac all but hissed. "Don't move a fucking hair."

The guy remained frozen. Really frozen. One arm bent at the elbow, the other thrust out mid-stride. It was a very adult version of Simon Says.

"Holy fucking shit, dude . . ." The guy's voice was an incredulous creak.

"Put your hands up where I can see them."

"I swear to God I'm not a burglar. Are you . . . what the hell . . . does Avalon have an armed guard now?"

"PUT. THEM. UP. Not going to ask again."

His arms shot up. So did the phone. Absurdly, the guy now looked like one of those idiots who aimed cell phones at concert stages in order to record them.

"Now turn around to face me. Really slowly."

The guy turned around. Slowly.

Two things happened at once.

Mac could plainly read the word *Dartmouth* on the sweatshirt.

And the lights of the balcony above and the flood-lights below switched on, and he was bathed in light.

Both he and the guy looked up at the balcony.

Avalon was peering over the edge. Her hair was spilling down around her and her face looked kind of grayish and taut in the bright light. Worried.

"Mac? Is that you? What's happening out there? Are you okay? Should I call the cops?"

"Call Eli, Ava. This pervert was creeping around your house."

The guy turned his face up to the balcony like a veritable Romeo, and plaintively said, "Avalon . . . for the love of God tell this guy who I am."

"Oh shit," she sighed. "Mac, this is Corbin."

Silence.

"Ah," Mac said.

And nothing else.

Which was astonishingly, almost thrillingly rude.

And he also didn't put the gun down.

"I'm coming down," she said tersely. "Neither of you move."

She found she didn't mind overmuch that Mac was aiming a gun at Corbin.

And she hoped he took her literally and didn't put that gun down.

She grabbed her Peace and Love sweatshirt and threw it on over her head and shoved her feet in her spaniel slippers and bolted down the stairs.

Crap crap crap. What the *hell* was Corbin *doing* here?

In the dead of night?

She emerged and truly got a good look at the tableau of Mac, spectacular in boxers, stubble, shoes and nothing else, aiming a gun at that asshole she'd lived with for four years.

And for the first time, Ava saw something truly unnerving in Mac.

Mac knew exactly what he was capable of in terms of strength and aggression, and that made him a universe different from Corbin.

Corbin wasn't easy to intimidate. But maybe he ought to be. He was charismatic. Not stop-you-in-your-tracks rakishly good-looking the way Mac was, but he was certainly used to getting his own way, which was in its way a form of confidence.

She studied him as though he were a stranger.

"Corbin, this is Mac. He's the groundskeeper for Devil's Leap and my . . . er . . . contractor."

Mac shot her a blackly incredulous look.

Corbin assessed Mac.

"Contractor, huh? You get guns like that from . . . what . . . carrying water from the well, swinging an axe?"

"Bench pressing skinny tech nerds. Do you guys come in a cord, like firewood?"

Corbin ignored this. "Your name is actually *Mac*? Like in a 1940s gangster movie?"

"Mac, as in Maximilian."

Mac wasn't blinking. His sense of humor had vacated and something very dark and palpable had replaced it.

"Wait. Coltrane? As in . . . Dixon Coltrane?"

"Yes."

"Didn't your father practically invent yuppies? And Ponzi schemes?"

"Corbin," Ava said sharply.

After all, Mac had the shotgun. And a temper.

"Not precisely." Mac's voice was now a lazy drawl. "But from him I learned what a fraud and a cheat looks like. Hence the gun aimed at you."

"Mac!"

She might as well have not been standing there. Testosterone was clearly making the two of them deaf to high-pitched voices.

She swiveled toward Corbin, clearly the weaker of the two. "Corbin, why don't you wait for me inside the house. I need to have a word with Mac."

"Yeah, why don't you wait inside," Mac concurred lazily. "You probably needed a change of underwear, anyway."

"Said the brave man with the gun," Corbin muttered bitterly.

"*Corbin*," Ava repeated sharply. "I swear. To. God."

Mac locked the gun and, with a flourish, put it on the ground. "Go right ahead and say more things to me, Dartmouth."

"*Mac*," Ava hissed. "Enough! For God's sake. Both of you. Corbin, you can wait for me in the house. The front door is unlocked. Just follow the flagstone path around. And don't let the dog out or I'll let Mac shoot you."

Faintly, they could hear the squeaky, beeping barks of Chick Pea.

A series of hard stares ricocheted among the three of them like a bullet in a closed closet.

"Going." Corbin flung up his arms and turned around and stalked toward the house.

"Nice meeting you, Corncob," Mac called after him.

Corbin shot a middle finger up in the air without turning around.

And suddenly Ava was alone with Mac.

They stared at each other in silence that felt portentous, and not in a good way.

"Mature," she said finally.

"But probably not wrong," he said mildly. "About the underwear."

His mood felt dangerous. The little hairs were standing up on her neck, as if in anticipation of a lightning storm.

"I hope Chick Pea bites him," he added. And he wasn't joking.

"She doesn't have enough teeth to do that."

He sighed. "Of course not."

Their faces in the floodlight from the balcony looked as stark as X-rays.

It wasn't a flattering light for anybody. Certainly not the be-stubbled.

"So . . ." Mac began with a blitheness edged all around in razors. "I'm your"—he bobbed exaggerated air quotes—"'er, *contractor*'?"

"You preferred me to introduce you as the guy I've been banging in between coats of paint?"

He considered this. "Yes."

She made a sound. Almost a laugh. Only much less amused.

"Avalon?"

"Yes?"

"Why is Corncob here at two in the morning creeping around your house before I could install the motion-sensitive lighting?"

"I don't know. I really don't. Cross my heart, swear on Chick Pea. I sure as hell didn't invite him."

"He knew where to find you?"

"Well, yeah. I wasn't trying to hide from him."

"So you're not worried about . . ."

Her voice softened a little. "I'm safe from him, Mac. I swear to you. He is mostly pretty harmless. In the physical sense."

"He looks like he'd bow like a twig if I handed him a barbell."

"But you should see him in limbo contests."

Mac was not in the mood to laugh. "So what am I in this scenario, Avalon? Am I like the gamekeeper from *Lady Chatterley's Lover*?"

She hesitated. "Isn't that kind of hot?" she tried. Weakly.

"That's beside the point."

"Did you actually read *Lady Chatterley's Lover*, Mac? Or just watch a porn version?"

"*Lady Chatterley's Lover is* the porn version of *Lady Chatterley's Lover*. Don't change the subject."

"What is the subject, exactly?"

Good question. Jealousy was not in and of itself a subject.

"No guy comes three hours out of his way in the dead of night for business reasons. He wants you back."

She gestured weakly to her sweat-shirted, pony-tailed, paint-splotched self. "Can you blame him?"

Her insouciance just seemed to infuriate him.

"He's a *dog*," he pointed out, slowly, blackly. "And not the fluffy kind needing rescuing."

Now she was really angry. "Thank you for the recap. You, on the other hand, are the . . . the Dalai Lama."

"I'm the *what*?"

"Or someone else with a stainless soul and fault-less motives who would never, ever hurt me."

The last few words were a trifle nasty and carried an implication that made Mac wary.

"Avalon, I just . . ."

He didn't know how he wanted to complete that sentence. Or rather he did. But none of those things felt safe to say, none of them added up to a defini-tive reason to keep her out here in the cold. They were things like: I *just* want to gather you up into my arms right now because it seems I can't stand it when you're upset, even when—especially when—I'm the reason. I just want to talk to you forever about noth-ing and everything, just ramble on and on, as if we existed in our own time and space. I just don't want to have this conversation. I don't want to decide any-thing. I just want to do you in every imaginable way and watch your eyes go hot, and then hazy, and then close when you come, and once in a while, if I get lucky, hear you say my name.

All of those things were true.

"Mac . . ." She sounded tense. "If you have something to say could you please just—"

Fuck the consequences. "Are you going to sleep with him?"

Her mouth dropped open.

"*What* do you think I . . . first of all, *how* is that any of your business? This whole . . . our whole . . . *thing* . . . with you and me was based on the premise that this, and I quote, doesn't have to be any 'big thing.' Because that's how you roll, right?"

Her sentence had begun sort of self-righteously astounded. But that last question, which she'd likely intended to deliver sardonically, faltered somewhere along the way. It became a genuine question. Almost an entreaty.

It rang there in the night air, alongside those little white ghosts of their breath.

Well.

Wasn't it just how he rolled?

He'd started this little encounter tonight, but he hadn't a clue how he'd intended to finish it. Because for more than the last decade all he did was start at the beginning of things and didn't abandon them until he was finished. He knew every step along the way.

And he always, always knew *how* they would finish.

"Maybe . . ." he said carefully. "I said that to give you room to decide what you wanted."

"Or was it to get what *you* wanted."

"What we both wanted," he corrected evenly.

She hesitated. "Fair enough."

And in that moment, nearly desperate, panicky *liking* for the person she was surged through him, brilliant and painful. She was not a bullshitter.

On the surface of things they were only talking about sex. He knew he was the one who ought to say the other things. The things about feelings and the future.

But just as there was something on her mind to-night that she didn't say out loud, there was something he wasn't saying, too.

And it was this that scared him into silence.

She'd wrapped her arms across the front of her. As if to keep herself from flying to pieces. Or to shield herself from him.

And he could feel invisible arms, too. Holding him back. Like that desperate nightmare he'd had where she'd thrown his stone heart into the water at Devil's Leap and vanished in after it. And he'd tried to get a word out, even if only her name. And he just didn't have a voice.

She turned around and went back to the house.

And he watched her go, until she disappeared inside.

CHAPTER 22

Avalon found Corbin sitting on the bargelike sofa petting Chick Pea, who was Buddha-like in her loving acceptance of all mankind, even cheating jerks.

"You got a dog?" he asked.

As the proper response to this was also "Duh" she said, "You couldn't find the front door? You had to creep around the freaking house? What the hell are you even doing here?"

"There aren't any lights out here. I mean, *any*. Almost didn't find the driveway."

"We're still installing the perimeter lighting."

A beat of silence. "We're?"

"Yes. You met my contractor."

"Big Guns out there? In more ways than one? Boy, for a Coltrane, he's sure come down in the world, huh?"

She leveled an amazed look at him, a look that contained such withering incredulity and scorn he dropped his eyes and began rubbing a nonexistent spot on his jeans.

Chick Pea moved over to lean against Avalon.

"Rented a car. A Prius."

She said nothing. Though that could explain why they hadn't heard him drive up. Priuses tended to move on little cat feet, to paraphrase a famous poem about fog.

"Lots of stars out here, though. Wow. Can't see them in San Francisco with all the lights," he added.

This was the kind of inane small talk two people who had never before met would struggle through until the bus arrived or someone they actually knew showed up at the same party.

If one of them had a pronounced hostile bias toward the other, that was.

She didn't reply to that, either.

She was still thinking of Mac out there, standing in his underwear and pointing a gun at Corbin as if it was the most natural thing in the world. Mac had been on watch somehow. That was his instinct. *All I want is for you to be safe.*

She drew in a shuddering breath. Her eyes burned.

"Avalon . . . that guy out there . . ."

She shot him another granite look. Daring him to ask some kind of question he had zero right to ask. She was in no mood to indulge guys tonight.

"Knows his way around a shotgun? Yes. Yes, he does."

He dropped it. He heaved a sigh. He looked around the place.

"This is that sofa from your parents' basement, isn't it?"

"Yes."

Mentioning the sofa, remembering it, was a crafty little move. Because it linked them to their shared history: two Thanksgivings ago, hanging out in her parents' basement with her siblings, playing Nintendo, drinking beer, and laughing.

All it did was make her sad, and the sadness swelled and morphed into fury, which flatlined into nothing but a wish for him to leave.

"This house is amazing. I can see why you snapped it up. I just roamed the downstairs a little. I had no idea there were houses like this out here."

"Yes." She was instantly protective of it. She did not like the idea of Corbin roaming around, assessing things.

"I talked to Rachel Nguyen. She was looking for a conference center property in the North State."

"I know. She's one of my best friends, Corbin, for God's sake."

He nodded shortly. He leaned back a little, as if to get a wider-angle look on her.

"Avalon, I have to say . . . you look . . . you look . . . beautiful."

He said it with great sincerity and the faintest surprise. He almost sounded a little affronted. Not as though he was just now remembering that he'd once had a beautiful girlfriend.

But sort of as if he'd expected her to have wasted away from heartbreak.

She scowled at him.

And she was going to be silent long enough for him

to realize he wasn't going to get a reciprocal compliment.

He looked fine. He looked the same as always. He *should* look like shit, thin from not eating with purple sleepless guilt shadows under his eyes. Maybe his hair should be a little thinner, since he had a tendency to tug on it when he was anxious.

Her diaphragm felt tight. It occurred to her that she was breathing shallowly. As if she begrudged the necessity to breathe the same air he was currently breathing.

He picked absently at the corner of the sofa cushion where it was already coming unraveled.

"I'm sorry to just show up like this. I would have told you I was coming up, but you would have told me not to."

"Corbin, I'd like to sleep. I've been working all day, actual physical labor. If you have something else to say, for fuck's sake, say it."

"I did something horrible," he blurted.

Oh, God.

"Are we referencing the horrible thing you did that led to my being here, or have you done a brand-new horrible thing affecting GradYouAte?"

She said this with utter dispassion and calm neutrality.

It badly rattled him, she could tell. Whatever his strategy was for coming up here, or whatever message he intended to deliver, it apparently depended on her giving a shit about him.

He drew in a breath.

"The first one," he said. With a ghost of humor, an attempt at his usual glib self. "But I'm here for two reasons. So I'm just going to talk business first. Because you wouldn't talk to me, and this requires your input. It's pretty critical."

Oh, crap. Concern twinged, and then the weight of that life she'd created almost without meaning to, a life with people who depended on her for their salaries, came and WHUMP—settled on her shoulders. She hadn't fully been aware of how much of a weight it in fact was until she'd managed, for at least a few weeks, to shift out from under it.

"The football tryout mod for GradYouAte is way behind schedule because two of the key programmers were deported to Canada for not renewing their work visas on time."

She knew what the cascade effect of *that* would be. Advertisers, subscribers. They'd shed them accordingly, and lose a huge chunk of income.

"Corbin . . . I *told* you to make sure everything is in order with their working visas! Twice! And you *know* you're supposed to review all that before hiring decisions are made. You *know* that but I made a freaking point of reminding you!"

"But there are so *many* teams working on so many things. And I usually just do the programming and interviewing."

She could feel tension like a noose around her forehead. "Yes, you do. While I do approximately a billion other fucking things. You know that about the *teams*, too. And if I can do all that, so can you. Unless you're saying I'm smarter and more capable than you are."

This was something she never would have dared voice aloud to him before. Part of the dynamic of their relationship had been the understanding that he was the brilliant one while she was the sparkly cute one who made it possible for him to be brilliant.

She wondered for one wild moment if he'd done this on purpose. So she'd have to come back and fix it.

"And I guess I've been feeling a little distracted by . . . what happened with us."

She stared at him. "By 'what happened'? You mean when I walked in on you mid-bang?"

He sucked in a sharp breath and continued. "There's more. The new programmers hired won't work for anything less than a hundred an hour. So it's either a hundred an hour, or a further delay in the rollout. And there's more trouble with the art for the cheerleader module. You know how we discussed the need for multicultural avatars and we had to have them redone? Well, they're of all ethnicities now. But turns out what they turned in and began implementing . . . well, all the cheerleaders look like this."

He made the universal gesture indicating giant bosoms.

Oh, good God. They would need to be redrawn to reflect the range of bosoms really possible in the real world.

"Anyway. The way it stands now, we can redirect

the ad spend for the football module, but in light of all this stuff, and to make a long story short, we still might not make office rent. Or meet all of payroll. So pick your favorite employee and they'll get paid. Ha ha ha."

She couldn't speak for a moment.

"*Jesus*, Corbin!"

"You know I'm not good with the money decisions." There was a whiff of passive-aggressive accusation here.

"What you actually mean is that you don't *like* to make the money decisions. You know that's not a reason to abdicate responsibility, right? 'I don't want to?' You know those aren't magic words, right?"

But she'd said this same thing to him in ways both pissy and diplomatic over the years. And in years past she'd made excuses to herself for him. "There are actual people *depending* on you."

Her mind was spinning. They'd had these kinds of blips once or twice early on, where the delicate balance of income and outflow had gotten away from them, where some surprise or snafu had resulted in them coming up short. They'd dip into their own earnings or savings to handle it; they'd foregone salaries for a few months more than once. They hadn't had an issue like this in *ages*.

They sat in silence, Avalon seething. Because he'd come all the way up here to force her to solve the problems he could have easily prevented.

And she was mad at herself, too. She'd needed time

away and to prove a point to Corbin. So she'd left him in charge, which shouldn't have led to anything like a disaster. She'd figured he'd rise to the challenge or . . .

. . . he'd do exactly what he ended up doing. Which was fucking everything up.

Now she'd need to go back into town and handle things from there. And she'd need to come up with money for payroll, because damned if she would let any of her staff go without a paycheck. Go hat in hand to their current investors?

She needed to sell this house as soon as possible.

She was absolutely silent. Resentfully, despairingly absorbing all of this. Already working on a solution.

"I wish . . . wish I did have magic words," he blurted suddenly. Sounding wretched.

"*What*?" she said. It felt like a non-sequitur.

"To . . . undo what I did to you."

She stared at him. Astonished.

He reached for her hand.

She slid it out of the way in time.

"Because . . . when I see you . . . I see this beautiful, funny, confident woman I've loved for four years . . . and I oh, God, just want to make it better. I want to turn back time."

Some part of her was amused by the specificity of this. They'd been dating for five years.

"Yeah, but you can't." That was pretty brutal, but it was exactly how she felt.

He took a long, deep breath. "I know what I did

was pretty unforgivable and . . . if I could take it back I would, believe me. We clearly have a few issues. I was hoping we could go to counseling, work something out, find a way to be together."

He had to be joking.

She stared at him wonderingly. For so long, she could see that he'd begun to hope.

"The problem, Corbin, is that when *I* look at you . . ." she said slowly, "I see an ass."

His eyes flared in split-second outrage. He drew in a long breath through his nostrils, and exhaled. Then he nodded rapidly in agreement. "Okay. I know. I know. I deserve that. I *have* been an ass. I was just hoping we could talk about how it—"

"No." She leaned forward, her hands clasped between her knees, and said earnestly and slowly, explaining it as if it were a compelling abstract concept that he might find fascinating, "An *actual* ass, Corbin. I actually see your white ass bobbing up and down between two sets of ten sparkly orange toenails. That's what I see when I look at you. An ass. That is what I'll always see when I look at you. From now on. Forever."

She let that ring in silence.

"And I can't go to counseling with an ass," she explained gently. "I'm sure you see the problem."

His face went a wash of different shades of red, then white again.

She had a hunch he was finally getting it. Because, God help her, she saw his eyes begin to shine with genuine tears.

"I love you, you know," he said.

She sighed, closed her eyes briefly, opened them again. "Maybe you do. But when I said we were done, I meant it. Full stop. Please do not ask me about it again."

He was motionless.

Pity stirred, because despite it all, there was some part of her that always ached for people and their foibles and their weaknesses, even when those weaknesses ended up hurting her.

Mac was in that category.

All she knew was that love was more than whatever she'd had with Corbin. She thought of her parents, and she thought of Morty and Helen Horton strolling along together, and she thought of Mac.

Mac, who even if he couldn't commit to another human, even if he was poised to run away from her, somehow hadn't thought twice about putting her safety above his.

Then again, at least Corbin could get those three terrifying words out. So she guessed he had that going for him.

Maybe the next lucky fool he dated would get to hear them, too.

He sighed bleakly. "Can I . . . at least stay here tonight? I'll sleep on this sofa. It was three and a half hours between San Francisco and here."

"Are you kidding me? There's a motel on I-5 about an hour from here. You're not going to want to stay at the one nearest here. It's pretty sketchy. You can try calling the Angel's Nest but they're already full up and

Rosemary and her husband work hard so I personally wouldn't be happy about you waking them up."

"Are you seriously kicking me out at three in the morning? I've . . . I've driven three and a half hours to get here."

"Are you seriously whining right now? Do I need to call Mac and have him march you out of here? Jesus, Corbin. Have some fucking pride."

She stared him down.

In a huff, he collected his Man Bag and turned around and stalked out.

She locked the door. She watched out the window to make sure he was gone.

And then she watched a little longer just to be on the safe side.

And then a little longer after that.

Even though she had a hunch Mac was watching, too. Whether he wanted to or not. It was just who he was.

While all this was going down, Mac lay as rigid as a board against his scratchy sheets. He felt pinned in place by that faint bar of light thrown down across his torso. But he was as wired as if he'd bolted a six-pack of Red Bull.

The lights were still on out there. Maybe that meant they were still awake.

Maybe they were having a reunion hump.

He flung an arm over his face as if the thought was an assault. He'd consigned the coconut pillow to a far corner of the bed.

In the deepest heart of him, he actually didn't think that would happen. Avalon was stubborn as hell, she had a lot of pride, and everything she felt went deep. She wasn't going to just cave.

And *he,* thank you very much, was *very* good in the sack. No woman wanted to eat a sensible main course, say, a steamed chicken breast, after a decadent flaming dessert.

He smiled sardonically at his own attempt at bravado.

Nevertheless.

He was worried. That spoiled twit had been horrible to her but he'd woken up next to her for the last four or five years. He was worried because even though Corbin didn't strike him as any kind of romantic hero—which was the kind of guy he had a hunch Avalon would hold out for—or even be worth fighting for, there was no accounting for the mystery of chemistry. Or history. History definitely exerted its own gravity.

Until tonight, he'd had those things in his favor with her—chemistry and history.

Until tonight, he hadn't even thought of the day after tomorrow.

Until tonight, "Corbin" had felt like something theoretical that didn't need to be addressed unless via sardonic jokes.

And Mac was man enough to own up to the fact that "spoiled twit" had once described him, too.

He imagined himself crawling out of bed to stand

beneath her balcony and falling to his knees and bellowing, "AVALON!" like Stanley Kowalski. He kind of understood the impulse now.

He just didn't know what he would say after that.

Making his way out to Avalon's balcony in fact seemed as possible as a mummy creaking its way out of a sarcophagus.

He'd successfully jettisoned everything that threatened to chain him in or make him uncomfortable or prevent him from moving precisely the way he wanted to.

And then he'd rebuilt himself from the ground up.

And he was free! He *liked* being free.

The light at the house went out.

And the bands across his stomach tightened, and something very like pain, but also very like fury, took up residence and burned in his chest in the vicinity of his heart.

He didn't actually *need* anyone, and that was indeed the definition of freedom.

The Cat, in his infinite wisdom, begged to differ, and jumped up and curled in the crook of Mac's arm.

CHAPTER 23

At about eleven o'clock the next day, as the mail truck trundled back down the road, Mac practically punched his hand into his mailbox. He swirled his hand around.

Nothing. Not even dust. Not even a spider.

He closed his eyes and swore softly. How much of this angst could have been avoided if Mike had just paid him back on time?

When he opened his eyes, Avalon was about ten feet away, heading toward the mailbox.

"How'd the visit with Corncob go? You kids patch things up?"

She stopped a good five feet back from him. As if she'd seen a dark object off in the distance, and she wasn't certain whether he was a tree trunk or a bear.

She said nothing. Her hair was gathered up in a straggly ponytail and there were purple shadows beneath her eyes. Her face was pale but her mood was palpably dark.

Clearly she hadn't slept any more than he had.

And despite himself the idea that she was feeling wretched made him restless.

She clearly wasn't glowing from a happy reunion, that was for sure. He knew a little unworthy thrill of pleasure at that.

"So did he leave?" He was conscious of pressing his luck but unable to help himself somehow. "You can't hear a Prius leave. Sneaky little car for a sneaky little man."

Before his eyes, her expression slowly evolved into one of black, incredulous amazement. It was like watching a time lapse of a bad, bad storm moving in.

She approached him, slowly. Slowly.

Very like she was stalking him.

She stopped at a distance he couldn't reach across without moving toward her. "At least *he* actually came looking for me," she said. With such wounded, resigned bitterness he blinked.

"What the . . . what the hell is *that* supposed to mean?"

She seemed to weigh whether to answer the question. "It means, Mac, that if I hadn't shown up here at Devil's Leap more than a decade after you last saw me, apparently you were perfectly okay with never seeing me again. And I'm pretty sure if I left today, the same thing would be true."

"What the—you disappeared on *me*, Avalon!"

He'd never said the words aloud to anyone in his life.

When he said them, he knew they summed up that

core of pain lodged inside him. It had never budged, never shrunk. He'd only been able to armor it. He'd never said them because they were his biggest weakness.

"Of *course* I disappeared!" Pain all but howled through those words.

He didn't think he'd ever known dread quite like this. Or maybe relief was a better word. It was whatever the guy facing a firing squad felt the second the triggers were pulled.

He had an epiphany then: He'd thought he was free before. And now he knew he wouldn't truly be free until she said what she was about to say.

"So you did have a reason. For disappearing."

The silence between them was seconds long, but miles dense.

"You remember that day . . . up in your parents' room?" she said finally.

"It's etched on my soul," he could have said. "It's the 'before' and 'after' dividing line of my life." He just nodded.

"I ran into your dad when I went downstairs. He was surprised to see me, too. I had to say something, so I told him I was looking for the bathroom. He gave me directions to it. Then the phone rang in the kitchen. You came down to take the call. And then . . ."

"You eavesdropped," he said with flat incredulity.

". . . Do you remember what you said?"

His hands iced as the blood fled the surface of his

skin. Disgusted with the boy he once was. Because he did remember.

He didn't answer. He couldn't get the words out.

"You basically said . . ." She drew in a long breath. ". . . you said, 'Avalon? Are you kidding me? Nah. She's just a hick from the sticks. Not Harvard material.'"

Yep. Just as horrible as he remembered. He made a pained sound. "And then you left without saying a damn thing to me and I never saw you again."

"What would *you* do, Mac?"

"*I* would have tracked you down and made you explain what you meant by that phone call, for fuck's sake."

"Bullshit! You never looked for me!"

"You were never anywhere I looked! You were never with your brothers and they would have given me merciless amounts of shit if I asked about you more than once. I . . . I just figured . . ."

"What did you figure?"

He recited it flatly, as if delivering it in a monotone could remove all the pain from it. "That maybe you saw something so irredeemable in me that you had to get the fuck away as fast as possible. Or maybe . . . maybe you'd just gotten bored. That all I was was a way to get through a summer."

He saw the words penetrate; she softened. Her fundamental kindness was warring with a righteousness she was wholly entitled to. She didn't speak.

"You weren't afraid of a damn thing back then,

Avalon. I'm surprised you didn't just go right up to me and deck me."

She whipped a stray hair out of her eyes. "Here's why," she said quietly. "I was shocked clean through. I thought you despised me. And I was ashamed that someone I cared about so much could think those things about me when I'd always thought the opposite was true. It entirely changed my view of myself and the world. It was the first time that I considered myself in that light . . . as somehow not *good* enough for someone. And hearing those words coming from *you* . . ."

He understood. And he really had no defense. Just pity and contempt for the boy he'd been. And an ache for the girl she'd been.

"I wish you hadn't heard them," he said wearily.

"Why *did* you say those things?"

He blew out a breath. "Because I probably meant them. That's how fucked-up I was back then."

Her expression . . . it was like he'd taken a shovel to her knees. "*What?*" Her voice was hoarse.

"Or thought I *should* mean them. I was told repeatedly that that was what you were and that was how I should feel. By my dad."

All the color had drained from her face. He could see her freckles starkly. Thirteen.

He took a step toward her, as if he could feel her pulling away. "I am bad at this, Avalon, so please . . . I'm going to try to explain. All my life, up until I was about eighteen, all I ever wanted to do was make my dad proud. I worshipped that man like he was a god. Everyone treated him like one, I thought—well, he *must* be a god, right? I thought everything he said was true and everything he told me was gospel. I wanted to be just like him and that's what he wanted, too. Didn't you feel the same way about your parents when you were a kid?"

It was clear she didn't want to concede any point or yield any understanding to him right now. But it would have been completely counter to her nature to lie. "Sure. Yes. I guess."

"And you can believe me or not, and you're not going to like hearing this: I was repeating things I knew he wanted to hear, because he was standing *right there*. I repeated them to a girl he wanted me to impress, because her dad was rich. And *he* did think you were a hick from the sticks who just wanted to get knocked up and get your hands on my money. And *every single time* he said something like that— and he said shit like that, horrible ugly things, so often and so blithely—I died a little inside. Because there was this . . . *chasm* between what I was told was true and what I knew was true about you. So I figured there must be something wrong with *me* for feeling the way I felt about you."

And now Mac was breathing as though he was waiting for someone to come along and help him pull a knife out of his gut. Ragged gulps of air.

Her eyes flared with a surge of compassion; he could see it move through her, in the drop of her shoulders; he could feel it as tangibly as a change in weather.

But she stood her ground. And he knew what the next question would be.

"How *did* you feel, Mac?" Her voice was quiet and even.

"I thought you were . . . beautiful. And . . . magical. And . . . and the world only felt right when I was with you."

She went still.

He'd hoped it was enough. But the corner of her mouth twisted; a faint cynicism darkened her gaze, as if he'd only just fulfilled her expectations.

"You know . . . those words . . . they blew my whole life off course. I feel like I've spent my whole life proving I wasn't what you said I was. No matter what, I would *never* have said those things."

"How . . . the *hell* do you know that?" A surge of frustrated fury sent the words out cracked. "The thing I don't think you realize, Avalon . . . is what a luxury it was to be allowed to be *yourself* your whole life. To just *be*, without someone dictating who they think you ought to be, without being forced to live up to what began as an impossible ideal that ended as a giant lie. I had to figure everything out from nothing. From *wreckage*. I made sure I did it scrupulously, one step at a time. I made sure I was straight with everyone. I never cut a corner, and I never did anyone dirty. And now I *know* who I am. And I just now told you the truth. Which you asked for. And apparently you don't like it. I'm sorry I hurt you, but I don't ever want to lie to *you*."

Her jaw got tauter and tauter as she listened to this.

"Okay. Fine, Mac," she said evenly, ironically. "I get it. But the problem is . . . you think cutting everyone and everything out of your life means you're tough. But I think all it really means is you're *scared*. Scared of loose ends, scared of complications, scared to be disappointed, scared to be hurt. And who could possibly compete with your true love? Fear."

"Guess it takes a coward to know one, huh?" he shot back.

There was a shocked little silence.

"What the hell is *that* supposed to mean?" It was practically a hiss.

"It means that I hurt you *one time*—and believe me, a lot of people go through life *collecting* hurt—and the rest of your disappointments or that twit Corncob or your other near misses are *my* fault? Much easier to blame me than yourself, I guess."

She reared back a little. Blinking in amazement. She stared at him for a second or two of assessing stillness.

And then the fight left her posture, like air slowly seeping from a balloon.

"You're right," she said, almost wonderingly. She gave a short, self-deprecating little laugh. "I *am* scared." It had the ring of finality about it.

"Avalon . . ." He took a desperate step forward. Her eyes gleamed with tears.

She shook her head implacably and stepped backward. "I'm heading to San Francisco this afternoon. Turns out Corbin made a hash of things and to make a long story short we now need an injection of cash to even meet rent and payroll by the end of the month. So I have a meeting with the potential buyer for the house while in the city. And all this means: you probably have about two days to offer me, in cash, what this house is now worth."

Too many emotions at once bludgeoned him into silence.

"I'll be back to wrap things up here by the weekend," she added. "And then that's it. I've decided I'll be going back to San Francisco after that. I think whatever I came here to do is done. But . . . thanks for everything, Mac."

She leaned forward then and punched him chummily in the shoulder.

And then turned around and took off at a jog.

He stalked back toward his cottage, his breath sawing as if he'd just been in an actual physical wrestling match.

He teetered like a drunk and sat down hard on the Adirondack chair in front of his house.

Then he bent his hands over his head like they tell you to do when the plane is heading into a nosedive. Won't help much if it's *determined* to crash, of course. It was really just a formality, in that case.

Kind of felt like a formality right now, given that the crash had taken place.

He breathed in and out.

The anger was bitter and caustic in the back of his throat. Where it mingled with a very nearly primal fear.

If she wanted to go, if that was her plan all along, then why should he try to stop her?

Finally, he heaved a huge sigh, sat up, and closed his eyes.

If only she understood how brutally hard all of this really was for him. How ashamed he was to even admit that to himself, let alone her. He didn't have the words to explain to her that his rigid pride, once his salvation, his armor, was a sort of bondage now, adhered to his soul like decades of paint adhered to a window.

But it had served him in life to date. It had gotten him *through*. It had formed the core of his personal credo, and for him, in the absence of any kind of safety net of a loving family, having a rigid credo had been like laying down a track under a runaway train.

Chaos had nearly crushed the life out of him when he was twenty-one, when he'd watched his dad hauled off by the feds, and then bore witness to the dismantling of his life in the light of public scorn.

All these years later, he thought he'd dug himself out of the wreckage of his life to get to this house. Which would be his way of getting back to himself.

He now knew in reality he'd been sifting through that wreckage in order to find *her*.

Himself. Her.

To his heart, it amounted to the same thing, in the end.

He knew it was killing her to walk away.

And still she was doing it.

His whole life system clearly had a flaw if Avalon Harwood wanted to get away from him. How could she not understand that he would literally rather die than deliberately hurt her? And yet apparently just being himself was guaranteed to bring her pain.

The Cat came and sat down next to him. Mac reflexively dropped one of his arms down. The Cat did all the work, rubbing his head to and fro all over Mac's distracted hand.

Breathing helped. So he just did that for a little while.

He might not be good at parsing out feelings. But he did know how to build things and repair things; he knew how to methodically solve structural problems. And now that his head was a little clearer he felt able to sort through the snarl of words, to peel them from their casings of emotions, feeling around intuitively for that beginning thread that he could follow out of the mess.

And he found both the cause and solution.

She was so scared to trust him that instead of staying here she was going right back to a life that didn't fit her. That in fact flattened her, dimmed her light. She knew and he knew it. She was going to be miserable.

He was scared, too. Standing-on-a-crumbling-cliff's-edge scared.

And yet he would do just about anything to make her feel safe in the world.

And in light of that, his own fear underwent an alchemical reaction akin to spinning straw into gold. His fear became courage. Her fear became his cause.

He knew how to fix this. And he knew how to do it the right way. A way that had such structural integrity and permanence she couldn't doubt it or him, or his feelings, or hers, ever again.

And whether she realized it or not, she was the one who'd already all but told him what to do.

Funnily, if Mike had paid him back the ten grand, he might not be on the precipice of getting everything he ever wanted. Next time he saw Mike, he was going to tell him he was basically a Fairy Godfather.

Mac was feeling a lot more like himself. His palms were a little sweaty, sure. But he could do this.

He reached for his phone, and pulled up a contact, and pressed a number he'd never even dialed from this phone.

Like they always said: go big or go home.

For Avalon . . . he would do both.

CHAPTER 24

She dropped Chick Pea off with her parents, then hit the freeway for San Francisco, driving at speeds that would have inspired feelings of rank betrayal if Eli had known. It was really kind of a miracle she didn't get caught.

She'd gotten just past Black Oak, an hour and a half or so into her trip, before the fumes of fury and blind ache and grief spent themselves, and something like sense seeped in instead, and when it did, she was seized with an urge to see Mac.

To tell him that she *did* understand him. That she thought he was a freaking hero for picking himself up the way he had. That he had indeed blown her off course, but that she also recognized that he'd just spent nearly the last month trying to steer her back onto it, trying to point out to her the things she loved, the things that made her truly herself, as only someone who *knew* her—and loved her—could.

So she found the nearest off ramp and roared back the way she'd come.

Screeched into her own driveway and leaped out of the car, very like the way she'd screeched up to the courthouse the day she'd bought this house at auction. And she didn't stop running until she was at the front door of Mac's cottage.

She thumped on the door.

It swung open immediately, which gave her a start.

"Well, Avalon! Hello there."

Avalon stared dumbly.

Morton Horton looked a bit awkward fully clothed. Kind of the way San Franciscans always look when they attempt to wear shorts out in public when the temperature in the city goes higher than seventy degrees.

"Oh, um, hello, Morty. Nice to see you again. Is Mac in?"

"Oh, Mac's gone off." He gestured airily toward the road.

"He's . . . gone off?" Like a carton of bad milk? Like a roman candle?

In an ambulance?

Her heart lurched. "Is he okay?"

"He seems just fine. He called me up and asked me to look after his animals while he was away. He was in a huge hurry, so I gathered it was an emergency. He called in a favor, so here I am."

"Where did he . . ." It wasn't really any of her business, of course. It was so unexpected, she was struggling with equilibrium.

"He didn't say."

She cleared her throat. "How long is he . . ."

"He just said he'd let me know," he said gently. "I don't think he'd leave his animals for long. He asked me to look after things here for a bit and to see if there's anything you might need. I can handle repairs or outdoor chores in a pinch. Helen will be by, too, and she'll be happy to help, if you're in the mood for a chat."

And just like that, she felt like her heart was on an elevator and the cable had snapped.

It was a feat of heroic proportions to just get the next few words out.

"No. Thank you, Morty. That's very kind, but . . . I *was* just on my way to San Francisco."

She couldn't feel her limbs again. Everything she was—all her thoughts and feelings—seemed to have retreated as far from the surface of her skin as possible and gathered in a tight, hard knot around her heart. The pain was so ghastly it was almost blackly funny.

Somehow she hadn't quite anticipated his *immediate* exodus. Whoosh! Like a cartoon character whose legs blurred as they scrabbled to get away.

She blindly turned to leave on her leaden legs and nearly ran headlong into a guy who was rocking a prosthetic leg, a huge smile, and carrying a big manila envelope.

Morty greeted him with a huge smile and a bear hug. "Hey, Mike! Long time no see, man! We were worried about you."

"I found work, man, and I just wasn't able to get away until now. Mac around?"

"Nope. He's out of town."

"Damn! I've got something for him, finally." He held up an envelope. "Ten thousand somethings, plus interest."

Three hours of freeway driving and slow traffic later, San Francisco expanded into view, spectacularly beautiful as always, as colorful and varied in scale as a carnival, and just as loud and lively.

And maybe just as sketchy.

And smelly.

The idea of San Francisco as a carnival made her think of circuses. Which made her think of tightropes, which made her think of "Don't Cry Out Loud."

Which ironically made her cry out loud.

Gulping, messy sobs that threatened to obscure her vision. So she got a grip, because that's what she did. She got a grip. She was a person who didn't believe in magic anymore, so why the hell should she cry?

Maybe someday she would find comfort in being *right* about Mac Coltrane being a terrible risk. Didn't it prove she had great judgment after all?

The excess emotion made her nauseated and a little dizzy.

But in the thirty hair-tearing, harrowing minutes it took to find a parking place within four blocks of her building (she finally double-parked) she didn't think much about Mac, which made her realize that merely getting around in San Francisco required every single one of her faculties practically every minute of the day; and who had time to dwell, or for emotions, or for love, when you were doing that.

But was looking for a goddamn parking place really a good use of the remaining minutes of her life?

She'd texted Corbin earlier to steer clear of her for the entire day she'd be in town, and he'd complied. She was in and out of the apartment inside an hour. She'd always kept the clothes to a versatile minimum in honor of the teeny closet, and for the same reason a good percentage of the rest of her stuff was made of fabric that could be wadded into balls. She didn't even feel the slightest urge to take a pair of scissors to Corbin's favorite ironic thrift store bowling shirt (it said "Bert" on the pocket), which was how she knew the spark, if they had indeed ever shared such a thing, was irretrievably extinguished.

She paused in the doorway for one last look around, but that only reminded her of pausing there and listening to the headboard bam, so she slammed the door quickly with a little shudder.

The next thing she did was shake Visine into her eyes then make a sweep through GradYouAte's offices to soothe the nerves of her staff with her sunny, efficient presence and a few brisk decisions, metaphorically tugging here and there at all the loose ends and straightening Corbin's messes as best she could.

Apart from the money issues. Those they would have to finesse together, somehow.

But the issues surrounding the work they were doing suddenly seemed irritating and pointless. She literally felt as if she were trapped in the midst of a boring dream.

In fact, after a month of feeling nearly everything on a symphonic scale—happiness and anger, peace and beauty, hilarity and admiration, orgasms—the entire day seemed muted.

San Francisco itself, arguably one of the most colorful places on earth in every sense of the word, seemed muted.

And it wasn't just because she was trying *not* to feel inconvenient emotions again. It was literally the difference between a banquet and a TV dinner, and about the . . . *ingredients* in a day. Specifically, the people. The situations. The work.

The presence or absence of hope.

Or love.

Avalon crashed on Rachel's couch in San Francisco's Richmond District that night and instead of sleeping, listened to giant buses groaning up and down the hills. Before that, she drove around for forty-five minutes before she found a place to park her car. The Thai food was awesome, though, and Rachel had a line on a possible flat Avalon could sublet, one that would let her keep a little dog. Things could be worse.

She was glad Rachel worked late and had to get up

early; Avalon could just barely handle the yawning hug and the few cheerful sentences they exchanged before they went off to their various sleeping arrangements. She missed Chick Pea. She missed knowing her sister could text for a favor and Avalon could get right in there and be a Hummingbird helper.

But the jobs were here, in San Francisco. Not only the one she'd created for herself, but the livelihoods she'd created for GradYouAte's (albeit transient, young and flaky) staff, and she supposed she felt some responsibility to the people who'd been kind enough to buy the game and play it. She'd only planned for Hellcat Canyon and the house at Devil's Leap to be an interlude, anyway. She knew Corbin was in no position to buy her out of GradYouAte, even if he wanted to—God only knew he didn't want to run the place on his own. The whole company would look more attractive to a buyer if they could actually meet payroll, for God's sake.

She exhaled. Then curled her hands under her cheek, and kissed her palm gently and thought, *Godspeed, Mac, wherever you are, you fucker. Thanks for demonstrating that you didn't run off with my heart, because I know now I never really got it back from you the first time.* For a few weeks there, she'd remembered how it had really felt to have one.

Maybe Mac had been right all along. Romance was a racket. And nobody with any sense believed in magic.

The next day, as San Francisco shrank again in her rearview mirror, no part of her looked forward to returning to her life there. That was a first. At the very least, she'd always looked forward to good Thai food.

But she'd be back, and she'd make it all work out, because that's what she did.

She currently just didn't see any other way.

She finally turned the key in the lock of the Devil's Leap house around four thirty that afternoon, and freed Chick Pea from her carrier to tinkle if she so chose. She chose only to sniff the flower beds and bark at a squirrel. She'd happily tinkled back at her parents' house, apparently.

The house glowed like a bride inside from the fresh paint. The smell was evocative in some ways of spring: new paint had always smelled like anticipation to her. Like the beginnings of things.

Maybe that's how she ought to look at it.

Rather than the end of a dream that, for one brief shining moment, she'd managed to capture.

Someone else would choose furniture for these beautiful rooms. See the rainbows sprinkle the foyer when the sun hit the chandelier just right. Walk across floors that glowed like amber. Wake up in the turret.

Maybe think twice about going in the attic.

The stuck or wobbly or dangerous parts—warped windows, creaky hinges, the stairs—now moved freely or, if they weren't supposed to, not at all. Scratches had been smoothed away.

For a little while, she'd been awake inside a dream.

She still loved this house with the same ache she had as a girl.

But now she knew that love was all tied up with Mac, of a piece. And the house did not mean a damn thing without him.

And for that reason alone she could, and should, let it go.

Still, her heart was pretty weighted when she carried Chick Pea with her up the stairs to drop off a load of clothes.

As she dumped them on the bed a text chimed into her phone. She glanced down and her whole being reflexively knotted up.

It was Corbin.

Call me. It's urgent.

Crap crap crap. She did not *want* to hear Corbin's voice right now, when the sun was at its most mellow and golden here in the turret. She didn't think he had the nerve to bother her with passive-aggressive requests just to get her attention, however. It must actually be urgent.

She punched his number. "What?" she said tersely, when he answered.

"Did you read that email from the venture capitalist firm? Coltrane Chatwick Forsyth? COLTRANE? What the hell, Avalon?"

Coltrane?

Her heart bounced like a rim shot.

She scrolled through her emails until she saw.

Dear Ms. Harwood and Mr. Bergson,
I write to you on behalf of venture capital-
ists Coltrane Chatwick Forsyth. We represent
an investor who is interested in purchasing
GradYouAte.

And then it listed a sum that stopped her breath.
It wasn't jaw-dropping. But it was better than fair.
It was . . . freaking the answer to her prayers.
After they repaid their investors, Avalon and
Corbin would be left with healthy chunks of money.
Avalon with more, since she owned more of the com-
pany.
Enough money to go back to school if she wanted to.

Alternatively, we are willing to discuss a
venture capital arrangement, but only if Ms.
Harwood agrees to stay on as CEO. We agree
her competence and creative vision have been
thus far key to the company's success.
We look forward to discussing this with you
at your earliest convenience. You may contact
me at the number listed above.

Sincerely,
T. Dixon Coltrane

P. S. Mac says hi, Avalon.
So do I.
And thank you.

The "T" stood for Tiberius.

Ty, Mac's brother.

HOLY. SHIT.

That's where Mac had gone. To see his brother in New York!

There could really only be one reason he'd done that.

He'd done it for her. *Because* of her.

Whoosh! Her crumpled, limp heart unfurled like a filled sail. She breathed joy instead of oxygen.

"Avalon, you there? The key to our success? Are they *serious*?"

The little voice in her hand gave her a start. She'd entirely forgotten about Corbin. "What the hell does that last part mean? The 'hi Avalon' bit?" Have you been planning this behind my *back*?"

"Shhh," she said rudely. "No."

Corbin was smart. He'd settle down and figure out this was about as lucky as he could get.

She pivoted abruptly when another email from "Martin Graybill Esquire" dinged into her mailbox. The subject line was: Devil's Leap.

Graybill . . . Graybill . . . where and in what context had she heard that name before?

And then she remembered. The guy from the auction! Mac's lawyer!

Her hands were shaking when she clicked it open.

Dear Ms. Harwood,
This is to inform you that the undeveloped

parcel of land known as Devil's Leap has been
deeded to you by Mr. Maximilian Coltrane.
You are now the official owner of record. Digi-
tal copies of the deed of transfer and relevant
documents are attached.

    No strings are.
    Mr. Coltrane insisted I make that very clear.

Sincerely,
Martin J. Graybill, Attorney at Law

She sat down hard on her bed.

She covered her mouth with her hand as little by little her vision began to blur with tears. "Oh my God."

"Avalon?" said Corbin's teeny voice from her hand.

Devil's Leap was *hers*? What did it mean? What was Mac *doing*?

And then she got it: not only was he giving her choices.

He was making the proverbial Grand Gesture.

And then both she and Chick Pea gave a little leap and a yelp when the floor began buzzing beneath her feet. An instant after that the entire room was vibrating from an enormous swell of sound.

Like the earth heaving an enormous sigh.

And it was nuts . . . but she thought she recognized that sigh.

"Ava, can you hear me? Shouldn't we *talk* about this?" Corbin, oblivious Corbin, obsolete Corbin, was still squeaking away on the phone in her hand.

She ignored him.

She drifted toward the window with almost as much trepidation as she had the morning a truck full of gourmet poop had been delivered to Mac, but with much more anticipation. She put her hand against it.

It was buzzing from sound.

And then she was positive. Because she knew this song the way she knew the sound of her own voice. How it sort of sighed into being, like a surrendering lover. The way the percussion slipped in, like a skipping heartbeat. The way the bass eased sinuously in alongside it, to give the melody shape.

How Bryan Ferry's voice was like a murmur from the next pillow.

She threw open the window.

And in rushed Roxy Music's "Avalon."

Heat rushed over her skin like a rain of stars. Which was exactly how she once thought she would feel if a wizard had waved a wand over her.

She drifted over to the next room. She closed her eyes and murmured something like a prayer before she stepped outside onto the deck, her heart pounding twice as fast as the beat of the music.

And like the spire on a church, or the ornament on the hood of a Rolls-Royce, there was Mac. Tiny, but visible.

Standing on top of Devil's Leap, holding a boom box aloft over his head à la Lloyd Dobler in *Say Anything*.

She clapped her hand over her mouth over a stunned laugh. "Oh, my God."

Whoops. It happened to be the hand holding her

cell phone. Corbin was squawking now. "Ava, what the hell is—"

She dropped the phone like a live coal.

She moved as if borne on a current of air, slowly at first, toward the stairs.

And then she walked sedately down them.

She managed to open the front door, even as her hands were shaking.

She closed it behind her.

And she followed the flagstone path. Walking. Like a grownup. Like the woman she was, who had learned to be cautious.

And then she couldn't help it. She moved faster.

And then she was running.

Hair flying out behind her, elbows pumping, the memory of the path in her body, she ran like a little girl. Down the drive. Past the mailboxes. A hard left up the gravel road for fifty or so feet, a swift scratchy plunge through some underbrush. Down the path lined with blackberry vines where he'd first kissed her, that narrowed to the sandy path that heralded the beginning of the little beach.

She picked her way through a collection of familiar stones, a dozen shades of gray from green to brown, and curved toward those slabs of stone that had helpfully been arranged over the centuries to form a sort of stairway for the nimble and brave, all the way up to Devil's Leap. But you had to know where to put your feet.

She hadn't taken this path since she was seventeen,

but rocks don't change much over decades. But they do indeed change. It just wasn't visible to the naked eye.

Kind of like stony hearts.

And then, at last, she was on top of the rock, flat and broad as a stage.

And she was next to him.

He eyed her wonderingly, almost cautiously, as if making sure she wasn't a mirage.

Then slowly lowered the boom box.

And settled it down at his feet.

It apparently was a prop, and he'd learned a few things about Bluetooth speakers.

Because thrillingly, he extended his arm and aimed a remote somewhere off into the distance, and the music lowered to a murmur, and the sun chose that moment to turn a streamer of cloud into tangerine, and he was like a wizard aiming a wand that could turn up the colors and sounds of the world.

A wizard whose hand was trembling as he stuffed the remote in his back pocket.

"You wanted choices."

He gave her a little lopsided smile.

"Mac . . . you're . . . you're just . . ."

She shook her head, because feelings were getting in the way of her ability to form words, and he was blurring from tears.

"Yeah," he agreed, with relief. "I sure am."

His smile faded. "Okay. I need to tell you something, all right?"

She nodded.

He drew in a breath. "That night when you blew a fuse? I knew the moment you did it. It was kind of funny. Suddenly everything was silent and dark, and the house was just this shadowy pile. And then I gave you the fuse, and I watched out the window as you went into the basement . . . and I waited. And I didn't know it, but I was kind of holding my breath. And when your house finally lit up again, it was the strangest feeling, but it was like watching actual magic. I felt like I was lit up, too."

This was hands-down the best story she'd ever heard, and it wasn't even over yet.

"And that's what I understand now: for me, you're like that fuse. You're the magic. For me, there's no point to this house or this town or possibly to any-thing, really, without you. You can laugh if you want, but that's as romantic as I know how to be."

It was as romantic as anyone had ever been in the history of the world, as far as she was concerned.

"I'm not going to laugh." She said it solemnly as a priestess. Her voice was shaking a little.

She watched his chest move in a huge sigh. As if he'd been dreading getting through that and he was relieved.

"I know this comes as a shock to you, Avalon, but I'm far, far from perfect. But I will be perfect at one thing: I will get you down out of attics and hand you ice and build anything for you, any kind of life you want. I know how to make you happy. No one will *ever* be better at that than me. And I know you. Not just how many freckles you have, but I know your heart. Not only that, but I have a plan. Because I will never *not* have a plan. Want to hear it?"

She nodded. He threaded his hands through hers and pulled her gently up against his chest, as if he sensed she was in danger of floating away like a dandelion from the sheer lightness of being.

And his voice got lower. And a little rushed, but to her, it might as well have been a spell.

"We live here. Together. You and me. In the big house. We raise goats and chickens and maybe get a horse or a donkey and other animals that need some looking after. We hold classes for kids, all kinds, for at-risk kids and programs for vets, too. About farming, ecology, animal husbandry. You get your teaching degree, if you still want it. We can get grants from the state and from other sources—I've looked into this—and invest our own funds, and if you choose to sell GradYouAte, you'll be pretty comfortable, too. I'm still working on it, and I already have a spreadsheet. Between the two of us, we can pull it off. We can even have outdoor concerts at a venue we build or other special events in the ballroom. Maybe even . . . weddings."

The donkey was kind of a wildcard but she was on board with every bit of this.

She wasn't going to mention the wedding part. They'd get around to that.

"Or . . ." he concluded. "You go on back to Grad-YouAte. I buy the house from you. If that's what you want."

He was a swirl of impressionistic colors, thanks to tears.

She swiped at them with a knuckle. "I choose staying with you." She didn't even make him wait. Her voice was thick.

She could literally see his breath stop then. His eyes closed and his head tipped back and his mouth moved in a word that looked like *hallelujah*.

The world was only his eyes, and his breath, and his hands twined in hers, and the river moving over the rocks as they stood high above it.

He raised their twined hands and collected her tears from her eyelashes gently on his knuckle. "I've loved you pretty much from the moment I laid eyes on you, Avalon. You have my heart. You can keep it or you can throw it off Devil's Leap. Devil's Leap's yours, too."

"Your heart is the most precious thing in the world to me," she could have said. But he'd already filled the air with romance and she knew he liked it when people said exactly what they meant.

So she said, "I love you."

Three words that contained worlds and the past and the future. They were as beautiful and intricate as the house, as basic as Mac.

He closed his eyes briefly and his head went back and he exhaled a breath. He folded his arms around her.

"And Devil's Leap is *ours*," she corrected on a murmur, as she melted against him, and looped her arms around his neck.

And her face turned up as his came down. They kissed each other like they'd invented kissing.

Somehow, deftly, as this was all happening, he'd managed to free the remote from his pocket and he used it to turn up the music again.

And they rotated in a slow circle, bodies fit together like gears, the length of him warm and strong against the length of her, like kids at a high school dance, there was no sound except Roxy Music and the river below them.

Until:

"You were right all along," he murmured into her hair, sounding only a little surprised. "This isn't ridiculous at all."

Don't miss the first two wickedly sexy and deliciously fun romances in Julie Anne Long's Hellcat Canyon series!

HOT IN HELLCAT CANYON

A broken truck, a broken career, and a breakup heard around the world land superstar John Tennessee McCord in Hellcat Canyon. Legend has it that hearts come in two colors there: gold or black. And that you can find whatever you're looking for, whether it's love . . . or trouble. JT may have found both in waitress Britt Langley.

His looks might cause whiplash and weak knees, but Britt sees past JT's rough edge and sexy drawl to a person a lot like her: in need of the kind of comfort best given hot and quick, with clothes off and the lights out.

Her wit is sharp but her eyes and heart not to mention the rest of her—are soft, and JT is falling hard. But Britt has a secret as dark as the hills, and JT's past is poised to invade their present. It's up to the people of Hellcat Canyon to help make sure their future includes a happily ever after.

WILD AT WHISKEY CREEK

Everyone knows the Greenleaf family puts the "Hell" in Hellcat Canyon—legend has it the only way they ever leave is in a cop car or a casket. But Glory Greenleaf has a different getaway vehicle in mind: her guitar. She has a Texas-sized talent and the ambition (and attitude) to match, but only two people have ever believed in her: her brother, who's in jail, and his best friend . . . who put him there.

Sheriff Eli Barlow has secretly been in love with Glory since he was twelve years old. Which is how he knows her head is as hard as her heart is soft—and why she can't forgive him for fracturing her family . . . or forget that night they surrendered to an explosive, long-simmering passion. But when a betrayal threatens Glory's big break, Eli will risk everything to make it right . . . because the best way to love the girl from Whiskey Creek might mean setting her free forever.

Available now from Avon Books!
Buy your copy today!

*G*ive in to your Impulses!

These unforgettable stories only take a second to buy and give you hours of reading pleasure!

Go to ***www.AvonImpulse.com*** and see what we have to offer.

Available wherever e-books are sold.

AVONIMPULSE